G000255374

Women Misb

Women Misbehaving

Five friends, too many lies,
and gossip that rocks a community

Victoria Bullimore

YouCaxton Publications
Oxford & Shrewsbury

Contents

Prologue

Journalists, photographers and vans with satellite dishes are causing mayhem in the road outside the school. Its motto, engraved in limestone above a polished oak door furnished with a gleaming brass knob, reads 'Industrium at Iustitiam', the irony of which hasn't been lost on those reporters who have translated it – 'Endeavour and Integrity'.

They tap on their tablets, exchanging notes. The fees at Kingsmead School start at 20k a year, the alumni are impressive, and the headmaster's wife looks fit in the photos. There is speculation as to whether she was in in on the scandal.

People have come to watch. Some of the reporters ask questions about the headmaster and his alleged crime but no-one can tell them anything they don't already know. Local teenage boys shove each other in front of the cameras, laughing and making hand gestures until someone tells them to push off.

'Mr King's a wanker!' yells one of the youths in retreat, 'I hope he gets banged up!' which is followed by an unruly chorus of approval from his mates.

Yummy Mummies in big shiny cars slow down to stare, shameless in their greed for gossip. A man with two black Labradors on leads is taking photos on his phone. A group of scaffolders sit in their van and watch the drama while eating sandwiches and sausage rolls.

When the door finally opens the throng of reporters stirs into life like an agitated nest of bees. A shabbily dressed woman with bleached hair steps out, not looking up. She walks quickly away, head down, lips tight.

'Just the cleaner,' someone says, and they lose interest.

Only one reporter decides to have a go, a woman from a local radio station who is hoping for a scoop.

'Excuse me! Excuse me! Do you work here?'

'No comment,' says the woman, like someone who's watched too many TV cop shows.

'Do you know Mr King, the headmaster? What's your understanding of what's happened here?'

'No comment.' Two red spots have appeared on the woman's cheeks. She grabs her bicycle from the rack and fumbles with the lock.

'Do you think he's guilty? What kind of a man is he in your opinion?'

'No comment.' She climbs clumsily onto her bicycle and pedals away, like the wicked witch from the Wizard of Oz, thinks the reporter, who is disappointed but wonders if she can make something of the fact that the cleaner is covering up for the disgraced headmaster.

The woman on the bike smiles to herself when she is out of sight, because she knows everything.

Or so she thinks.

1. Minty

Shame, Champagne and Custard Creams

I wake with a start, heart thumping, wet with sweat, feeling sick. I'm in my own bed, still in my red dress, but Simon is not next to me... where is he? I squint at the digital glow on the clock – 07:50. I can't remember how I got back home, or in to my bed. I have a vague memory of looking for my keys to the front door, but that's it.

I stagger to my beautiful white ensuite and throw up in the loo, tears washing the grit of last night's make-up from my eyes. I struggle with the zip of my dress, which is tight and clammy, and I wriggle out of it, relieved that at least I still have all my underwear on, even my tights, the feet of which are black. Where are my shoes? Where is Simon?

I strip naked, discarding my clothes in a pile on the under-heated floor, pull on my white fluffy bathrobe, the one Jack got me for Christmas, and walk gingerly to the stairs. The lights are on. It's quiet. The door to Jack's room is closed. Jenny stayed with one of her friends last night, Phoebe probably, I think they said they were going to watch the fireworks on Midsummer Commion. I hope she's alright. Oh God. My head is spinning, there is a sharp pain behind my eyes and the nausea fills my stomach again.

Slowly I go down the stairs, my hand on the polished bannister, my dirty feet luxuriating in the thick carpet. The chandelier appears to spin, like a kaleidoscope, the lights bright and splintered.

Why have I allowed myself to get into this state again? Why, why, why? I'm angry, and the anger feels as if it's been there for a long time. Then I remember, Simon and I had a massive fight last night, oh God, a proper big one, it started in The Cross Keys, in front of everyone.

Fuck.

I know that Simon is not in the house. I can feel his absence. The lights are all on in the kitchen too (Jack is so careless like that), and there's a sticky jar of Marmite and a used knife on the chopping board, crumbs, the butter dish with the lid off, half a cucumber, I feel sick at the sight of it, at the thought of food.

My bag is on the rocking chair. I rummage blindly inside it and find my phone, thank God. The screen is full of messages, Facebook, Happy New Year texts, WhatsApps, Snapchats, I call Simon but it goes straight to voicemail. I can't leave a message. It would sound too pathetic. I need to speak to him, face to face. I know where he'll be.

Am I safe to drive?

Guilt, Fear, Shame, my faithful friends, the old gang, they play with my emotions and I feel the tears welling. *Simon. Simon. I'm so sorry. Forgive me.* How many times have I asked for his forgiveness? How many times has he granted it?

I hope Jack hasn't hidden my car keys. He did that once, but I was so mad with him I don't think he'd do it again. I grope my way to the pot where they're kept. I lift the lid on the pot and fish them out with relief. My pink Birkenstocks are by the back door. I slip them on.

I'm as quiet as a cat. I steal out of my own house like a thief. Like someone bad.

I take deep breaths of the cold air, steam comes out of my mouth, the dawn is breaking and another year has begun. What will it bring? I clamber into the leather driving seat of my Porsche Cayenne, no-one can see me here on the drive, the house is shaded by enormous elms and cherry trees, and anyway the Huths, my next door neighbours, are in Germany until next week. It feels odd being in my bathrobe. Perhaps I should have pulled on a coat. I hope to God I don't see anyone I know.

I'm longing to see Simon, desperate to tell him I'm sorry, but maybe this is the day when he tells me he's had enough and that he can't forgive me again. Maybe this is another tragic date in my life that I will never forget. The first of January. The thirteenth of August.

I cruise down to the junction and turn right out of Elm Road slowly, carefully, the pain in my head squeezing all the sense from me. My foot misses the brake, shit, finds it again - I stop at the mini roundabout, check the deserted road then pull away, heading towards the city centre. Christmas lights spangle the shop windows and festoon the deserted street. I pass Boots, Kate's Tea Rooms, NatWest, Oxfam, Hardy's the butcher's shop, Hambleton's Estate Agents, the Post Office – the lights at the pelican crossing are green, the colour I imagine my face to be right now.

I see a man and a woman in Hi-Vis Lycra up ahead. Fuck. It's Sarah and Gary. I turn left. Shit. Have they seen me? What the fuck are they doing out at this hour? Don't they ever give themselves a break? It's New Year's Day for fuck's sake. They were in The Cross Keys last night, but left early, they always do. They don't drink. Imagine that. In my rear view mirror I see them disappear round the corner.

I turn right. Then go over the second mini roundabout. Down the road for a mile or so, nearly there.

The allotments are next to Kingsmead's little railway station, the ugly, dusty end of the town. I park the car on the kerb, relieved to be here. I take a few more deep breaths. *Don't be sick. Don't be sick.*

Pulling my robe tight around me I step down from the car and head towards Simon's patch, the one with the biggest shed, painted blue, and the Union Jack. It's cold. The earth is lumpy and hard beneath my Birkenstocks and the long grass is making my toes wet. I'm shivering.

I knock on the little blue door. I know he's in there, I can sense his presence. I knock again, because he sleeps deeply, even in a shed. I have no idea how much he had to drink last night. I don't even know what I had myself.

I hear the lock turning, I step back, the door can only open an inch because the thin, rolled out mattress is blocking it. Simon looks at me as if he has been expecting me, like bad news. His eyes are red. I can smell his breath, booze and garlic.

'Simon…' I sound like a beggar, pleading. Pathetic.

'Yeah, yeah, I know, you're really sorry, you won't do it again, you're going to cut back on the booze, blah, blah, blah…'

I'm shivering uncontrollably now. Jackdaws are calling in the mist. 'Can I come in?'

He sighs, forces the door open a little more and I step inside, into his reluctant embrace, my face pressed against his cashmere sweater, the beat of his heart against the thumping of my headache and I thank God, or someone out there, that today is not the final judgement day after all. I have been given another chance. *Thank you, thank you, thank you.*

'You stink,' he says.

'So do you,' I reply, smiling, holding on.

When Jack was born I was totally blissed out. We were living in London then, in a flat off Finchley Road, Simon had just got his accountancy qualifications and I'd graduated with a 2:2 in Business Studies (hurrah, bloody miracle), so it felt like everything was ahead of us, careers, children, holidays, a home with a garden, Christmas with grandparents, etc. etc., there was so much to look forward to, and Jack was a happy, smiling baby, a proper bundle of joy, it was as if he knew it too, that we were blessed. We were starting out on a path paved with good fortune, rose petals, love, and all that baloney.

Simon was a brilliant Dad from the start, so patient and laid back. Too laid back sometimes. Jenny was born two years after Jack, and when she was six months old I had to have an emergency appendectomy. Simon's mother had died four years previously (lung cancer, sixty fags a day for forty years is not good for you apparently) and his father was sweet but hopeless, so with my parents off spending my inheritance on world cruises, boats and safaris, etc. etc. we were left to cope on our own. When I came home from hospital the flat was a mess. Amongst the teetering pile of festering crockery in the sink I spotted the Garfield mug I'd abandoned just before the ambulance had taken me away. A thick skin of green spotted mould had formed on the tea I'd never finished. There were no clean sheets on the bed, no dry towels anywhere and only a couple of Sainsbury's pizzas in the fridge. 'I got your favourite, American pepperoni,' he said. I sent him out for a couple of bottles of Chablis while I tidied up. Jack and Jenny were perfectly happy though, well fed and clean, which I had to admit was more important than coming home to a spotless flat. Still, clean sheets would have been nice.

We moved to Kingsmead when the children were six and four. An old school friend of his, Gary Simpson, had just bought a business there and was living in the town with his first wife, a ball breaker who left him eventually for a career in the City. When he asked Simon if he would take on his accounts we went up for a visit and fell in love with the place. It was the perfect environment for bringing up children. More inevitable bliss was surely to follow. Simon quickly built up a strong client list and I enrolled in evening classes to train as a beautician. I'd spotted a gap in the local market, Kingsmead is full rich housewives but when I came it only had two beauty salons which were constantly booked up. So within three years I'd opened my own retro style beauty parlour and I loved it.

There are excellent state schools in Kingsmead, and Cambridge which is only ten miles away, and because of this we had our first proper disagreement. Simon wanted Jack to go the local pre-prep school where all the precious little darlings wear grey shorts with red and green striped blazers and caps (like the little Scottish one out of the Krankies), there was no way I was going to subject Jack to such a fate. It wasn't just the god-awful uniform, it was the whole feel of the place. Too much one-upmanship and snobbery, I just wanted Jack to feel free to be himself and not have to compete for everything at such a young age. I got my way in the end. Jack and Jenny thrived at the local primary school and eventually Simon got over his fear of fat Dads in football shirts and Primark Mums with orange faces wearing tee shirts with slogans on. They weren't all like that, I made some really good friends there, but inter-school football games were a bit much for Simon. The parents were full on. A proper fight broke out once. I thought it was funny but Simon was terrified. He wanted Jack to take up tennis or swimming, but I love football (all my

Dad's fault) and I told Simon to lighten up. 'You know sweet FA about the beautiful game,' I told him, which was quite witty I thought.

When Jack was eleven we had the same debate about which school to send him to. He was a bright boy, sporty and outgoing and I had to admit I was impressed when we looked around Kingsmead School. I gave in. I figured I'd had my way for long enough, and Jack really wanted to go there, but we needed help from my parents to meet the 20K a year fees, and the rest. Kingsmead School is co-ed so Jenny followed him two years later. It's still a bit too stuck up for my liking but they were really happy there.

Getting pregnant for the third time wasn't part of our blissful plan. Neither was giving birth to a stillborn baby at twenty-six weeks. Jack thought it was gross that Simon and I were still having sex (he was fourteen at the time) but he and Jenny were both upset when I was so ill afterwards.

It was a girl. We called her Joy, because I'd just seen the Tess of the D'Urbervilles movie, and Tess had called her dead baby Sorrow. Maybe I thought that if I called her Joy then I wouldn't grieve for her every day for the rest of my life.

She's buried in the cemetery on the edge of Cambridge, under a sycamore tree. I thought at the time, here I am, burying my Joy in the ground.

The night of her burial I drank two bottles of wine and Simon had to undress me and put me to bed.

In the words of the magnificent Forrest Gump, 'that's all I have to say about that.'

It's nine o'clock by the time Simon and I get back from the allotment. Jack is frying bacon and eggs in a big pan on the Aga. He doesn't turn round when we come into the kitchen and doesn't ask where we've been. His broad back doesn't look welcoming. I had half a Thermos of black coffee and a packet of cheese and onion crisps in the shed (I know, I know, but needs must) so I feel better, but really it's Simon's forgiveness that has cured me.

'Happy New Year, darling,' I say, going to kiss Jack, but he pulls away from my touch and the pain of his rejection is like a kick in the stomach. It hurts every time. The atmosphere between us is thick and I know it's my fault. I look to Simon for support but he says something about taking a shower and leaves without catching my eye.

It's the feeling of being alone that I can't stand.

'How's your finger?' I ask. He broke it last week in a football game and it's strapped up.

'What do you care?' He turns round and glares at me, just for a second, as if he can't bear to touch me even with his eyes. He pushes the bacon around in the pan with his good hand, shakes his head, 'I can't believe what you did. In front of everyone,' he says, 'Jesus.'

'What? What did I do?' I go to sit on one of the outrageously expensive designer chairs at the table, gingerly, like an old woman, dreading what he's going to come out with. Simon didn't say anything about last night or what I actually got up to, but then I wasn't exactly in a hurry to ask him to fill me in on the details. Perhaps it won't be any worse than last time, a bit of singing, some crazy dancing, everyone's seen me like that before, they know I like a good time, they love me for it, I'm the life and soul of the party, it was New Year's Eve for fuck's sake.

'You really can't remember?' demands Jack, knowing full well I can't, it must be written all over my wrecked face. 'Shall

I give you a clue? Let's just say I think you might be known as Paula Radcliffe from now on.'

What?

Oh God. I get it. I put my head in my hands.

'Who told you?' I ask, as if it matters. It will be all round the town by now.

'I saw you!' He shoves the pan away from the heat. 'I was on my way home from work and there you were, pissing in the middle of the fucking road outside The Cross Keys with everyone looking on, and that dickhead Bertie-fucking-Hambleton telling me that 'maybe it was time I took my mother home.' Jesus...' he shakes his head.

I look at my son and I don't know which feeling to give rein to. He's twenty-two years old, six foot, blonde, handsome, clever, on his way to getting a first from Edinburgh University, he has a sweet girlfriend called Maddie and works as a waiter in The Olive Tree restaurant during the holidays. Everyone loves him. Of course they do. I'm so proud of my little boy.

Yet here he is, judging me, telling me off as if our roles have been reversed, letting me know that he's ashamed of me, that I'm letting the family down; but he's never had a bad day in his life, everything came easy to Jack because I made sure of it. I sent him to Kingsmead School and supported him in everything he did, I worked full time in the salon and spent all my wages on him and Jenny, holidays, clothes, a new car when they were seventeen, I protected him from bullies at school when he was small, put healthy food on the table, sat up with him when he had childhood nightmares, watched him play football and cricket weekend after weekend, paid his mobile phone bill, made his appointments at the dentist and physiotherapist, cried at his brilliant A level results, sat through all those parents' evenings and did all his worrying

9

for him, and yet he's ashamed of me. He towers over me, a wooden spatula in his hand, waiting for me to say something pathetic.

'I'm sorry...'

'No you're not.'

'I am.'

'Not sorry enough, Mum.'

I feel a glimmer of hope at his gentler tone.

'I love you, Jack.'

'I'm not coming back home again until you sort yourself out.'

'What?' I feel the tension in my face as I look at him, aghast.

'You've got to get some help, Mum. You're killing yourself.'

'Don't be dramatic.' I try to sound cross, motherly, but it's just a poor imitation of a better mother than me, the sort of mother I once was.

'I mean it, Mum. I hate seeing you like this....'

'Oh, poor old you, my heart bleeds.' Even I'm surprised by how nasty my sarcasm sounds, and he withdraws from me again.

'I'm going back to Edinburgh tomorrow.'

I contemplate begging. I could do it easily. I'm only a tiny step away from throwing myself at his lovely feet, I could cry in a heartbeat, put on a really good show, but I feel empty now. I can't be bothered. What's the point.

My baby Joy left me. And now my little Jack is leaving me too.

By the time Simon comes back to the kitchen I'm trying to eat the toast and poached eggs that Jack has put in front of me, like an apology or a peace offering. He's also made a pot of coffee and is pouring it into my cup. Simon puts a couple of paracetamol on the table and tells me to take them. They are both looking so serious that I want to laugh, which is awful, nothing is funny here. I put my hand over my mouth to hide the smirk.

'You're not going to throw are you?' Jack is horrified.

'No! I'm fine. Why don't you put some music on Jack, it's too miserable in here.'

Jack scrolls through his phone and Ed Sheeran starts playing through his Bluetooth speaker on the dresser behind him. He knows it's my favourite album and I want to hug him. I don't think he means what he says, about not coming home again. It's just a childish reaction, like a sulk.

'Jenny just called,' says Simon, 'I'm going to pick her up from Phoebe's in a bit.'

'I can't believe you drove this morning,' says Jack, folding his arms, 'you would have been way over the limit.' Here we go again, mother/son role reversal.

'I'm going to take a shower and go back to bed,' I say, getting up.

I know they will talk about me now but I don't care.

They have no idea what it's like, being me. I'm comforted by the thought of Simon going to Cambridge to fetch Jenny, he'll probably take her out for a late breakfast somewhere before coming home. Tonight we'll cook that joint of beef that cost me thirty quid from Hardy's and I'll open that bottle of Bolly that Sarah and Gary brought over on Boxing Day.

Everything's going to be ok. Last night was just another blip. Like they said in the film The Best Exotic Marigold Hotel, 'Everything will be ok in the end. If it's not ok, it's not the end. ' But actually, I think it was John Lennon who said that first. And for him it really wasn't ok in the end after all.

The shower is bliss. I sit on the floor and let the water run over me. I love that scene in the Bond film where Daniel Craig and Eva Green are sitting on the floor like this in the shower together, fully clothed, and he's being so gentle and nice…which one was that? Casino Royale I think.

My head is thumping. The water is too hot. I stand up and notice that my thighs are bright red and my legs need waxing. Not much like a Bond girl then. I know I've put on weight over the last year or so, I don't know how much, I don't weigh myself, I only know that all my clothes are too tight. Simon still wants to make love to me though, so that's good, I can't look all that bad. Poor Simon, I told him not long ago that he wasn't very imaginative in bed, I think I'd read something in a magazine about sex after years of marriage and I recognised too much of us in it. He was really mad and went to spend the night in the shed again. I guess I could have handled it better.

Sex is over-rated anyway. I've always thought so. And at my age I'm not likely to have a moment of sexual awakening, like Geena Davis did with Brad Pitt in Thelma and Louise, which is one of the saddest films ever.

I hear the front door slam. I think Jack is working at The Olive Tree today, that must be him leaving, without saying goodbye. He works double shifts as soon as he gets back from Edinburgh, he even worked on Christmas Day, though I begged him not to. It's as if he'd rather be there than at home with his family.

I get out of the shower and dry myself on the thick, warm towel. Simon pops his head round the door, he looks so tired, poor thing. It's hard work being married to me.

'I'm going to pick up Jenny,' he says.

'Ok. Take her to Brown's if you can get a table, she won't have eaten properly.' I'm thinking, I don't want them back until much later, that way I can spend the rest of the day in bed. Simon asks me if I'm alright. I tell him I'm fine, give him a kiss on the cheek, the towel wrapped tightly around me because the light is cruel in here and I don't want him to see my red, hairy legs.

When I hear the car start up and pull out of the drive the thought flashes through my mind that I could have a quick glass of wine, just enough to settle me, to get rid of this foggy feeling that I have, but no, I must try to be good, show Jack that he's wrong about me.

I climb in between the sheets and doze off, comforted by the sound of wind and light rain buffeting the window.

I'm woken by the slam of car doors, voices out on the drive. It's dark outside. I look at the clock. Shit. I've slept for three hours. I haul myself out of bed, pull on my 'slouch pants' and an old sweater of Simon's. I hear Jenny chattering away like a starling, as she does. Bless her. She always brings sunshine to the house. My little girl. I have no make-up on and I know my hair is a mess because I slept on it without drying it properly, but who cares. It's only family here tonight.

'Hi Mum,' Jenny squeezes me when I appear in the kitchen, 'I hear you were on it last night!' She grins at me. I wonder what they've told her.

'I'm going to ignore that remark,' I say, aware that Simon doesn't want to look at me. He's filling the kettle. 'Did you have a good time?' I ask Jenny.

'SUCH a good time. The fireworks were AWESOME.' She perches on the table, scrolls through her phone, squinting slightly. She needs reading glasses but is always losing them. She looks like I did when I was her age, skinny, blonde, pretty. I watch her with love. She puts a strand of hair behind her ear, laughs, says, 'Phoebe is such a nutter! Look at this, they went on for ages, it was SO COOL.'

I look at the wobbly video of coloured explosions in a dark sky and say the right things. Simon puts a cup of coffee in front of me, like a statement. I don't need coffee. He also finds a packet of custard creams, my favourites, and puts them on the table. I help myself, the delicious vanilla sweetness is a moment of bliss as I listen to Jenny talking about her night. Soon be time to open the Bolly.

I hear the front door open. Jack is home. He walks in, shrugging off his jacket. I go to hug him. He stiffens but at least he doesn't pull away. 'Here we all are at home together,' I say, stupidly cheerful, 'Simon, why don't you open that Champagne Gary and Sarah brought? It's time to celebrate!' Simon gives Jack a look, as if they have cooked something up between them. Jenny, oblivious, is still playing with her phone.

'There's no booze in the house,' says Jack, staring straight at me, challenging me.

Jenny looks up. 'You what?'

'Me and Dad got rid of it all.'

'We don't need to drink tonight,' says Simon, 'I've got loads of Coke, and that elderflower stuff that you like –'

They are all staring at me. I recognise a feeling of panic in the wings, then something else, anger, boiling and bubbling like lava. My brain works quickly. My nails are digging into my palms. The sweat glands in my armpits prickle.

'Fine!' I say, forcing a smile. Simon looks instantly relieved but Jack is stony faced. He doesn't trust me.

How dare they treat me like a child. All I wanted was a couple of glasses of Champagne. It's New Year's Day, and we are all gathered together as a family, it doesn't happen very often, it's worthy of a celebration.

Jenny looks puzzled. 'You threw out all the booze?' she asks. 'Bit harsh.'

'No, it's fine,' I say, 'totally unnecessary, but fine.' Already I know what I'm going to do. I will outwit them, not because I'm so desperate that I can't go for twenty-four hours without a drink, but because I refuse to be patronised like this. It's a fucking outrage.

It takes a colossal effort to be civil, but I realise it's in my best interests to go along with this ridiculousness. I ask Jack if it was busy in The Olive Tree, if there was anyone we know in there, just by way of conversation. He's moody and monosyllabic. Jenny says she's not hungry, they had pasta and salad in Brown's, but Simon is determined to create a happy family occasion. He finds some vol au vents in the freezer, some mince pies, smoked salmon and various half eaten blocks of cheese, and goes about arranging them on to plates as if we're having a party. He even digs out a few crackers left over from Christmas Day. I don't remember having those.

The tins of Coke on the table are laughing at me. I'm a big fat grown-up child at a tea party. Jenny's endless chatter and choice of music lightens the atmosphere, and I'm so grateful to her, for her joy and her naiveté, but most of all for her lack of interest in alcohol, which means that the half bottle of Marks and Spencer's Champagne with chocolate truffles (a Christmas present from a hopeful admirer) will still be in the wardrobe of her bedroom - If Jack and Simon haven't got to it first.

Who's a clever girl then.

Why, you are, Araminta Morgan.

I wait for a while to allay suspicion. Then I exit like this:

'Why don't we play that Kingsmead Monopoly that Jenny bought us for Christmas? I'll go and get it!' I go to the door with something like a skip. Treat me like a child and I'll behave like one.

'Let's not.' Jack spears a vol au vent with his fork.

'Good idea!' Poor Simon.

'Shotgun I get the boot,' says Jenny.

'Don't eat that last mince pie!' I call as I leave the room, as if I care.

I run up the stairs. My heart is thumping hard, partly because I'm so unfit and partly because I'm being devious and don't want to get caught. Also, I admit, because I'm afraid the Champagne won't be there.

At the top of the stairs I tiptoe towards Jenny's room. I love it here. Her window overlooks the back garden and in the summer the room is flooded with light. There's a tiny Victorian fireplace stuffed with fairy lights, a big, fluffy, pink rug on the floor, hundreds of pictures and photos on the walls, many of them are team photos of the Kingsmead School netball A team. Her double bed looks so cosy with its Kath Kidston covers and cuddly toys still held on to from her childhood.

I go to her pine wardrobe, the one Simon and I bought for our bedroom in our first flat. Pine was all the rage then, everything in the bloody flat was made of pine. The wardrobe reminds me of our first years together. I know every crack and knot, and recognise the slight honey smell of the resin.

I open the door and squat on the floor, pull out one of the wicker storage baskets and see it immediately. It's a small but significant thrill. The room is in semi-darkness, lit only from the light on the landing. I can hear their voices downstairs.

The cellophane box is impossible to open. I look around for something sharp, grab the nail scissors on the bedside table and start hacking at the infuriating plastic with its pink sparkly bow. It tears suddenly and the chocolate truffles fall out, tumbling onto the wooden floorboards. I pull out the bottle, tear the foil, twist the wire free from the cork. I hear Jenny's laughter and I panic. I squeeze the cork tightly in my hand, easing it out of the neck of the bottle, and with a sigh it comes free.

Like someone lost in the desert I guzzle the fizzy, sweet liquid until I choke, bubbles popping in my nose. Coughing, I pick up the truffles, gather the bits of ribbon and card, the cork and the cellophane, tuck the bottle under my arm – where can I hide this? Back of my wardrobe.

I continue to drink and splutter as I make my way back across the landing and into my room, where I stash all the evidence behind the hat boxes at the bottom of my built-in wardrobe. I lean against the wall and drain the bottle, surprised at how little there is. But it's enough, it's enough. I feel elated. The fizz inside me is dancing.

I go quickly back to the stairs but then remember I don't have the board game. Silly me, nearly gave myself away. I fetch the game from the spare room, where lots of other Christmas gifts are stacked, waiting to be put away, a box of shoes, books, a scarf, the usual assortment of scented candles.

Guilt and Shame are watching me from the shadows as I go back down the stairs with the Kingsmead Monopoly under my arm. I ignore them.

'Here it is!' I say, going to the table and opening the box.

Anyone looking at us now would think we were just an ordinary, happy family.

2. Sarah

Secrets, Sex and Sadness

Gary and I are out on our early morning run, our breath billowing in the cold air, our brand new trainers (Christmas presents to each other) springing off the damp pavement, when I see a familiar Porsche Cayenne turning the corner ahead of us.

'Isn't that Araminta?' I ask, just as it disappears from view.

'I doubt it,' snorts Gary, 'she'll still be in bed sleeping off her hangover.'

'I could have sworn it was her car.'

'Maybe it was Simon, going to pick up one of the kids from somewhere.' Gary checks the pedometer on his wrist.

'Maybe,' I say. But I know Jack is at home. I know because he has texted me in the early hours of this morning. He was working late at The Olive Tree last night and had to scoop up his drunken mother from outside The Cross Keys on his way home. I also know that Jack's sister, Jenny, is staying with her friend in Cambridge. I don't say any of this of course. I would have to explain how I know. There are many things I don't say any more.

Araminta's an embarrassment to Jack. I wish I could take her in hand, get her off the booze, introduce a fitness routine and shift those extra pounds she carries. Jack doesn't know that she smokes when he's not around, and I'm not going to tell him. I know the rules, it's ok to moan about your own mother but when someone else joins in…it's different. I have secrets from Gary and secrets from Jack. Knowledge is power.

We avoid a puddle, he going round one way and me the other.

'How's your knee?' I ask him, wanting to change the subject from Araminta's 'kids'.

'Not too bad.' Gary is puffing out his cheeks on every breath. He looks like a pufferfish. Or a toad. He's very good looking, and knows it, but when he pulls those faces it turns me off. He'd hate it if I told him that. He worries about the age gap between us - he's fifty one, I'm thirty two - and he works hard to keep that gap as narrow as he can. He overdoes it sometimes. That's why his knee has flared up again. The pain slows him down and makes him short tempered. I've no patience with him when he's like this. I'm different with Jack. He broke his finger playing football last week and I was all sympathy. He's so delicious.

'Minty was so wrecked last night,' Gary says, in between puffs. Everyone but me calls her Minty. 'I don't know how Simon puts up with her.'

I say nothing. Araminta's drinking is often a subject for discussion between us. Gary's friendship with Simon goes back a long way. It's complicated for me now, with all this business between me and Jack. I know it's a dangerous game I'm playing, but I'm in control, and nothing has happened. Not yet.

We run past The Cross Keys, which is closed up, lights off, all evidence of New Year's Eve revelry cleared away from the tables outside. We left early last night. We don't drink and it's no fun being surrounded by drunks when you could be at home watching Jools Holland on telly. Plus, we always get up early to run, five miles usually, depending on whether we're in training for a biathlon. We need our run in the morning like other people need their caffeine.

Araminta's an alcoholic. There, I've said it. Everyone knows she drinks too much but nobody talks about it like it's a bad thing. Quite the opposite in fact, she's very popular. I looked at her last night, singing and shouting and making an exhibition of herself as usual and I thought, you don't deserve your beautiful children and your long-suffering husband. When I think of all that I went through trying to get pregnant, all the failed IVF, the ruined hope…and Araminta gets everything she wants, just like that, without any effort. She doesn't appreciate her good fortune. I know she had a miscarriage when Jenny and Jack were teenagers but I don't think it affected her much. It was probably the drink that caused it anyway.

We run past the little railway station with has just had a refurb and looks very quaint. There's a train that runs direct to St Pancras from here now, it doesn't go very often but I use it when I can. I go to London regularly, usually for work meetings but also to have my hair done and visit friends and family. The hanging baskets of winter pansies at the station are an impressive effort. I check my watch. We're bang on target. Pretty good considering Gary's bad knee.

We run in silence for a while and my mind moves on to the week ahead. I'm going back to work tomorrow, I've got a hundred and one things to do and I'm keen to get on. I'm glad Jack is going back to Edinburgh. Although I love the thrill of his attention he's a distraction I could do without. My feet pound the ground in synchronised rhythm with Gary's. It's the only time when I feel in complete harmony with him.

I look down the lane towards the allotments and notice the Porsche Cayenne pulled up on the kerb. I can see the number plate from here so there's no doubt that it's Araminta's car. Something's not right.

'Look,' I tap Gary's arm, point to the car, 'Do you think we should go and investigate?'

Gary stops running and checks his pedometer again, making a show of the fact that I've interrupted the training. He puts his hands on his hips. I used to think he looked sexy when he stood like that.

'Simon's got an allotment with a man-shed,' he says, shrugging, his breath fogging in the cold air.

'I know, but what would either of them be doing there at quarter past eight on New Year's Day?'

'Maybe Simon's come down for a bit of peace.' He restarts his pedometer and runs off.

I don't get it. I'm sure it was Araminta driving, and she was alone. Maybe I'm wrong, maybe it was Simon. It all seems mighty odd to me.

'Simon's murdered Araminta and now he's going to bury the body parts amongst the potatoes,' I shout to Gary's retreating form. He laughs, not turning round. I hesitate when a black cat appears from under a hedge, but it takes one look at me and fortunately darts back into the undergrowth without crossing my path. Phew. Close one. I run on.

When we get home Gary goes up to take a shower and I check my phone while Bruce and Sheila, my Siamese cats, mew and rub themselves against my puddle-splashed ankles. There are two more messages from Jack. He's going back to Edinburgh tomorrow and wants to see me before he leaves. I tell him it's not possible. He answers straight away, pleading. I feel like something is falling inside me, a hot liquid sensation from my neck through my stomach and into my loins. I can hear the shower running upstairs, the radio playing, the background noise of my husband and my conscience. I reply ok, I'll see if I can get away tomorrow lunchtime, push my meeting back, see him for ten minutes before he leaves.

He says thank you and then sends a row of emojis, hearts, flowers, winky smileys.

I delete the messages, lock my phone and get myself a glass of water, staring out of the kitchen window at the drab, damp garden which looks so neat and pretty in the summer. A single magpie lands on the lawn and I look anxiously for his mate. When none appears I salute him. 'Aye, aye, Cap'n.'

I can feel the warmth of the underfloor heating and I'm looking forward to a relaxing soak in our Jacuzzi bath. Jack's texts always make me jittery, like a shot of adrenalin. He has no idea of the effect he has on me. I'm completely in control of my life but when it comes to sex…It's my only weakness. That's why I have to be so careful. I don't want to be controlled by anything or anyone, not anymore. I'm through with all that. I was controlled by the desperate need for a child once, it completely took me over, it nearly ruined me, but after the seventh miscarriage I made up my mind. No more. It's done. So I won't allow this to take me over. As I said, I'm in control.

Gary comes into the kitchen, naked but for a tiny towel round his waist, his skin damp. He loves his body, he's in good shape for his age, but I look away because my head is full of Jack right now.

It never used to be like this. Our relationship was founded on sex and for years it was hot, hot, hot. It was all the trying for a baby that killed it for me. Sex was no longer reckless fun, it was something serious, and it was something that was failing us.

'I've just had a call from Bertie,' he says, giving Bruce a shove off the leather armchair. 'He wanted to know if we can join them and the Dixons for lunch today at The Olive Tree, one o'clock. They had someone drop out.'

'Charming as ever.'

'And he's paying. So obviously I said yes.'

'Fine.' I'm glad he can't see my face. Jack's working there today and I'm quivering with anticipation at the thought of surprising him. I know exactly what I'm going to wear.

I always thought I'd live in a city. I grew up in London and took a degree in law at Cambridge University. Yes, exams came easily to me but I worked hard too. I pursued a good time with the same ruthless ambition and had as much sex as I wanted when I was a student. I have a strong libido and I'm attractive. I'm slim waisted with large, nicely shaped boobs and thick, dark hair. I tan easily, I've never been fat, I have perfect teeth, green eyes and nicely shaped brows. My parents weren't short of money so I always had nice things to wear, even when I was at Uni. I get on alright here because I talk with the right accent and dress expensively. Kingsmead is a stuffy, parochial town, they pretend to embrace outsiders as 'refreshing' but it's all part of the bullshit. You have to fit in or you're screwed.

I met Gary when I was working for a law firm with a swanky office in Cambridge. My boss was handling his bitter divorce. The sexual chemistry between us was instant and lethal. I thought, he's on the rebound, this won't last, but we totally fell in love, and the age gap only made us feel sexier. It was crazy, how we were. I look back on those days now with wonder. What happened?

Gary's wife took what she could from him but he managed to keep his business going. It's called The Wellington Boot Company (fancy wellies, individual designs, modern and funky, not the flowery crap you see everywhere) and it's doing ok. It's not cheap to live here, but everything is easily accessible, good schools, countryside, close to London…Oh

God, listen to me, I sound like a sales pitch for one of John Dixon's new houses.

We live in one of them. Built to a high spec, four bedrooms, three ensuites, a small but pretty garden, double garage, electric gates, built with local stone and slate and quality fittings, personally designed kitchen, oak doors, all of that. We bought it on a massive mortgage thinking that eventually we'd have lots of children to fill those rooms.

Now here we are, six years later, still not married (the ex put him off all that) and still no children. Just us. And the cats. We have pots of money, three empty bedrooms, and an obsession with biathlons. Does that sound sad?

As I undress I catch sight of myself in the mirror. I often imagine other men looking at me, lusting after me. I do have a beautiful body.

I think of Jack.

I feel wired when we arrive at The Olive Tree, as if I'm on a first date, despite the fact that Gary is with me. I'm wearing a green, silk wrap-over dress, it's divine, it feels like cream against my skin, my boobs look fantastic in it. It falls just below the knee, flattering my shapely calves and skinny ankles. It's just started to rain so I trot quickly in my heels across the gravel car park, avoiding too many wet spots on the silk.

The Olive Tree is rammed as usual. It's owned by a middle-aged gay couple, camp as anything (very modern for Kingsmead) who greet everyone by name and remember favourite drinks and tables. They're so charming and brilliant at it. They're raking it in.

Bertie Hambleton and his wife, Sally, are at the bar and we make our way over through the crowded tables. We see familiar faces, and although I feel eyes following me with interest I pretend not to notice. I'm looking forward to the thrill of seeing Jack, surprising him. Bertie greets us loudly and tries to kiss me on the mouth, as he always does, the dirty old goat, but I'm ever ready for this and turn my head. Sally and I greet with air kisses and exchange the obligatory compliments. She's dressed in the usual country clobber, it's a uniform round here, cashmere sweater, boring jeans, comfortable leather shoes with tassels. I see Jack over her shoulder, emerging from the kitchen with plates of food, just as I am telling her how much I love her ear-rings, 'a Christmas present from Bertie,' she tells me, dead chuffed that I've noticed them. When Jack catches sight of me his expression changes. We exchange a fleeting look. I'm going to enjoy myself this afternoon. He's going back to Edinburgh tomorrow after all. I may as well have some fun. It's only a game, and I'm totally in charge.

I think Sally recognises my sexual greed, even though she looks like she's never had a good shag in her life (the thought of sleeping with Bertie…Oh my), and it makes her nervous. I wish there was some way of making it clear to her, without being offensive, that if I were to steal anyone's husband (which as yet I have no plans to do) it certainly wouldn't be hers. I win her round by paying her lots of attention. She's alright really, just a bit dull, and I don't suppose she can help that.

Bertie, as usual, is dressed in bright, mismatched clothes, a yellow shirt, straining over his gut like muslin over a Christmas pudding, and trousers of an indeterminate red/orange/tan colour. He has the essential brown brogues on his little feet, a classic watch on his fat wrist as well as a plastic charity wristband to show how on-trend he is. He is so blond that what's left of his hair looks like spun candy and when he drinks his cheeks go red. On the plus side he always smells nice and his clothes are well-made, expensive if badly fitting, so he is at least making an effort not to look too revolting. Everyone knows Bertie, the go-to estate agent, and Bertie knows everyone worth knowing and is first to dish the gossip. It's amazing how much he knows, and he always knows it first. If you have a secret, best keep it tight.

He tells me I look ravishing, I thank him sweetly and Gary looks at me appreciatively. I see Jack going back into the kitchen, his body language tense and angry, and I long to speak to him alone.

Bertie hates it that Gary and I don't drink and he tries to convert us every chance he gets. Sally is slowly sipping her way through a glass of Champagne and tells Bertie to 'stop being a bully'. Gary orders two lime and sodas, Jack re-appears and I give him the smallest of smiles. He catches it and moves on.

Let me explain how it is between me and Jack.

Jack turned up at my office one day last summer, asking for advice about a career in law. 'Mum said I should talk to you,' he said, sitting awkwardly in the chair in front of my desk, 'I wondered if maybe I could shadow you for a while, see what it's like.' I was charmed by his looks and his public school polish, I couldn't believe how much he'd grown up. It had been several months since I'd seen him last and to me he had always just been Araminta's son, another ex-Kingsmeadian in the same old Abercrombie & Fitch/Hollister/Jack Wills get up. That day in my office though, on my patch, with him looking cute and dressed up (he was wearing a suit and looked devilish handsome and at least five years older than he really was) I saw him differently. I remember noticing the delicious smell of him left behind after he'd gone, and for a while I swivelled slowly in my chair, thrilled by something I hadn't felt for a while, thinking how nice it would be on a dull day to have Jack around.

And it was. He surprised me with his keen, intelligent interest, both in my job and in me. I quickly sensed he was attracted to me and I was flattered, I'm a good ten years older than him after all, and I flirted with him gently. I just wanted to make him a little nervous, not scare him to death.

In between appointments we had lunch together. Usually I have something light in Kate's Tea Room if I'm in town, but I took Jack to pubs in nearby villages and we soon starting sharing confidences. He told me about Araminta's drinking and how worried he was, and I told him about the damage done to my relationship with Gary by all the years of failed IVF. He listened. He looked like he cared. It was strange that I could talk to him in a way I hadn't been able to talk to anyone else. He assumed that Gary and I were on the rocks and I didn't put him right. I'm not sure why.

I hated it if someone we knew saw us and interrupted us. 'Jack is thinking of taking up a career in law,' I would explain to any nosy gossiper who wanted to know what we were doing together, and Jack would back me up and talk charmingly to them about his options on leaving Uni; but soon it started to sound like a lie, as if it were a cover for something else, something as yet unspoken.

It was only ever a two-week arrangement. It wasn't practical for me to work with Jack constantly in tow and he wanted to get back to working full-time at The Olive Tree. When we parted on his last day I went to give him a kiss on the cheek, a kind of good luck gesture, but to my surprise he held me there in an embrace that was sensual beyond his years and surely beyond his experience. It took my breath away, and when he went to kiss me on the mouth I couldn't resist him.

His mouth was delicious, soft and strong, it was a confident kiss full of restrained desire and it set me on fire.

I needed to come up for air and some common sense, we were in my office and my business partner, Heather, doesn't wait after a knock to come barging in. Jack apologised profusely, running his hand through his hair, he looked as shocked by the kiss as I was, but I just said something about having to forget this happened, it was nothing. It was incredibly arousing though. Obviously it couldn't go any further. I'm trying to hold on to a damaged relationship with Gary, and Jack is the son of friends, two very good reasons to take back control and knock it on the head.

So the summer passed, he texted me a few times but I didn't reply, and eventually he went back to Edinburgh. I thought nothing more of it. Then one day he called me, it was a wet, cold, Monday morning some time in November and said he was feeling low. He said he'd messed up some exam, and on top of that he was worrying about Araminta. He said he was sure she was going to drink herself to death. We talked for an hour and I agreed to meet him later in the week for lunch, I suggested Leeds because it was half way between us and easy on the train, so we met like star-crossed lovers and spent three and half hours talking at a small table in a nice restaurant where nobody knew us.

We held hands. We briefly kissed. I told him he was gorgeous but that there was no way we could have any sort of relationship other than friends. He looked downcast but said he understood. He told me he had an on/off relationship with some girl called Maddie and my furious jealousy took me by surprise. We parted like friends but there was a charge between us that we both knew was dangerous.

Sometimes I dreamed about him at night. I would wake up next to Gary, drenched in desire, but I wouldn't wake him for sex, I wanted to keep it to myself. Silently my fingers drew the shuddering, agonising longing out of me. My attraction to Jack was powerful but I still wasn't worried. I was in control.

I knew he would come home for Christmas and I looked forward to it. It was nothing more than an amusement. A bit of fun. He texted me the minute he got back. Light hearted, funny texts, but they soon turned into something different and I told him off. 'Naughty boy', I would say, 'Go away' or 'Leave me alone', 'Stop teasing me' and even 'How's your Mum?', thinking, that will do it, mention the Mum and it's like a bucket of cold water in the face.

I'm still in control. It won't go any further and it won't last.

So that's how it is between me and Jack.

For the moment.

John and Shona Dixon arrive, looking more like father and daughter than ever. Shona is wearing a tiny, sequinned black dress with a feather trim. She must be freezing. John is filthy rich and tiny, five foot five at the most. He's hard as nails and ruthless. Last summer he left his wife of twenty-five years and married Shona, who is the same age as his daughter. I wonder if John struggles to keep up with her, she appears to have a lot of energy, but he looks fit, like a flyweight boxer, his eyes are beady and alert, he has a nasty gold watch on his wrist and a diamond stud in one ear.

Bertie is all over him, pouring him Champagne and ordering another bottle. John is Bertie's best customer you see, because every time a Dixon's housing estate goes up somewhere, Hambleton's gets the job of selling them.

Shona greets us all enthusiastically with air kisses. She smells strongly of Opium perfume, cigarettes and booze. Her long, white-blonde hair gets caught temporarily in my earring and we untangle ourselves while Bertie looks on.

'I love seeing two pretty girls getting close,' he says, his eyes shining on us like torches. Shona, free at last, slaps Bertie on the arm and calls him a devil. She's a sexy little thing; I could almost fancy her myself. I imagine her and John having sex, the older man and the young siren. John's ex-wife Carol is in bits since he left her.

The men are soon talking business. John is celebrating the fact that his piece of land on the edge of Cambridge has just been granted planning permission for a development of ten Dixon homes. More millions for him then, and more business coming Bertie's way. The Champagne is going down easily. But not with us. We see the changes. I would never drink. It makes you lose yourself.

Shona asks me and Sally if we had a nice Christmas.

'It was lovely, yes, thank you,' says Sally, who is still Carol's best friend so it must be hard for her to be civil to Shona, but Sally is like that, a proper lady, she never puts a foot wrong. It makes up for the god-awful behaviour of her husband. 'What about you?' she asks the marriage-wrecker, 'Did you have a nice Christmas?'

'Oh, it was great,' Shona says, knocking back the Champagne, 'we went to Johnny's villa in Florida, it's *fabulous*, everything in it is white, and I mean *everything....*'

'I know,' says Sally, fidgeting with her glass, 'we've been. John and Carol invited us over last Christmas. You're right it is lovely. Very lovely.' Good for you, Sal. Stick it in. Shona, the pro, carries on as if Carol's name has never been mentioned, as if she doesn't even exist.

'We went to Disney World,' she says, her smoothly made-up face lighting up at the memory, 'have you ever done Disney?' We both say we haven't, and she tells us all about it while I sip my lime and soda and cast my gaze around the room, hoping for another glimpse of Jack. Gary is talking sport and Bertie is shaking his head at him.

'All that exercise is bad for you,' he says, emptying his glass and looking around for the bottle.

'I've got Shona to keep me fit,' says John.

'You talking about me, Johnny?' Shona slips her arm though his and I catch Gary appraising her enticing cleavage.

'Do you think our table is ready?' asks Sally, looking for a waiter, clearly wanting to avert any danger that the conversation might turn to John and Shona's hot sex life. 'Excuse me, is our table ready?' I didn't notice Jack behind me, and Sally has collared him. 'Oh, Jack! It's you!' she says.

'Hiya,' Jack says, not looking at me, but I see the colour rise ever so slightly in his lovely ears. 'Your table is the one in the window. I'll bring the Champagne over for you.'

The temptation to touch him almost overwhelms me.

'Poor kid,' mutters Bertie when Jack is out of earshot and we're seated at our table.

'What do you mean?' I ask, a little too quickly.

'His mother has a problem holding her drink, as I'm sure you know. Jack had to peel her off the road last night -'

'As usual,' says Gary, rolling his eyes.

'Apparently she pissed herself in the street,' says Shona, wrinkling up her pretty nose. Like *she's* such a lady. Bertie is about to say something else but everyone falls silent as Jack comes back with seeded bread and a pot of herb butter on a black slate. I just want to take him away and smother him with kisses. And the rest. Poor Jack. I try in vain to catch his eye before he disappears again.

'The demon alcohol,' says Gary, looking smug as he pours sparkling water into his glass.

I excuse myself and head towards the ladies, my heels clicking on the quarry tiled floor. Jack appears suddenly, his hands full of wine glasses.

'Nice surprise,' he says in my ear as he passes. He doesn't look happy and I put my hand out to touch him on the arm but he moves quickly away.

There's expensive soap and hand moisturiser in the ladies, I love it, I help myself liberally, washing my hands in the big basin and drying them on one of the fluffy white flannels from the pile on the window sill, before chucking it in the wicker basket. I check my face with a sigh. Yes, I look good, but what's the use? For the hundredth time I wonder what my children would have looked like, those seven children I lost when they were just beginning on their journey of life. I imagine pretty little girls, sassy or shy, clever or maddening, chunky, sporty or skinny, and boys with cheeky smiles, boys who maybe had my green eyes, my long limbs or Gary's big feet, boys who would grow up to have girlfriends, drive cars, go to university.

None of them exist. They never will. I look at my face. It all stops here.

I walked in to this place buzzing, and now I feel like crap. I want to march into that kitchen and steal Jack away for a night of total sexual abandonment.

I pull myself together.

Back at the table Gary puts his hand over mine.

'You ok?' he asks. I nod, smiling.

Sally asks me where I got my dress from. 'It's beautiful,' she says, 'although I could never wear something like that.'

'Why not?' I say, 'you have a lovely figure.'

She blushes, which is sweet, and protests, saying she's all skin and bone and doesn't have nice curves like me. Bertie perks up at the mention of nice curves and give me a wink, as if we're in on something together. He is beyond gross. Poor Sally.

Shona is telling us the story of the dress she is wearing, which John bought her for Christmas. Apparently she'd pointed it out to him in a magazine ('I wasn't dropping hints, no really, I wasn't!') and we are all asked to imagine her surprise when she opened it on Christmas morning. 'Isn't that just the most romantic thing *ever*?' she coos. We all agree that it is, but Sally is spreading herb butter on a tiny piece of bread and I wonder that she doesn't get up and bop Shona on the nose. ('This one's for Carol!')

As we eat our starters John and Bertie talk about the entrance exam to Kingsmead School.

'My nephew is sitting it next week,' says John.

'Good luck to him,' says Bertie, pulling a peculiar face as if he has something stuck in his teeth, 'we were nervous as hell when ours went through all that. Tense times.'

John shrugged and poured himself some more wine. 'I've no cause to be nervous,' he says, 'my nephew will get in alright.'

'Oh? Clever boy is he?' I sense some indignation in Bertie at the implication that nerves are only for the parents of dunces.

John grins. 'We'll see,' he says.

I'm ok with talking about other people's children. I listen to Bertie and Sally boasting about their kids' successes,

33

they have two teenagers at Kingsmead who are brilliant at everything. I know far more people with children than I do without, so it's just something I've learnt to live with, it's part of life. It's the pregnancies and the babies that get to me. It's as if I've had something stolen from me and no-one has been brought to justice.

Unless you've been through IVF you won't understand the pain and the stress it causes. It made me ill, both physically and mentally. It drove me and Gary apart, at a time when we should have been the closest, because we needed to support each other. I was a bitch to him, and he withdrew. I think that's when the obsession with running and biathlons started. He had to immerse himself in something in order to escape all the crap in our house, and the prospect of a future without children.

We considered adoption, but I don't think I could commit myself to a child that wasn't our own. Plus, you're never quite sure where they've come from, if you know what I mean. We agreed on that at least.

It's two years now since the last failed attempt and our decision to give up. I should have got used to it, accepted that I'll never be a mother, but I can't. I still have some weird innate belief that some miracle will happen. I haven't told Gary this. He thinks I'm fine. I overheard him telling his parents how 'amazingly brave and pragmatic' I am. He has no idea what goes through my head and I won't tell him. I feel more remote from him now than I have ever done. Maybe that's why Jack has got to me. It's like Gary's left the room and Jack's walked in.

Bertie and Shona are getting drunk.

'I went to the school of life,' says Shona, pleased with herself, as if no-one's ever heard that expression before.

'Excellent establishment,' says Bertie, and Shona laughs.

'I think University's a waste of money,' she says, 'unless you're going to be a doctor or something, or a lawyer,' she looks at me coldly, like she doesn't want to give me any credit.

Jack appears and begins to clear the tables. I catch the faintest whiff of his familiar, gorgeous smell and watch his back as he leaves, carrying our plates to the kitchen.

It's too hot in here. There's a log fire crackling in the grate, every table is full, the conversation is loud and lively and the staff move hectically here and there. A different waiter brings our main course, and I wonder if Jack's contrived a way out of serving our table.

Gary is talking about Simon's allotment because John had his eye on the land for development.

'He loves it down there,' says Gary, 'he says it keeps him sane.'

'I don't get it,' says John, 'they're an eyesore.'

'I agree,' chips in Shona, 'why go to all that bother growing potatoes and stuff when you've got a Waitrose in the town. Tide's out, Johnny.' She waves her empty glass in the direction of the wine bottle.

'I don't think it's about growing stuff,' says Gary, 'not for Simon anyway. He's got plenty of room to grow vegetables in his garden. He goes to the shed to escape. He spends the night in it sometimes.'

'Is that legal?' asks Sally.

'Escape what?' asks Shona.

'Poor chap,' says Bertie, looking genuinely sympathetic.

'You're so *posh*, Bertie,' giggles Shona. 'I love the way you talk. *'Poor chap...'*

I take another trip to the ladies just to cool down, but a text comes through from Jack and it floors me.

What time/ where? x

I reply, giving him a time and place tomorrow. It's crazy. But I go back to the table feeling elated.

I make small talk with Sally. I'm sure that everyone around this table would be shocked if they knew how I was carrying on with Jack, not that anything's happened, not really, only that one kiss, a few texts and phone calls. It's nothing.

I know I have to draw a line under all this crap, get Jack out of my head, and then I can go back to working on my relationship with Gary, and a life without complications.

The thought of it drains me. I look at Gary and I'm sad. We just assumed that life was going to be perfect for us. I have no idea where, when or how we got to this impasse, this dead relationship.

Sally is talking about her cleaner, Jules, who works for me too, and everyone else it seems. Good cleaners are in such short supply that they're often the topic of heated debate. I join in with my experiences, I'm sure I've told all these dull stories before, to someone else, at some other time. Shona glazes over, Bertie tops up the wine, Gary gets up to go to the loo and me, I just wish I was somewhere else.

3. Bridie

Angels

Ah, what bliss.

I am lying under a tree in the park with my eyes closed, listening to the birds and enjoying the breeze on my face. It's unseasonably warm for April and the park is full of daffodils. I open my eyes to squint at Martha in her pushchair, still fast asleep with a grumpy expression on her face. She looks so adorable! She's wearing the red dress that Mum bought her for Christmas, purple tights and her new red shoes. Her little fat legs are splayed out and her beaker is clutched in her hand. Poor Martha, she's teething, one of her cheeks is bright red. We're not getting much sleep at the moment. Now where's that daft dog of mine? There he is. Heading straight for the stream as usual. That's the trouble with children and dogs, you can never totally relax.

I know I shouldn't say it, but I breathed a sigh of relief this morning when I dropped the other five off at school. They've just had two weeks off for Easter and what with Martha's teething and then all the chickenpox I have to confess it's been challenging, even with a GP as a husband. I've left the kitchen in a total mess but hey-ho, 'third world problems', as Jeremy would say. I give a silent prayer of thanks for my lot. This is such bliss, to have a little moment to myself....

'Bridie!'

I jump out of my skin. Sarah Simpson is standing there in head to toe Lycra, wired up to some sort of gadget attached to her arm. 'Doing a spot of sunbathing are we?' She's panting, resting her hands on her hips. She does look amazing. I feel really dumpy under her gaze.

'Just grabbing some 'me' time!' I smile up at her, shielding my eyes from the sun.

'Isn't the grass a bit damp?'

'Only a bit.'

She looks at Martha, who is still asleep, exhausted after her school-run screaming session. Sarah went through years of IVF and it makes me feel guilty for having so many babies so easily. 'Are you going to the ladies' night on the 30th?' she asks, doing some leg stretches.

I have no idea what she's talking about and I really haven't thought that far ahead but I don't want to sound simple so I say that I'm sure I can make it while at the same time noticing that Wes, our stupid black Lab, is hurtling towards Sarah dripping wet and carrying an enormous stick in his mouth. She turns round just in time and gives a shriek of surprise as Wes drops the stick at her feet and shakes himself vigorously, spraying her. I scold him half-heartedly for Sarah's benefit, while suppressing my giggles.

'Sorry!'

'No problem,' but she is rubbing the muddy splashes off her legs, making a show of it. She wouldn't last two minutes in our house. We exchange a friendly good-bye and off she goes, with her bouncy ponytail, I feel exhausted just watching her.

Martha stirs sleepily and for a moment looks startled at her surroundings, then she sees me and her face relaxes into a smile. 'Hello, my angel,' I say. Gorgeous, gorgeous girl. I am so blessed. I yawn, stretch and stand up.

'Right, come on Wes, you horrible wet dog, let's go.'

We walk home, a rag-tag trio.

I love this town. We can't afford to send our children to Kingsmead school (Jeremy may be a GP but I don't have any earnings and we have six children), but they'll do alright, more than alright, at the Catholic Grammar School in Cambridge. I'm not ambitious in the way lots of the mothers are around here. Maybe it has something to do with Daniel, my little brother, who was a star, brilliant at everything, but was killed instantly when he fell from a tree aged just thirteen. It changed us all. I watch my children too closely I know, I can't help it. I hope Daniel and our guardian angels are watching over us, but all the same, the fear hasn't left me. Whenever I hear a siren my blood runs cold. I always think it's one of mine.

I have to take a breath now.

The facilities at Kingsmead School are amazing though - immaculate cricket pitch, enormous indoor pool, well-equipped gym, theatre, library, beautiful assembly hall, ancient chapel, tennis courts and rugby pitches, plus boarding houses that look like hotels. Jack and Jenny Morgan (Minty's children) both went there. They babysit for us sometimes and the children adore them, they're so lovely.

All I want for my children is for them to be happy, safe, healthy and *nice,* and have lots of friends. Mind you, if they are also very clever and earning pots of money that would be a bonus for me and Jeremy in our old age!

So there's the school, and there's the park, where I try to go every day to walk our stupid black Lab, Wes. The park is lovely, you always see someone you know, like I did today, Sarah Simpson, putting me to shame with all that energy she has.

The High Street is sweet, with lots of privately owned businesses, like Minty's beauty parlour and Kate's Tea Rooms, plus some nice but expensive gift shops, like Kirsty's, great for birthdays and Christmas etc. If you want more choice you have to go in to Cambridge.

The Catholic Church is across the road from Kingsmead School's tennis courts, and is where I drag my little angels to Mass every Sunday. I grew up in a village in a County Clare and have fond memories of tedious Masses with my family. I believe that giving your child a faith is part of their all-round education, like making them clean their teeth or being careful on the road. My middle son, Patrick, is preparing for his first Holy Communion right now but he's not taking it very seriously. He says it's cannibalism. He's a bit of smarty pants is Patrick and a handful for the teachers, but he's a softie underneath.

The Cross Keys pub is at the bottom of the High Street, it's nice enough, but on special occasions Jeremy and I will go to The Olive Tree for a meal. It's the best place around her, but a bit pretentious. Jeremy says you shouldn't have to ask for a translation of the menu in an English restaurant!

Jeremy and I came here from Newcastle, which is where we met as students. He is much, much cleverer than me, I fell in love with his brain before I noticed his lovely knobbly knees and his skinny white chest! I dropped out after my first year, wasn't up to it, but I stayed in Newcastle so I could be with him, I got a job in the toy department in John Lewis which I loved but when Jeremy finally qualified we knew we wanted to get married and live in the country with lots of children.

So here we are. We took out a massive mortgage (Jeremy's Dad chipped in) on a big end-terrace house five minutes from the town centre, it's the perfect family home and we couldn't be happier. It was also a wise investment I think, as there are only eight houses in this row and Bertie Hambleton is always telling us that if we ever decide to sell he's got a whole list of people who would fight over it. It's very shabby our home, there's always something that needs attention, a leaky tap, a dead bulb, a loose door knob, scribbled on walls, a wailing child! All the rugs downstairs are shredded round the edges where Wes chewed on them as a puppy, and his dirty scratch marks are on the doors. I try, I work really hard, but sometimes I feel like King Canute, trying to hold back the tide. I have a brilliant cleaner, Jules, who comes once a week, she works for practically everyone around here, I don't know how she fits us all in.

The garden is long and narrow, overlooked by the neighbours' upstairs windows but pretty nevertheless, with an apple tree and a broken greenhouse and enough lawn for picnics and a paddling pool.

So this is where I live, this is our home, and this is where I belong. I am lucky. I wouldn't swap my life with anyone.

I've got an appointment with Minty in her Beauty Parlour at eleven (a manicure, a gift voucher from Jeremy for my birthday, which was sweet of him, but I can't help thinking it's wasted on my hands) so I have about an hour to clear up.

Upstairs in our bedroom I pick up Jeremy's book from the floor and put it on his bedside table - Death Comes To Pemberley by P D James, a second hand copy he bought from a charity shop. Funny old Jeremy, he spends his days trying to keep people alive and healthy but at night he likes nothing better than to lose himself in a good murder mystery!

As I work I keep an ear out for Martha. I know she's perfectly safe in her play pen but my maternal instincts kick in when leave her there and my hearing is super sharp. She's being as good as gold now, bless her, the Calpol's kicked in I guess.

It's quarter to eleven by the time we're ready to leave the house again. Wes looks at me with reproach when I chuck him a Denta-Stick and tell him we won't be long.

The earlier sunshine is veiled by a layer of thin, grey cloud, but the birds are singing, and there's a feeling of summer waiting in the wings. It's going to be a good day. Our road is lined with lime trees that have just been pollarded. They look offended by it, like they've been given a bad hair-cut they didn't ask for.

As we make our way towards the town centre I think of my youngest boy, Patrick, who's got a wart on his knee and was worried that the other children would tease him about it when he puts his shorts on for P.E., so I put a Spider Man plaster on it and told him to say he fell over and cut his knee. I know I shouldn't encourage him to lie, but I'm sure Jesus will forgive. He'll be in P.E. right now. I imagine him in his little blue shorts, scrambling over equipment, with his Spider Man plaster hiding his secret wart. How much do I love him? I love my children so much it hurts. The pain of it frightens me.

I cross the road at the pelican crossing. Sally Hambleton stops at the red light in her shiny black Audi and gives me a wave. I wave back. I like Sally. I don't know how she ended up being married to such a pompous oaf. That's unkind of me. Maybe there's a side to Bertie that only Sally sees. You never know what goes on behind closed doors.

Ah, I remember now, the ladies' night Sarah talked about is at Sally's house. I think the invitation is stuck on my fridge. Sally and Bertie live an old village rectory four miles out of town, it's absolutely divine. It's got a tennis court, an outdoor pool and a stunning orangery at the bottom of a beautiful garden. Hopefully Jeremy won't be on call that night and will be able to stay home with the children.

We get to the Beauty Salon bang on time, and Krystel, the girl who works on reception, comes to hold the door open for me so I can push the buggy in. She makes a big fuss of Martha who looks at her with suspicion and I can't say I blame her, Krystel has blue hair today, and nose piercings, as well as tattoos of spiders on her wrists. Minty appears, rubbing hand cream onto backs of her hands. She greets me with a big hug and she smells lovely. I give Martha her book and a bread stick and pray she'll behave with Krystel, just for half an hour.

'Don't worry about her,' says Minty, pulling out a chair for me, 'my next client's not for another hour so she can scream all she likes.'

I feel a little piqued at the implication that Martha is a screamer but Minty always says what she thinks. It's one of the reasons she sometimes gets across people but exactly why I like her. I grew up in a big Irish family, I'm used to blunt talking, bad language and boozy bust-ups (Minty likes a bevvy or three!), and she is honestly the most understanding person I know, if ever I'm having a little moan or a worry she just gets it straight away and always comes up with something funny or practical to make me feel better. She's a good friend.

She settles herself opposite me and takes a look at my poor washer-woman's hands.

'What the hell have you been doing, Mrs Gray?' She always calls me that when I'm in the salon.

'The usual. Looking after five children and running a mad house.'

'Tsk tsk, you must wear gloves you naughty girl. How's Jezza?' No-one but Minty calls him that. She soaks the cotton

43

wool in blue liquid and wipes it over my nails one by one. 'He's fine, thanks. A bit worn out, but nothing new in that.'

'And the ankle-biters?' More cotton wool, more blue liquid.

'They're good, thanks. Although Martha's teething. I told you they all had chicken pox didn't I?'

'Yes you did. Did you have a chicken pox party?'

'No, I couldn't face it.'

'Don't blame you.'

'One of the Mum's at school suggested it because her daughter is ten and still hasn't had it, but the last thing I wanted was hundreds of other people's children running riot round my house.' I glance over at Martha. Krystel is reading the book to her in a loud, peculiar voice.

'Do you know what colour you'd like?' I ask Minty to choose and after some consideration she selects a deep bluey-pink, which apparently will 'complement my skin tone and my hair'. Considering that I'm pale and freckly with what I like to think of as 'strawberry blonde' curls I don't know how she's come to this conclusion, but Minty is the expert and she's insisting.

'I saw Sarah in the park this morning,' I say, as she starts to shape my nails. Her hands are trembling slightly but I think nothing of it. My Dad's hands are always shaky, and he's a brilliant pianist and always wins at Jenga, so there you go. 'She was out running and caught me lying down for a rest under a tree.'

'Hmm.'

'Are you going to the ladies' night at Sally's on the 30th?'

'Probably. It's for charity isn't it?'

'No idea. I can't remember. It was Sarah who reminded me. Hopefully Jeremy won't be on call. How are Jenny and Jack?'

'Good thanks. Although I miss them of course, now that they're both at Uni.' She starts to work on my other hand. 'Guess who came in this morning,' she says, without looking up.

'Who?'

'Shona, wanting a bikini wax.'

'Oh. That's awkward.' Shona is the local vamp/gold-digger/marriage-wrecker who lives with the millionaire John Dixon, who is twice her age. His company, Dixon Homes, built all the new houses on the east side of Kingsmead.

I try not to think of the intricacies of Shona's bikini waxing.

'As it happened I had a cancellation,' says Minty, 'so I squeezed her in, but Carol was booked in after for an eyebrow shape so I was nervous as fuck about them meeting in reception. I had to do a rush job but I don't think Shona noticed.'

'Poor Carol...' I say, my heart sinking as it does every time I think of her. Everyone feels nothing but sympathy for Carol, the abandoned wife. Jeremy told me she'd come into his surgery not long after John walked out on her, she was so damaged and incoherent that Jeremy was really concerned. I wonder how John could be so heartless, and how Shona can live with herself, but it's not for me to judge. Let he who is without sin.. etc. etc. 'Did you get Shona out in time?' I ask.

'Only just. Jesus, can that woman talk. She didn't draw breath. Sorry for the blasphemy.'

A thought occurred to me.

'She won't be at the ladies' night, will she? Not with Carol there, surely?'

'God, no. Sally wouldn't do that to Carol.'

'No, of course not.' Sally and Carol have been friends since school, or Uni or something like that. Ages anyway.

'I just kept thinking,' says Minty, 'as I stripped the wax off her bits, that this is what John left his wife for. You know. Her crack, basically.'

I laugh. 'You are awful, Minty!'

'Although I'm sure those splendid silicone knockers had something to do with it as well.' She unscrews the lid off the base coat and begins to apply it carefully, resting the side of her hand on the table to steady the shake.

'There must be more to it than that,' I say, 'I mean, he and Carol had been married all those years, he wouldn't just leave her for–'

'Boredom. The monotony of a long, tired marriage. And men have most of their brains in their dicks I'm sad to say.'

'Jeremy doesn't.'

'Apart from Jezza.'

'Or Simon.'

'Ok, ok, but you're not trying to tell me John Dixon wanted Shona for her wit and conversation.' She raises an eyebrow in challenge. She is wicked!

'Are they really fake?' I ask, lowering my voice.

'Shona's tits? Come on, Mrs Gray. They look like a pair of grapefruits shoved down her bra.' She dips the brush, applies more base coat.

'I hadn't really noticed,' I say truthfully, 'I just hope when I'm fifty Jeremy doesn't get bored of me and run off with some bimbo half his age.'

'No offence, but your Jezza isn't a multi-millionaire with the pick of the young gold-diggers, more to the point, he's a totally lovely guy who loves you to bits, and you know it.'

I feel myself blushing and make a mental note to be especially nice to Jeremy when he comes home tonight. I look across at Martha again, who is now squealing with pleasure at all the attention she's getting from Krystel.

Minty starts to apply the first coat of polish. She manages to get a lovely straight line, in spite of the shaking.

'And how was Carol?' I ask her.

'Not good. Off her face on all those pills she's popping.'

'Oh. Poor Carol.' It was Jeremy who prescribed those pills. Best not to say anything else.

'Got the lovely Karl Huth coming in later,' says Minty. Karl lives next door to Minty with his stunning wife, Petula. He's from Berlin and teaches German at Kingsmead. Minty is smirking.

'What on earth is he coming in for?' I ask.

'Keep it to yourself?' She throws me a warning look but she knows I don't betray confidences. As the wife of the local GP I'm sometimes privy to things I shouldn't know but I never breathe a word to anyone. I promise her that my lips are sealed.

'Back, sack and crack,' says Minty, 'and the rest.'

'What does that mean?' Although I'm beginning to guess.

'The whole lot. Bald as a baby.'

'No...stop it.' The image that comes into my head is not a pleasant one.

The door opens. 'Talk of the devil and his wife will appear,' Minty whispers, for who should be walking in but the lovely Petula. She's petite and blonde, like a perfect little doll. She waves at Minty, says something to Krystel then comes over, her heels clicking on the hard floor. She teaches art at Kingsmead School but couldn't look less like an artist if she tried. She looks more like a footballer's wife.

Minty breaks off from doing my nails to greet her, they exchange air kisses and the usual exclamations, lovely jacket/

hair/shoes etc. etc. while I just smile and say hi when Petula acknowledges my presence. She wants to know if Minty can fit her in today for a manicure, and while they're talking I take in her tiny, pale pink jeans with little diamante spangles on the pockets, her shimmering silk blouse which is ever so slightly see-through, and her soft-looking black leather jacket. Her hair is literally golden and shiny, her eyes are as green as a cat's and her teeth are like tic tacs. I wonder if it's possible for anyone to look more perfect and I wish suddenly that I'd made some effort with my appearance when I left the house this morning. I probably have grass stains on my M&S jeans and I pulled on yesterday's jumper before leaving the house without checking whether or not it was spotted with milk/ketchup/toothpaste/Play-Doh.

Minty says she can stay late at the salon and do Petula's nails at 6.30, and Petula is so grateful you'd think someone had saved her life. She gives Minty another light squeeze, and as she leaves (with lots of waves and smiles and cheerios) I notice her perfect, pert behind which unleashes a riot of unwelcome mental images of all the things that her apparently rampant husband does to her in the bedroom, or any room in the house quite probably.

When she has gone, leaving wafts of her perfume behind her, I can't help myself.

'Is it true they have an open marriage?' I whisper, to my shame helping to spread a rumour I heard long ago.

'Oh, definitely. It's common knowledge,' replies Minty.

'Really? But how does that work? I mean…what do they…?'

'Don't ask me!' Minty laughs. 'Just take my advice and don't accept any invitation to get into their hot tub with them. You might find yourself in trouble.'

'Why? Have you got in their hot tub with them?'

'Are you kidding? Not likely. Sarah and Gary have though.'

'Have what?'

'Got in the bleeding hot tub, do keep up! I've heard that's their code for wanting to wife swap.'

'No! You mean…Gary and Sarah…? I don't believe it!'

'Don't tell Sarah I told you.'

'As if I would!'

It's too shocking. I don't want to think about it.

For a moment we're silent, locked in observation of the mesmerising ritual of nail polish application, which is strangely soothing. My troubled imagination goes back to Karl, and the waxing he's having done this afternoon, and by Minty! His friend and neighbour!

'How can he?' I say.

'What? Let another man shag his wife?'

'No…I mean, yes, that, of course, too weird and awful to contemplate…'

'He likes to watch apparently.'

'Stop it!'

'It's true, he told me himself.'

I feel faint. 'But how can he ask you to do all that intimate stuff with him, I mean, you're neighbours! You feed his cat!'

She laughs.

'Will you see everything?'

'Yep. The complete tackle.'

'Do you think…he won't try anything with you will he?'

'Possibly. It wouldn't be the first time.'

Well, this is all news to me! I'm offended that Minty hasn't told me all this before but she says it was just one drunken suggestion Karl and Petula made one evening round at their house, about the four of them all going to bed together, and

Minty and Simon didn't want to make a big deal of it, least said soonest mended and all that, and they like Karl and Petula, they're good neighbours and friends, a good laugh, it's no big deal, says Minty, who was so drunk at the time she can hardly remember it anyway. 'English people are so uptight about sex,' she says.

So are Irish people apparently, because my cheeks are burning with all this talk of Karl's bits and pieces and foursomes or whatever it is they get up to - I'm blushing like a nun.

'But…you didn't though, did you? You didn't do it with them?'

'Of course not! It's a game I'm not the least bit interested in playing. And can you imagine Simon going along with it?'

No, I can't imagine that at all. Poor Simon. I think Minty is a bit much for him sometimes.

'Well, we certainly won't be inviting the Huths over for dinner any time soon,' I say, haughtily, stupidly, as if I'm some kind of sex goddess that Karl wouldn't be able to resist. 'I don't know why he wants other women when he has a wife like Petula. And if he loves her how can he stand the thought of another man…' I can't say the words. 'And why bother to get married in the first place?' My cheeks are now so hot with indignation and prudery that you could fry an egg on them. 'Their marriage vows obviously mean nothing to them at all, 'Forsaking all others –"

'Keep your hair on.'

'Til death us do part.'

'Calm down.'

'Well. I think it's gross.'

'And I think you're adorable, Mrs Gray.'

'You mean boring, old fashioned and uptight about sex,' I say, deflating. Minty puts my right hand under the LED lamp.

'Not that uptight, Mrs Gray, how many children do you have now? Or have we lost count?' She grins, and as if response Martha lets out another squeal.

I calm myself with a deep breath, like a child getting over a tantrum. The bluey-pink is looking lovely on my nails and it cheers me.

'Changing the subject,' says Minty, dipping the brush in the bottle, 'fancy coming over for a movie night on Thursday? Simon's staying over in London so I'm on my own.'

'I'd love to, as long as Jeremy's at home. That would be really nice.' Minty is mad about movies and sometimes I go over with popcorn and Coke and we watch something nice on her enormous screen, lights down, feet up on her sofa while she drinks white wine out of a pint glass ('saves on trips to the fridge').

Martha is getting bored. Krystel is losing her audience. 'Mummy's nearly done!' Minty calls over to her.

Krystel asks me if she can take Martha out of her buggy. I say yes, and watch as she manages to figure out the clasps on the straps. My protective instincts kick in as she lifts my little angel out, her adorable, plump body tensing as she leaves the security of the buggy. Krystel is on her way over to me, carrying Martha in her arms when suddenly, so suddenly that it seems to be happening in another time frame, the world crashes in on me, the bang is deafening but we have no time to jump, the noise fills my head, it booms between my ears, the sound of screeching tyres, scrunching metal, broken glass, a woman screaming in the street, and the surreal sight of the car bonnet sticking through the door of the Beauty Parlour with glass and debris scattered everywhere, a deflating air bag visible through the windscreen, the woman at the wheel, head rolling backwards, I see it all in the few seconds that it takes to happen, but my brain can only register one thing. The buggy, in which Martha had been sitting just a few seconds before, is a crumpled wreck beneath the wheels of the car, crushed as if it were made of match sticks, and standing in front of me is Krystel, her face as white as milk, holding my baby, my baby who is safe but screaming with fear, and I take her in my arms and hold her tightly and rock and howl in shock and relief, thank you, thank you, Jesus, Mary and Joseph, Oh dear God, thank you, thank you……

Minty has dropped the bottle of varnish and is staring wide-eyed at the driver of the car which has careered into her shop.

'It's Carol…'

Amongst the screams, the shouts, the unaccountable hiss of water, the plumes of smoke, I hear the gentle, beating wings of Martha's guardian angel.

4. Sarah

Men, Mysteries and Miracles

My mind is in turmoil, not even the running is clearing away all my confused jumble of thoughts, I've only just turned in to the park and already I'm tired. I have no energy. I've been feeling like this for weeks, months even, it's as if I'm coming down with something, but it never goes away. I'm tired and bloated, I've lost my appetite and I can't sleep properly. Last week I googled the symptoms, freaked out (renal failure, bowel cancer, hepatitis) and immediately made an appointment with Jeremy Gray, my GP, for this morning at 10.45.

I'm just pondering this when who should I bump into but Jeremy's slightly loopy wife, Bridie, who is lying under a tree, as if it's a boiling hot day in August.

Bridie has six children, more than her fair share, and there's her youngest, Martha, in the pushchair. As I approach I realise that Bridie has her eyes closed, and out of concern that she is actually just having a rest and hasn't collapsed in exhaustion from having so many children, I call out to her, which makes her jump. It's hard to look at Martha. Even now, after all these years, I daren't look at her for too long in case the pain shows in my face.

Her vile dog has been in the stream and shakes himself all over me. Bridie obviously thinks this is funny, which doesn't improve my mood. We pass the time of day before I say goodbye as cheerfully as I can and run on.

When I get home the silence of the house greets me. My cleaner, Jules, came yesterday so the place is even more spotless than usual. I think about Bridie's little girl, her cute podgy legs, her adorable chubby cheeks, and I imagine a pushchair here in the hall, toys on the rug in front of the fire, little shoes by the door, school blazers hanging on the coat hooks. Then the images disappear, and the house is empty. Like me.

I check my emails, rub a towel over my face, pour myself a glass of water and drink it at the sink. A text comes through from Gary.

We don't have to go through with it tonight if you don't want to x

I sigh and look out at the garden. It's as neat and as tidy as the house and I hate it. Bridie's garden is messy, overgrown, with mismatching garden furniture and a small plastic slide that's faded from years in the sun. I wonder, if Bridie came here, would she envy me my neatness and my solitude?

I doubt it.

I look down at my phone and tap in my answer.

I want to x

Which is a lie. I don't want to go through with it at all, but I feel I owe Gary and he's been so stressed with his business recently, tonight has given him something to look forward to. He won't talk to me about what's bothering him, so maybe a night of sexual oblivion will do him good.

I think about what's in it for me. I enjoyed it before, but I was different then. Everything was different then.

When we first met Karl and Petula I immediately had the feeling that they had more than just a friendly interest in us. They live next door to Araminta and Simon, who introduced us to them at a party. They're teachers at Kingsmead School and I often wonder what the parents would think if they knew about what they get up to in private.

Karl phoned me one day, unexpectedly, saying he wanted to run something by me. We'd been flirting whenever we met, I enjoyed it, he's attractive and funny, but when he called it was my lunch hour, I was in Kate's Tea Room eating a tuna salad and I was completely unprepared for such an explicit invitation.

'Would you and Gary like to play with us?'

It took a while for the penny to drop. I was thinking, Monopoly? Scrabble? I was confused because he didn't sound at all embarrassed, he was upbeat and confident.

'Adult play, I mean...' he said, in a tone of voice that cleared away any doubt as to his meaning, and my heart started thumping like a jack hammer. I remember Bridie coming in with Martha in a buggy, she smiled and waved at me just as Karl was beginning to warm to his subject and tell me all the things he wanted to do to me. He couldn't have known that Gary, while shagging me, had been expressing similar ambitions concerning Petula. I wasn't jealous, it turned me on, but I didn't for one minute think anything would actually happen.

So there I was, surrounded by the locals and regulars enjoying their healthy, organic, locally sourced lunches - an elderly couple, a table of three yummy-mummies, two Kingsmead sixth form girls playing with their phones and Bridie, buying scones - while in my ear Karl was talking about licking and sucking, tongues and fingers, and promising to make me scream. Afterwards I thought how astonishing it was that he had such confidence to approach me like that. I could have blown the whistle on him, Gary could have gone round to his house and thumped him, but he was so charming with it. He didn't make it sound pervy, just sexy and completely harmless, a bit of adult fun. Why not?

My cheeks were burning and I prayed that the volume was sufficiently turned down on my phone so that the young waitress bringing my bill couldn't pick out any of Karl's words.

I told him I was surprised and flattered by his request, I tried to sound cautious but interested, enough to give him hope, I clearly wasn't rejecting him and I sensed his excitement going up a notch. I asked him, knowing the answer already, if Petula knew he was making this call, if she was in on this, which of course she was, they had a completely open and honest relationship, he said.

What could go wrong? Four consenting adults, discretion, mutual respect. And more to the point, lots of no-strings, deception-free, fantastic (probably) sex. Even then, in the middle of a working day in Kate's Tea Rooms, the thought of watching Gary with Petula was exciting me. Karl isn't my usual type, but he has a great physique and I guessed he was quite expert. It was funny, the way he talked about it, with his trace of a German accent, as if he was presenting me with something that I'd be mad to turn down, like a deal on a new car or an insurance policy. I said I'd talk it over with Gary. I spoke in a neutral, professional voice, so no-one in the café could possibly have had any idea that I was discussing the possibility of an orgy. 'I'll run it by him and get back to you ASAP.' There I was in my work clothes, with my document bag on the floor and my iPad in front of me, as if I was just doing a work deal.

When I ended the call I was wild with excitement. It was amusing, a diversion from another dull day in this dull little town. I love sex, and if it can come to me in a neat, diverting and tasteful package then so much the better.

Gary and I didn't know then about all the years of IVF and miscarriages that lay ahead of us. We thought the future was on our side. We thought we were in control. What a pair of idiots we were.

I knew Gary would say yes. I put it to him over dinner that night, and he tried to hide his excitement but I could tell he was overwhelmed with lust at the thought of it. Who could blame him? Petula is wildly sexy, and I already knew that he liked the thought of watching a good-looking man turning me on, taking me, doing to me all the things that Gary knew I liked. We fixed a date to spend the evening with them at their house, two weeks away, and the anticipation was almost unbearable. Gary and I tried to save ourselves for the big night but every time we talked about it we ended up having fast, greedy sex. Even so, we were still hot for it by the time we finally arrived on their doorstep.

I wasn't concerned about Simon and Araminta next door seeing us arriving and leaving. For all her faults she's not the spying kind, and anyway, I guessed she would already be lying on the sofa well on her way to the bottom of her first bottle. Even if she had taken a glance out of the window we just looked like we were going round for dinner as we walked up the drive and rang on the bell, dressed up a bit, me in a little red dress and Gary in a nice shirt and close-fit jeans. We were like school children in a secret society, making up the rules as we went along. I look back on that now and I can't believe how blind we were. We thought we were so close, when in reality we were just giving each other away.

It was a warm night but I made Karl close the window when I realised how noisy he and Petula were. Gary and I laughed about it afterwards.

'He bellows like a bear, I wondered what the hell you were doing to him,' said Gary as we drove home.

'She sounded like a porn star,' I said, then added, wondering why I wasn't in the least bit jealous, 'she looks like one too. Lucky you.' I was as high as a kite, satiated with sex, endorphins, adrenaline and cocaine. We hadn't expected the cocaine, but as we don't drink it was a welcome addition to the evening. Karl expertly arranged it in long, fat lines on the glass top of the coffee table, and all the while he was stark naked, unashamed and completely hairless, everywhere. My heart had raced, my blood felt thin and hot.

I shudder now at the memory.

Shake it from my mind.

I have to go through with it tonight, I really do. It will help to assuage the guilt over what I did with Jack, because of course, inevitably, Jack and I did end up having sex after all.

What's the time? Nearly ten o'clock. I go upstairs to shower and dress (a pencil skirt with a cashmere sweater, suitably sensible for a doctor's appointment) and while I blow-dry my hair the memory comes back, unwelcome, of the time Karl spunked in my face, it went everywhere as he let out his deafening bear-like bellow, in my ears and in my hair, I was amazed at the amount of it and how quickly it went cold. Afterwards he proudly rubbed it across my cheeks with his thumbs, as if he was giving me a beauty treatment. I couldn't wait to wash it all off, it felt ridiculous on my face, as if someone had splatted me with a mud pie.

'But sex is funny,' Gary had said, laughing, when I told him on the way home.

Maybe I don't have a sense of humour.

Still, it didn't stop me going back for more, we met up with them regularly after that, we were mad for it, all four of us. I wondered if it showed in my face at work. Sexual images were constantly flickering in the back of my mind, like a cine reel left running, of Gary taking Petula from behind, stroking her smooth, pert buttocks, his face contorted with lust, her shoulders ramming into the pillows, Karl playing with me before he entered me, so brilliant with his fingers, driving me crazy, and Petula watching, smiling, knowing how good he is at that. Then Petula kissing me, taking me by surprise, 'Karl likes watching me with a girl,' she purred, and Karl telling us that his greatest turn on was engaging in 'double penetration' with Petula. She and Gary obliged him happily in his fantasy, many times, and it was a marvel that Araminta and Simon didn't call the police with all the noise she made as they took her simultaneously. Karl generously offered me the same treatment but I declined. One at a time is enough for me.

Wow, when I think about that now....We were crazy, totally crazy. Then after a couple of years I began to think about the family that we'd planned, and I stopped wanting the sexual thrills. Sex became an act of procreation instead, something magical and private just for me and Gary. After all the madness it was nice to feel back in control. When we told Petula and Karl that it was over, they took it so well that I wondered if they'd already got other people lined up, but Gary said it was just the way they were. They're cool about everything, he said. Nothing seemed to ruffle them.

Then came the dark years, the years of trying for a baby, the agony of failure.

If ever we saw Karl and Petula in the pub we would talk in a cheerful, friendly way as if none of it had ever happened. It's difficult to make small talk though, when you know what someone looks like without their clothes on, limbs akimbo, bellowing like a bear or (in Petula's case) squealing like a piglet. I honestly didn't think we'd ever do it again. I thought we'd got it out of our system.

Then last week Karl and Gary got chatting, and somehow, here we are again, and I know it won't be the same, because my stomach is churning with dread instead of lust, and I'm seriously beginning to wonder if I can go through with it because this means I'm going backwards in my life not forwards, and worse, it means that Gary really has given up on the prospect of us ever having a child. The sex will be mocking me and my failure. Here you are, Sarah Simpson, you sad, empty, hopeless vessel, right back where you started. Worth a useless fuck, but not good enough to be a mother.

I have to go through with it. I have to. I owe Gary this after what I did with Jack. I pour myself a glass of water and drink it.

It's only a ten minute walk to the surgery but I feel so tired I take the car. This is what I'm talking about. It's not like me. I usually walk everywhere.

Jeremy is everything you'd want in a GP. Old enough to be experienced, young enough to be enthusiastic. He wears the uniform of old faithful chinos, checked cotton shirts, brown lace up shoes (very comfy looking) and black rimmed glasses which are a bit too trendy for him, as if the optician persuaded him to have them and they weren't really his choice. He has thick dark hair, cut in no particular style, and the nicest navy-blue eyes. He has photos on his desk of Bridie with their children and dog. His green anorak and small rucksack hang on the back of the door. He probably goes home for lunch, hearty soup and homemade bread, or door-step sandwiches lovingly assembled by Bridie. His surgery smells faintly of cinnamon and I notice an orange diffuser lurking behind his computer screen. Probably a Christmas present, still hanging around, something to get rid of the smell of sickness and leaky babies/toddlers/old people.

He smiles at me as if he's genuinely pleased to see me but with just the right amount of professional reserve. We exchange the usual pleasantries as I take the green upholstered seat at the end of his desk. He swivels to face me, all genial and receptive, waiting but not rushing, and for a moment I envy Bridie having this man all to herself. I feel like I could tell him everything.

'What can I do for you?'

I tell him I'm tired all the time. I tell him I'm bloated and nauseous, sometimes I feel faint, I'm having trouble sleeping and I've lost my appetite, except for yesterday when I guzzled four tubs of cherry yogurt in one sitting. He listens to me, but his attentiveness begins to make me nervous. He asks me questions about my lifestyle, if I'm under any stress, if my periods are normal. I answer him truthfully. No more stressed than I usually am, and periods as irregular as ever. They've always been that way, right from the start. It could be something to do with my 'unexplained infertility'.

His expression is unreadable. He says he'd like me to give a urine sample, and then he might take some blood tests, 'process of elimination' he says with his lovely, reassuring smile. He gives me a sample pot and sends me out to the patients' loo.

Five minutes later I'm back.

'I couldn't manage much,' I say, handing him the pot apologetically.

'Oh, that's plenty, take a seat, we only need a little bit.'

I sit in silence as he dips test strips into the pot.

'Well, well,' he says, throwing all the bits and pieces in the appropriate bin, and washing his hands with the rigorous thoroughness of a pro.

'What?'

He comes to sit down, folds his hands in his lap, puts his head to one side and beams at me, maddeningly, because he knows something I don't.

'You're pregnant,' he says.

The room shifts. Quickly he leans forward, as if he's afraid I'm going to fall out of my chair. My face must have gone a deathly pale because he asks me if I'm feeling faint and when I don't answer he gently guides my head down between my knees to let the blood flow back.

'Are you sure? Are you absolutely sure?' I ask, from the hidden shadows of my awkward position.

'Quite sure,' he says, sounding triumphant, 'especially as I suspect you may be some weeks advanced. Are you feeling any better?'

I raise my head, nod mutely. He smiles at me. He thinks he's just given me the best news of my life, and it is, it is, or it would be, if only…

Oh God. What have I done?

'How can you tell how many weeks I am?' I ask him. I sound like a frightened child.

'When you first walked in I thought you looked pregnant. Lie down, I'll give you a quick external exam, but you'll need to have an ultrasound scan to find out for sure, with your irregular cycle it's difficult to tell. When was your last period?'

I move over to the examination bed and lie down, lifting up my sweater.

'I don't know…' I cast my mind back, but all I can see is…. Oh God. 'It was months ago. Which isn't unusual for me. I can't remember. I never take any notice of them anymore.'

Jeremy palpates my tummy. He has nice hands. I think of them on Bridie. He's concentrating. Then he gets a tape measure and stretches it over my bulge, which suddenly looks bigger than ever. Eventually he tells me, 'off the record', that I could be as much as twelve weeks gone.

He says I can get down, he goes back to his computer and begins to type while I retake my seat, frantically trying to do the mental maths.

'I'll arrange for an ultrasound scan to be carried out as soon as possible.' His nimble fingers tap away at the keyboard. He's still smiling.

He turns to face me again. 'Congratulations,' he says.

Twelve weeks. That takes it back to January. Oh god.

'Will the scan tell me everything? I mean will it date it for sure?'

He tells me yes, it will date the pregnancy and other things which I don't quite catch, about making an appointment with a mid-wife as soon as possible so I can discuss screening, diet, folic acid.... my mind is reeling, I can't take it in. I ask how this is possible. He laughs. I say no, I mean, after all those years of trying, and he says sometimes, when a woman has given up all hope, she can fall pregnant naturally when she least expects it. He says he's seen it before, more than once. He tells me about a couple who adopted two Chinese babies after years of trying for one of their own, and six months after bringing the babies home the mother fell pregnant. The body is a marvellous, mysterious machine, he says, beaming, quite ok with it all.

After a while there is nothing more to say. We sit in silence, me staring into the middle distance, at the white sink in the corner, the anti-bacterial cleanser, the box of vinyl gloves, the poster explaining body parts, and all the while Jeremy witnesses my symptoms of shock with barely concealed joy.

He breaks with protocol to give my hand a friendly squeeze.

'Go home and break the good news to Gary,' he says.

I am sitting in the car in the surgery car park, wondering if I'm in a fit state to drive. There is a row of poplar trees in front of me, rustling in the breeze, such a peaceful, timeless sound. Birds are chirping and playing in the branches. The earlier cloud has lifted and a thin, April sun has broken through. Life goes on.

I look down at my belly and place a hand over it, as if it will tell me something. For weeks I thought I was just bloated. I thought it was fluid or gas or a gluten intolerance, any number of things, but I never for one minute thought that it might be because there was a baby growing inside me….Oh God, it hits me so hard that I begin to sob, I put my head in my hands, the tears spill, copious and sudden, my mascara stinging my eyes and running down my cheeks.

I'm pregnant. I'm pregnant!

I'm going to have a baby.

All the years of agony and despair rage inside me like a tornado, swirling up and away into the ether, leaving me at last. I cry so hard that I feel that I won't ever be able to stop.

The door to the surgery opens and Jeremy comes running out. For a sickening moment I think he is coming over to tell me he was wrong, I'm not pregnant after all, it was a mistake.

'There's been a car accident on the High Street,' he says to me through my open window, 'are you ok?' He's fishing his car keys out of his pocket, already moving away.

'I'm fine,' I say, smiling, pulling myself together.

I watch Jeremy drive speedily away in his Land Rover Discovery with a flashing green light stuck on the roof. I hope no-one I know is involved in the crash.

I take more deep breaths, find a tissue in my bag, wipe my face, put some lip salve on, run my hands through my hair.

This is it, the first day of the rest of my life.

I have to take a detour to get home because of the accident in the High Street. I wonder where Gary is, but I can't contact him until I've decided what I'm going to say to him. There is no way I can go through with tonight. No way. The thought of trying to get high on sex…Oh God. The whole thing is totally insane.

My house is the same, but different. Same vase of lisianthus on the polished side table, same tasteful lamps, all ready to come on at the flick of a single switch. The glass I had my water in just before I left for the surgery is by the sink, a trace of my lip gloss on the rim. Everything looks like a relic of my former life. The life before I knew.

I still can't take it in.

I kick off my shoes and collapse on the sofa. I can hear a siren some way off. Imagine if Gary's been killed in that accident today, imagine the irony. Killed on the same day that his wife found out that she's carrying a longed-for baby.

Stop it, Sarah. If Gary had been hurt or killed you would know by now. Jeremy is at the scene, he would have contacted you.

Right. Enough of this. Time to get practical. What's the next step? I cancel my appointments for the rest of the day. I need space to organise my emotions, my head, my new, suddenly unpredictable life. I get a pad of paper and do what I always do when the pressure is on. I make a list of salient points. I get as far as 1) tell Gary he has to cancel tonight because I'm not well, but I can't think of what to do next. I sit for a moment, thinking.

Whatever happens, I'm not giving up this baby.

I feel better for the clarity of this statement. It's one thing I'm certain of, so everything else can come from that. I'm keeping the baby. Now all I have to decide is, when do I tell Jack? Now, later, or never?

I pick up my iPad. I go on to Google and type in: *can I determine paternity before birth*

I quickly read the replies. It's easier than I thought, and paternity tests after the baby is born are easier still. I can do it without Gary ever knowing.

You're keeping the baby, Sarah, hold that thought. Whatever happens, you're keeping the baby, with Gary or without Gary, you're going to be a mother. If the paternity test goes the wrong way, if Gary kicks you out, no-one is taking this baby from you. You're going to be a mother.

The first wave of euphoria floods me.

I put my head back and stare at the ceiling. Poor Jack. It was my fault really, I'm old enough to know better. It was only the one time, the day he went back to Uni in the New Year, in his father's shed on the allotment of all places. He wanted to use a condom because he's an intelligent, well-mannered, modern young man, but I told him not to bother. I'm infertile, I told him, we don't need to bother with that, we're clean and safe enough.

Poor, lovely Jack. The sex wasn't even that good.

It's true what they say, that God laughs when man makes plans.

5. Carol

Falling

I'm getting ready to go out. It's the first social engagement I've had in months. I suppose I ought to be nervous about it, but the pills take care of that.

I'm like a Victorian widow, suffering with my 'nerves'. Except that my husband isn't dead, he's alive and kicking, or should I say alive and f***ing (excuse my language). Living with a tramp young enough to be his daughter. A rich man leaving his loyal, boring old wife for a younger model. A gold digger. My (ex) husband has reduced himself to an embarrassing cliché.

If he were dead it would easier. I don't think anyone understands that, and it's too shocking to say it out loud.

My arm still hurts from the crash. I'm trying to put on a cardigan but it's awkward. Maybe it's shrunk in the wash, it seems to be too small. Or is it just twisted, inside out? Perhaps I won't bother with the cardigan. What's the weather like anyway?

I walk over to the window. Nothing much to see. A dull sort of day. No rain, I don't think it's cold, but I don't know, I haven't been outside all day.

The grass is beginning to grow. It needs cutting. We used to have a gardener but he retired. Or so he said. He's very religious and Bridie said he still cuts the grass outside the Catholic Church. There are people who don't want anything to do with me anymore. I'm an embarrassment. People don't know what to say. They wouldn't admit that of course.

Bridie is nice. The nice sort of Christian. Not like the gardener, whose name I've forgotten. I'm forgetting a lot of things these days. It's the pills. And that's a good thing. I don't want to remember anything anymore.

If I don't wear the cardigan I'll have to change my dress. I can't have bare arms, not at my age. And I still have bruises, yellowing under the skin. My arms look like uncooked pastry. Shona's arms don't look like pastry. I bet Shona's arms are firm and brown all year round.

Do I really have to change my dress? It's all such an effort. I can't be bothered. I don't want to go but I promised Sally. I bought this dress from M&S in Cambridge, ages ago, before John decided to let his dick dictate his life.

Dick-tate his life. That's funny. If I wasn't on pills I would laugh at that. Sally would laugh at that. We used to laugh a lot. I suppose Sally still does. Her husband hasn't betrayed her. Or has he? He is a terrible flirt. Who would know? I heard Bridie say once, 'it's the quiet ones you have to watch,' but that might not be true. You can never tell.

Your husband might be cheating on you *right now.* Look at me. *I had no idea.*

I wonder what the time is? I shuffle in to the kitchen and see the green luminous figures on the microwave – *19:00.* The microwave is covered in greasy finger prints. That must have been me. What did I have for lunch? There's a plate in the sink, and a knife and fork, but the plate has been licked clean. No clues there then. Oh well. I'm not hungry so that's ok. Jules will clean the microwave and load the dishwasher when she comes tomorrow. Jules isn't frightened of a bit of scandal like the gardener is. She still comes every week. Otherwise I would be like Miss Havisham by now. It's quite an appealing idea.

I'm not going to bother with the cardigan. Who cares if people stare at my fat, bruised arms? I don't. I don't care about anything anymore. I suppose that's the pills too. It's ok.

My phone bleeps. It's a reminder that Sally is coming to pick me up at 19:00. It's so kind of her, considering she's the hostess and must be very busy. She's says that's what friends are for.

I've been banned from driving since the accident you see. Not officially. It's Dr Gray and all my friends who've told me I shouldn't drive while I'm on all these pills, and my children have taken the car keys (I still call them children, although they're all in their twenties now). Poor Dr Gray. He was the first on the scene. I think he blames himself because he was the one who prescribed me the pills. He didn't have much choice. I went into his surgery that time, screaming and crying and making a fool of myself, as if John hadn't done a good enough job of that already. I was at breaking point. Living on your own with your memories and your anger can send you to the edge.

I can't remember what happened the day I drove my car into Minty's Beauty Parlour. I don't even know where I was going. Dr Gray says I may have fallen asleep at the wheel, which is ironic, considering how I can't sleep at night without a fistful of pills. Anyway, I ended up in the reception area, crashed right through the glass doors. The place was trashed. They had to close the road. No-one was hurt, thank God. I found out later that Bridie was in there with Martha at the time. It could have been a tragedy of terrible proportions. And it would have been their fault, John and Shona. The tramp. They would have had blood on their hands, the blood of an innocent child, because I wouldn't be on these pills if

69

it wasn't for them. I wouldn't be driving around in a stupor, running into buildings, forgetting things.

My arms were badly bruised, Dr Gray said it was the air bag flying off that did that, and I had a hell of a headache for a few days, but it's all a bit of a blur. Dr Gray figured out that I had been taking double doses of the pills. I remember him talking to the police woman and the paramedic about it. He changed my prescription so now I have to pick them up on a weekly basis instead of every month, to stop me from taking too many. Perhaps he thinks I'll 'do something silly'.

'Silly' is the wrong word, but people always use it. What's 'silly' about despair that runs so deep and darkens your life so completely that the only prospect of peace is in death? But I'm not suicidal, not yet anyway. The irony is I haven't even got the motivation to kill myself. I can't be bothered.

He's a lovely man, Dr Gray, very kind. (He's always Dr Gray to me, not Jeremy). No wonder Bridie looks so happy all the time. She's a very lucky woman.

I pick up my little hand bag, and I wait. I don't really need a bag. I look at it. A small, brown leather clutch, I can't remember when or where I bought it, I've had it for years. It has my phone in, which I hardly ever use, a packet of tissues, and my purse, which I won't need tonight. I'll leave the bag behind. I chuck it on the little green upholstered chair and sigh.

I am standing in the dim hall of our old family home, which looks dated now, a bit nineties. It has a parquet floor. On the wall there is a mirror which I don't want to look in, and a still life of a bowl of fruit in a brass frame. A typical present from John's mother. I should sell it. I've never liked it. There is a space where another picture used to be, a family portrait which is too painful to look at, so I took it down.

70

I shouldn't be living in this house. I should be living in the house John now shares with Shona. We were doing it up. It has a beautiful garden. I think of them there together and I feel my chest tighten as if in memory of the pain.

The dust motes play in the thin beam of daylight that comes from the glass above the front door. It's quiet, except for the sound of Radio 4 playing in the kitchen, I never switch it off, it keeps me company. The children have gone, the husband has gone, even the cat's gone, run over by a plumber's van at the end of the road. This house is too big for one person. John's company built it for me when we were first married. Like the Taj Mahal, he said. A labour of love. I don't think he laid a single stone.

I hear a car horn pip. Sally.

Whenever I see Sally she discreetly gives me the once over. She tries not to let it show but I can tell. We've known each other since we were eighteen. She's thinking, *how is she today?* The same as yesterday, Sally, my friend.

We hug. I smell her regular perfume. She's thin and small. I'm thin too, but taller that Sally. We can't share clothes, we never could, we would only swap them for fun, for a laugh, when we were students. Her feet are size four and I'm a giant eight. She looks like a clown in my shoes.

She tells me she likes my dress. I call her a fibber and she protests.

'What are we going to do with you, Carol?' she says, but nicely, 'how are we going to get your self-esteem back?'

When she's kind to me I feel something like self-pity snatch at my throat. I don't recognise my feelings anymore (the pills again) because they are all pretty much the same. Self-pity, sadness, anger, jealousy, despair, fear, loneliness, confusion, all stirred up in one big pot and disguised by the medication

71

into a generic feeling of emotional malaise. They're all bad feelings anyway. Nothing good in there.

I get in the passenger seat of Sally's car and feel like saying, 'Let's just drive. Let's just go somewhere, see where we end up.' I'd happily never come back to this house.

Sally is talking about the food. She's thinks there's far too much, which is a fault on the right side, she says. My mother always used to say that.

'My mother used to say that,' I say.

'What?'

'"It's a fault on the right side"'.

'How is she?'

'The same.'

My mother is in a care home in Cambridge. She has dementia. What a pair we make.

It's nice, just sitting here with Sally, being driven through the town, watching the world go by. The light is fading. The shops are all closed. There's an old man walking a stiff, old dog. A teenage boy on a bike, going too fast and without a helmet. Everything carries on as normal. I see the lady with the wobbly head who works in Oxfam. There she goes, wobbling along. I wonder where she's wobbling off to.

We pass the **John Dixon Homes** sign, up-lit, arrow pointing to the left, "Fifty new quality homes, 3 & 4 bedrooms with gardens, show home now open". I've thought about defacing that sign, but I haven't the nerve, and I can't be bothered. Knowing my luck I'd get caught, and then I'd look even more of a fool than I do already.

There's Mr King, headmaster of Kingsmead School, and his wife in their swanky Range Rover.

'She's coming tonight,' says Sally, nodding towards them, 'I hope he realises it's a ladies' night. I don't want to have to ask him to leave.'

'That would be funny.'

'I'm sure he's just giving her a lift.'

'I've forgotten her name.'

'Michelle.'

We sit in easy silence at the lights. I can see Kate's Tea Rooms from here, with its Union Jack bunting, and three or four young men who look as if they're on their way to The Cross Keys, strolling along the pavement. They look carefree. Happy. Untroubled. I watch them with something like envy.

'Carol, I've been thinking.'

'Uh-oh.' I smile at her, unconcerned. Nothing really fazes me now. Nothing she says can change things.

'I think you need to talk to someone.'

'What about?'

'About you. About your life, and what's happened to you.'

'I talk to you.'

'Yes, sometimes. And I'm your friend, and I'm always here for you, but I don't know how to make things better for you. You can't stay propped up by pills for the rest of your life.'

'I don't see why not.' It sounds appealing.

'Ok, look at it this way. From a selfish point of view, I've lost my friend.'

'I've lost my husband.'

'Yes, I know,' (that's thrown her) 'but you still have the rest of your life to live, you can't just lie down and give up.' That too sounds appealing.

'Why not? Why can't I live how I want to live? I don't tell you what to do with your life, do I?' She sighs, and I know I shouldn't talk to her like that. Sally is a good, loyal friend and a really sweet, lovely person. 'Sorry.'

'I know a really good therapist –'

I groan. 'Oh, please.'

'Give her a chance. Please, Carol, for me. For your family.'

'Such as it is.'

We're out of town now, on the road to the village where Sally and Bertie live. I wish I didn't have to go to this wretched party. I wish Sally had never talked me into it. *If wishes were horses, beggars would ride.* That's another thing my mother used to say.

'Go and see her once, and if you don't like her you don't have to go again.'

A crow is tugging at a dead rabbit in the road. It hops lazily out of the way as we pass. I let out a big sigh.

'Alright. I'll go just once.' It's a waste of time.

'Good!' Sally looks delighted. She obviously has a lot of faith in this woman. It's easier just to say yes. I don't want to argue with her and she means well.

As we approach the house she slows down, turns into the drive, zaps open the electric gates. Without looking at me she reaches over and gives my hand a squeeze.

She really is a lovely person.

It looks like every woman in Kingsmead and beyond has turned up. There are cars parked all over the gravel drive and on the front lawn, shiny, big, new, expensive cars. I recognise a few, and I also spot Jules' push bike propped up against the wisteria to the side of the house. It's the old fashioned sort, with a wicker basket on the front. She goes all over the place on that bike doing her cleaning rounds.

'Why is Jules here?' I ask.

'She's answering the door and waitressing with Jenny Morgan. Are you ok?'

I nod mutely. She smiles at me, and we go in.

I love this house. It's pure class, so different to any John Dixon house. It has big sash windows and solid, internal doors, painted in deep grey. An Italian glass chandelier hangs from the hall ceiling (Sally and Bertie bought it while on holiday in Tuscany), there are family photos on the walls, tasteful, beautifully framed, and glass vases of lilies on the antique furniture, inherited from Bertie's family. It's a peaceful house, but not silent and dead like mine.

Jules, as usual, is taking her position seriously. She appears out of nowhere as we enter the cool, spacious hall with its original black and red tiled floor that echoes the steps of the guests.

'Oh, it's only you,' she says, as if we were trying to play a trick on her. She's wearing a black, shapeless skirt and a white blouse that looks two sizes too big. Her dreadful, bleached hair is scraped back into an untidy pony tail and I notice a small ladder in her black tights. That's Jules. There is nothing at all feminine about her. No make-up, no heels, no bust and no hips. She has a perpetual earnest, wary look and she frowns when she cleans, as if she's puzzling over some problem. Her limited conversation is brisk and defensive and she has a habit of narrowing her eyes when you talk to her. She's a very good cleaner, everyone in Kingsmead wants her (*too many chiefs, not enough Indians* as my mother would say), she's even got a waiting list. The strange thing is, she's been coming to my house for four hours a week over the past ten years and yet I hardly know a thing about her. She has a husband, I forget his name, and one son who went to the Catholic primary school (the same one that Bridie's children go to) and she lives on the council estate on the edge of the park, but that's the sum total of what I know. I like her though. She's reliable and doesn't pry. When Bertie left she just carried on as if nothing had happened, even though half the women in town were calling on me to 'make sure I was alright', which actually means they wanted in on the scandal, the inside line, to come and witness the abandoned, devastated creature for themselves and then go away feeling relieved it wasn't them. Once, when I was having a particularly wretched day, Jules went to answer the door without my prompting and I overheard her telling my nosy neighbour that 'Mrs Dixon is indisposed to receive any visitors at present' (she watches Downton Abbey). I was grateful to her. There is kindness in that rather stoical, taciturn frame. We never mentioned the incident. I pretended I hadn't heard, and she doesn't go in for chit chat, which is a good thing. I don't pay her to gossip and drink my tea. She's of the *ask me no questions and I'll tell you no lies* variety.

'Is everything ok?' Sally asks her. Sally has switched now from being my friend to being the hostess and she follows Jules towards her beautiful, enormous kitchen. This 'Ladies' Night' is for a local charity, Sally is brilliant like that, always busy, always doing something worthwhile. Thirty-five pounds a ticket for all you can eat and drink, plus a string quartet by the sounds of it. Sally will have done most of the food herself, and no doubt struck a good deal with The Cross Keys over the wine. I realise as I enter the enormous drawing-room that the musicians are students from Kingsmead School, probably doing this for nothing and adding the charitable hours on to their Duke of Edinburgh Awards.

I see Minty leave off entertaining a small audience to greet me. She's wearing a tight, black dress and leopard print stilettoes. She's never been slim but she looks fatter than ever and judging by the expression on her face she's already half-cut. Her Champagne flute is empty. It's nice of her to come over, seeing as I'm on my own and probably look desperate. Poor abandoned first wife that I am.

She greets me with a kiss on each cheek and says how lovely it is to see me. I return the compliment. I say I like her shoes and she laughs and says she can't wait to kick them off. She asks me how I am, with a serious face, and while I'm trying to formulate an answer she looks around for a top up. She thinks I don't notice this, but my father died of drink and I know the signs. Jules, ever vigilant, appears at her side and fills her glass, the bubbles stopping just short of fizzing over. I ask Jules for orange juice and she goes in search of some.

'You should have a proper drink,' says Minty, almost crossly, 'God knows you deserve one. If Simon had left me for a younger woman I'd be under the table every night.'

I think, are you not already? You have to hand it to Minty. She comes right out and says what everyone else is thinking.

'I can't drink on my medication.'

She shrugs, downs half her Champagne, 'I guess not,' she says.

I notice Michelle King, the headmaster's wife, a bit of a celebrity round here, has just arrived and Jules is offering her Champagne. She's being greeted by the delectable art teacher, the one who's married to the big German, what is her name? Petronella? Petunia? She's wearing a very short skirt and has fantastic legs. Lucky her.

'Hey, have you heard Sarah's good news?' Minty draws my attention back.

'Erm…remind me.'

'She's pregnant!'

I'm blank. 'Oh, yes, I think I did hear that. Wonderful news. After all they've been through. They must be over the moon.'

'You'd think so wouldn't you,' Minty looks over at where Sarah is talking to the owner of Kate's Tea Rooms, 'but she's still got a face like she's chewing a wasp.'

I smile. 'She has a hard kind of beauty. Are Jenny and Jack ok?' Jack was in the same year as my son at Kingsmead and they're still friends.

Minty reaches inside the shoulder of her dress to hitch up a scarlet bra strap. 'Jenny's over there,' she says, nodding towards her beautiful daughter who is walking around topping up Champagne, 'and Jack's graduating next month of course.'

'How time flies.'

'Your lot ok? Still all doing brilliant things?'

I fill her in as best I can. I know where my children are living, what jobs they have, how long left at University, but I've forgotten the name of my son's new girlfriend. It doesn't matter. It's the pills. Minty smiles at me encouragingly. She is definitely three sheets to the wind and the evening has only just begun. I see Sarah making her way over. She's stunning as ever in a red, lacy dress, but she's far too lean. It can't be healthy. She has a small, neat bump. I congratulate her and her face changes briefly into something less severe.

'We were just saying how quickly the children have all grown up,' I say, 'so make the most of your little one, enjoy every minute.'

Minty agrees and raises her glass as if in a toast. Pretty little Jenny takes it as a sign and makes her way over to us with her bottle just as Jules puts a glass of orange juice in my hand. Minty gives her daughter an unsteady hug, nearly knocking her over. Jenny doesn't seem to mind, but I see Jules frowning as she moves away.

'Your children are so good-looking,' I say to Minty, smiling at Jenny, who beams back at me. She has the twinkliness of a twelve year old and I can't believe she'll be off to University later this year.

'Aw, thanks,' she says, 'but I'm the brains of the family! Jack's the good-looking one, he has all the girls after him!'

Sarah shoots her a strange look which I can't fathom.

'I miss them as little kiddies,' says Minty, pulling a sad face, 'I can't wait to have grand-children and do it all over again.'

Jenny laughs. 'Not yet, Mum! Not me anyway! Go and tell Jack !'

Sarah has gone suddenly pale and looks as if she wants to be somewhere else. It's the hormones I guess.

'Brains AND beauty you are,' says Minty, holding out her glass for another top up. Jenny extricates herself charmingly and goes in search of more empty glasses. 'Let's have a toast,' says Minty, 'to our children. All of them,' her voice wobbles, 'those no longer with us, and those yet to come.' It's an awkward moment, I guess she's referring to the baby that she lost, and I ask Sarah if her pregnancy was an IVF success story, just to divert the situation because I don't want Minty to get all emotional about her miscarriage while Sarah is here, no doubt worrying herself sick over all the possible complications now that she's finally fallen pregnant. I'm not good with over-emotional people. I never know what to say.

'No, we gave up on the IVF,' says Sarah, so quietly I can hardly hear her. I wait for her to elaborate but when she doesn't, Minty chips in.

'Isn't it weird?' she says, 'all that trying, then just when you've given it up as a lost cause, BANG! She gets up the duff. It's a miracle.'

'Every baby is a miracle,' I say.

'The miracle of life,' agrees Minty, philosophical with all that Champagne inside her, 'got any names yet, Sarah?'

Sarah suddenly says she's going to catch up with someone on the other side of the room and quickly disappears. 'Can't stand still for a minute that one,' says Minty, 'that poor baby will be born with trainers on.'

I circulate as best I can but I feel no connection with anyone, or with planet earth quite frankly. Michelle King asks after my children. Her husband has an impressive way of remembering the names of all the students and parents who've passed through the school but Michelle obviously finds it a struggle. I sympathise. I can just about remember my own name at the moment. I go through the whole rigmarole again, the universities, the career prospects, the sporting achievements, and she nods and shows an interest and says all the right things. I appear to have her undivided attention. It's a brilliant effort and I salute her. Every ambitious parent in Kingsmead wants to be her friend because of who she's married to. Minty doesn't like her, but I can't remember why.

Minty is only a few paces away, her voice carries sharply over the hum of conversation and the string quartet. She has her arm around Bridie who has arrived late (apologetically, something to do with the children's bath time and a lost rabbit). Minty says Simon bought her a rabbit once for her birthday, but it's not until she starts talking about a flat battery and a lost charger that people realise she's talking about some kind of sex toy. Minty makes people laugh. She's honest and loud, two things you don't get much of around here. She shouts 'Bollocks!' at something someone has said and Michelle glances over at her with interest. She's one of the untouchables is Michelle. Cool as a cucumber. The sort of woman for whom nothing ever goes wrong. Her husband won't ever walk out on her, her father won't die of drink and her mother won't end up in a horrible nursing home forgetting her own name. She won't end up dazed on pills, old before her time. Her life will never go wrong, I guarantee it.

I should go and visit my mother. I can't remember how long it is since I've seen her. The good thing is, neither can she.

Some of the ladies are queuing up at the long tables for food. I'm not hungry. Sally appears from nowhere and asks if I'm alright. People ask me that a lot these days. She introduces me to two ladies called Fiona and Liz (I will have forgotten their names in two minutes). They live in the village and have 'done wonders' with the food, Sally says. She doesn't know what she would have done without them. Then she disappears to 'rescue' an apple pie which has been left in the oven for too long.

Fiona (big face, thin hair, lots of white linen, pink chiffon scarf and comfortable shoes, the kind that a child would wear) asks me if I live in Kingsmead. I say I do, but don't elaborate. I don't want to give too much away, I dread the moment when they realise who I was married to and what's happened to me. I ask her how long she's lived in the village. Six years, she says. Liz says she's a newcomer too, she's only lived here for twenty years, and they laugh. Liz has a very pretty face but an unfortunately large nose. Her hair is black and very straight and she's thin, in an attractive sort of way, like a model.

I'm exhausted. The effort of making small talk is crushing me. I'm just wondering how I can extricate myself and find sanctuary in one of Sally's nice, cool bathrooms, when the sound of raised voices coming from the hall hushes the room. Everyone turns to look. The voices get louder, it's an argument, two women, one of them I know to be Jules.

The door bursts open. Some of the ladies gasp in shock but me, my heart just about implodes at the sight of Shona, looking furious, scanning the throng of stunned guests who all stand quite still as if they're playing musical statues.

Jules is shouting at Sally across the room that 'she just came barging in' and I feel a sensation of falling, as if the blood is draining from my body. I'm sure that if it wasn't for all the pills smothering my emotions I would have died of shame there on the spot, because I knew, I just knew, that she was looking for me.

'Fucking bitch! Where is she?'

I'm rooted to the spot, it's like my shoes are nailed to the floor, but every fibre of my being wants to flee, to hide. Sally (and possibly Minty too?) makes an ineffectual move to calm her, and bizarrely the musicians carry on playing, like on the Titanic, while every Kingsmead lady in the room stands and stares, with Champagne flutes in their manicured hands, their jaws agape, their fascinated eyes riveted to the scene. In the corner of my eye I see that a few of them have turned towards me. They know the history between me and Shona.

She has a bundle of clothes in her hands, silky, expensive looking clothes, but they're torn and cut to shreds. I notice some sequins falling on Sally's Persian rug. She's waving them around and asking again where 'that bitch is hiding.'

Then she sees me. It's hopeless. There's no escape. Her face contorts and reddens horribly. She's not that attractive when all is said and done.

She marches over. Fiona and Liz move away (thanks) and although Minty makes an effort to hold her back she gets right up close. I can smell her perfume, I can see the shine of sweat coming though her make-up, I can see the tic-tac whiteness of her teeth as she snarls in my face.

'You did this didn't you? You fucking bitch!' She pushes the ruined clothes in my face and I back away. I have no idea what she's talking about but I have lost the power of speech as well as movement. The sequins have scratched my cheek. Minty grabs Shona by her arm and tells her to back off but Shona shakes herself free, telling Minty to 'fuck off or I'll deck you and all!' Class.

It's very quiet now. The musicians have petered out and all I can hear is the sound of my rapid breathing, and Shona calling me every name under the sun, 'you fucking jealous bitch! No wonder he left you, you dried up fucking cow, look at yourself!' and Minty grabbing her again and pushing her, telling her to 'get the fuck out of this house!' and someone else getting upset at the language and leaving the room, and Sally saying she'll call the police if Shona doesn't get immediately out of her house, *right now*.

Shona tells her to 'fuck right off' and says she'll leave when she's good and ready and has had her say. She's on an unstoppable rant and I'm just waiting for it all to be over. It's like the roller coaster I went on when I was thirteen years old. *Just hold on, keep breathing, it will all be over soon.*

Sally goes out of the room, I assume to phone the police, which would just seal my mortification. Shona is screaming at me, accusing me of breaking into her house. *Her* house? She hasn't got a penny to her name. She was working as a waitress, just like the Spandau Ballet song, when John picked her up and decided she was a better woman than me, the woman who'd loved him for all those years and born him three children and given herself completely to her family. I think all of this, but I can't speak.

Minty asks her 'what the fuck' she's talking about, she says, 'Carol's been here all evening, every woman in the room is an alibi.' She sounds quite sober now and looks like she's up for a fight. Shona is still livid.

'She fucking did it,' she spits, jabbing at me with the shredded clothes, 'she still has a key and no-one broke in, who else would do this? Every piece of clothing, all my shoes, the fucking bitch has ruined everything and I'll make her fucking pay....' on and on... 'You need to take a good look at yourself,' she advises me as she runs out of breath, 'you're a fucking loser, a total fucker loser! You're *never* getting him back, and pulling these sad, pathetic little stunts will only make him hate you more!'

I didn't think he hated me. He never said he hated me.

'The police are on their way,' says Sally, coming back in to the room and sounding so like an extra in a TV detective drama that I wonder if I'm dreaming. It's all so surreal.

'Don't worry, I'm leaving,' says Shona, and the relief in the room is palpable, as if the walls themselves are breathing out at last. 'Any more fucking about, you stupid bitch, and I'll have you!' She pushes me. I wobble, and when I realise she's left the room, finally, I collapse.

Minty and Sally grab hold of me as I fall to the beautifully polished floor, wishing that I could close my eyes, shut it all out and sleep forever.

6. Minty

Classy Connections

I pop my head around the door of Simon's office. The smallest bedroom in the house on the top floor has been kitted out so he can work from home most days. I would hate to be stuck in there all day without a proper window to gaze out of (there's one small skylight in the roof) but Simon says it keeps him concentrated.

'Bridie's here,' I tell him, 'I'm off. I'll see you later.' Something about the awkward way he's sitting at his desk rings alarm bells. 'Are you alright?'

He's slumped, with his head in his hands. He lets out a big sigh.

'I'm fine,' he says, 'off you go. Have a lovely time.'

'Hey, this is me you're talking to you. Stop playing the martyr. What's up?'

'Gary's business is in a bad way,' he says gloomily. 'He's probably going bust.'

Rather uncharitably I just feel relief that his despair has nothing to do with us. Except for the loss of a client of course. 'Shit,' I say, 'that's bad. And crap timing, with the baby coming and everything.' I tap my fingers on my thighs.

'He's got this idea for personalised wellies. You know, photos of yourself or your pets and stuff –'

'Like you have on mugs and cushions?'

'Exactly. What do you think? Is that a good idea or not? It means borrowing yet more money to invest in new equipment but he's convinced it's going to make a mint and get him out of this mess. I'm not so sure.'

'It could work.' I'm not much interested in Gary's Wellington Boot Company, why should I be? He's never shown the slightest interest in me or my salon. He's a good friend of Simon's though and was his first client when we moved to Kingsmead, so I suppose I ought to show a bit of gratitude. 'Can we talk about this later, Hun? Bridie's waiting.'

He waves his hand at me in a vague gesture. 'No worries. And darling, please, keep it to yourself?' He makes me sound like a gobshite, always mouthing off. I raise my chin in self-righteous hauteur and promise him I won't breathe a word.

Bridie is waiting in the hall and she smiles up at me and tells me I look 'really nice'. I'm wearing a new dress. I've had to buy new clothes because I've put on more weight (why, why, why?) and I gave my hair some extra special treatment today, so I'm feeling alright. Bridie is looking the same as she always does, wholesome, organic, as though she's made entirely out of 100% unbleached fairtrade cotton. I do love her.

'Thanks for picking me up,' I say, clambering into the Land Rover Discovery, sweeping crumbs off the seat and kicking a tiny pair of Cinderella trainers out of the way. Little pink lights flash briefly on the soles in protest. Multi-coloured loom bands strangle the gear stick. She apologises for the mess as she always does, and, as always, I ignore her. She asks if I've remembered the DVD and I pat my handbag. We're off to Carol's house to watch *Spy,* the Mellissa McCarthy movie which I've seen before but can easily sit through again. Bridie is my 'movie buddy'. Sometimes she comes to my house and we pick something off NetFlix but tonight Carol has asked if we will go over to hers and 'help' her with 'something awkward on the web'. When I suggested making a night of it with a DVD and some nibbles she agreed enthusiastically. She doesn't socialise much these days and after what happened at Sally's (fuck me, what a show that was!) she's become even more reclusive. Poor Carol. We have no idea what advice she's after. It's all very mysterious. I think Sally is coming too.

Bridie asks after Simon and I tell her all about Gary Simpson's Wellington Boot Company being on the point of going bust. It's okay, Bridie never tells. Her lips are sealed, which is a good job, because she must get all kinds of juicy stuff from Jezza.

I've brought two bottles of white wine and I can feel their iciness against my legs. I can't wait to crack one open, although I've already had a bottle of Sol. I have to hide alcohol now, ever since the episode on New Year's Day. It's ridiculous, but there it is. If you can't join them, beat them. Ha ha! If my family insists on treating me like a child then I will behave like one. We've reached an understanding (or so they think) which allows me to drink wine with our evening meal, but no more than two glasses, and never anything before 6.30 (in the *evening*…ha ha again!). Jack was the driving force behind this new incentive, and I resent the hell out of it. I don't show it. I love my son and I want us all to be happy, so I go along with their idea of what's 'responsible' drinking, but they have forced me into secrecy. It's their fault.

It was fun coming up with a brilliant hiding place. I wanted somewhere easily accessible but where neither Jack nor Simon is likely to look. Jenny isn't a concern. She agrees with me that they're being far too heavy-handed and I think if she found my secret stash she could be relied upon to keep quiet. She's my girl. I wonder if Joy would have been like her.

At first I hid some bottles of Sol in my wardrobe and some wine in my bottom drawer, but there are hot water pipes running behind the skirting boards in our bedroom and the bottles were getting too warm. So after some purposeful tours of all the nooks and crannies in the house I decided upon the picnic basket in the garage. I emptied it of all the plastic cups and plates, filled it with the booze and put the cushion covers for the garden furniture on top. No-one would ever look in there. Even if we decide to go on a picnic it will always be me who fetches the basket. Every time I secretly open the creaky wicker lid it sounds like a party. I've been sneaking off to the garage for my top ups for nearly six months now and no-one has rumbled me yet. It gives me great satisfaction.

Bridie is upset about Gary's predicament, because she cares about everyone.

'That's terrible,' she says, 'and now they've got a baby on the way. Poor Sarah. What's he going to do?'

Poor Sarah my arse. She's hard boiled that woman.

I tell her about Gary's idea for personalised wellies and Bridie is enthusiastic, she thinks it's great. Her house is full of The Wellington Boot Company wellies in various sizes, decorated with flowers/puppies/Union Jacks/cup-cakes. If this plan comes off she'll no doubt buy a whole load more with pictures of the children and Wes the dog on them, bless her.

She drives very carefully down the High Street and I know she's thinking what I'm thinking as we pass the Beauty Salon. The door and windows have been replaced, it looks as good as new, but we can still remember the almighty bang when Carol's car came crashing through, and I'm sure Bridie will never forget the sight of Martha's pushchair, crushed beneath its wheels. We stay silent in the shared memory as we drive by. Bridie is so holy that she forgave Carol immediately for nearly killing her child. Apparently Carol was off her face on prescription drugs. There but for the grace of God…

Carol's house is on the edge of town, part of a small, leafy estate in red brick. Hers is the biggest. It's ugly and depressing, I can't think why she stays there. 'At least he left me the house,' she said to me once, and I thought, a double blow.

Sally's car is already on the drive. The garden is shabby, the grass is overgrown and there are weeds poking out between the paving stones.

'The gardener hasn't had a change of heart then,' I say, thinking it would drive me mad to look at that jungle every day. I have a gardener twice a week (on top of what Simon does in his spare time) and I think Jules does more hours for me than anyone else I know because I can't stand things to be untidy. Tidy house = tidy mind, so they say.

Bridie says he's a difficult man with some 'controversial opinions.' Actually, he's a bigoted, sexist 'Christian' who think it must be something Carol's done wrong to make her husband want to leave her. Carol's the victim, not the perpetrator. I mouth all this off to Bridie but she's the best advert for religion there is and it's not her fault the gardener is a twat.

A face appears in the window of the house next door then quickly goes back into the shadows. As we walk up to the front door I feel tiny, invisible eyes on me from all directions. I don't know how Carol can stand it, living here. I turn round and stick up my middle finger at anyone who might be watching. Bridie doesn't see. I smile to myself.

Carol answers the door bell, looking thin but quite happy, happier than when I saw her last anyway. She greets us warmly, accepts the wine off me and we follow her into the gloomy hall saying how much we like her dress and has she had her hair done differently? The dress is new, she says, from the very expensive shop in town where all the yummy mummies from

Kingsmead go. I always say there's one uniform shop for the kids and another for the parents. They all dress the same. Still, she looks nice.

We go into the kitchen where Sally is sitting at the table with a laptop in front of her. I notice the wine is already open. The house is warm from the Aga and there's a whiff of garlic in the air. There are candles burning in tins on the dresser and a red glow from a faded lamp throws an unusual hue on the scene.

'So - what's happening?' I ask, taking a seat as Carol goes to fetch wine glasses.

'Just tea for me please, Carol,' says Bridie, rooting around in her bag and producing a purple tea bag, 'here, I brought my own.'

'I need your advice,' says Carol, putting a wine glass in front of me and filling it, irritatingly only half full. I raise it to the room.

'Cheers!' Ah, the bliss of the first mouthful. I resist the urge to down it in one. 'Come on then, spill the beans.'

'I hope you won't be shocked,' says Carol, flicking on the kettle. She's blushing. I'm intrigued.

'I doubt it,' I say. It's bound to be something really lame.

Sally gives me a look, a hint of a warning.

'Is this blackcurrant?' Carol sniffs the tea bag.

'Can I tell them?' asks Sally. Carol gives her the go ahead with a coy smile, still holding the purple tea bag up to her nose.

'Blackcurrant and elderflower,' says Bridie, 'do you want to try one?'

Sally turns the computer screen towards us and I quickly take it in.

'Oh my God, Carol, *really?*'

'What is it?' Bridie leans in for a closer look and reads out loud. '*Classy Connections, international encounters offering you discretion, security and fun with people just like you...* I don't get it.'

'Whatever gave you this idea? I don't want to be negative Carol, but *Classy Connections*?' Honestly.

'I know. The name is a bit cheesy, but-'

'Is it a dating agency?' The penny has dropped with Bridie and she looks appalled.

The kettle whistles. Sally, Bridie and I read the *Classy Connections* extremely un-classy home page in silence as Carol talks with her back to us, filling the mug with boiling water. I can smell the steam from here, sickly blackcurrants. I reach for the bottle and give myself a top up. Looks like Sally's drinking tea too, so all the more for me.

'Sally advised me to go and see a counsellor,' Carol is saying, 'and it's given me a new perspective on life.'

'You can say that again.' I've clicked on 'saved favourites' and a picture of a fat middle-aged man on a boat grins out at me, lots of blue sky and sea is the promise he gives. Good times aplenty. Fun. Laughter. Wining and dining followed by middle-aged divorcee sex.

'My counsellor, Jayne with a y, has been teaching me how to take back control.'

'Lose it more like,' I say, and Sally gives me a reproachful nudge under the table.

'I hope you're never in my situation, Minty.' Carol is looking at me straight on. I've never known her to be so challenging. I apologise. It's just a bit of a surprise, I say, it seems so out of character.

'That's just the point,' says Carol, putting a white, china mug with 'I'd rather be in Norfolk' on it in front of Bridie who doesn't notice because her wide eyes are fixed to the screen. 'I couldn't go on the way I was.'

I click on the next 'saved favourite'. A tanned, good-looking man gazes moodily out at us. He's an improvement on Fat Boat-Man but I can't even for a second imagine Carol going out on a date with him.

'That's Sebastos,' says Carol, 'he's Greek.'

'I can see that,' I say, reading the screen. 'He's thirty-five and 'likes working with wood'. I bet he does.' No-one picks up on my wit.

'He's likes carpentry. But he's an optometrist by profession, as you can see.' Carol sounds defensive and I try to curb my cynicism for her sake.

'Do you really want my advice?' I ask. She says yes, although she isn't sounding so sure. I want to scream *what the fuck are you thinking*? But then, what reasons do I have to be so negative? Sebastos the Greek is watching me. Carol is watching me. Sally is staring at Sebastos with something like despair and Bridie is probably praying for Carol's lost, misguided soul.

'Just…be careful,' I say, like I'm talking to Jack or Jenny.

She smiles. There's a child-like gleam in her eyes and I think, maybe I'm wrong. Maybe Fat Boat-Man or Sebastos the Greek will make her happy again. It would certainly put two fingers up to her deserting ex and that bitch Shona.

'Was this your counsellor's idea?' asks Bridie.

'Not directly,' Carol says, 'but I'm not going to sit in this house and play the role of victim anymore.'

Oh God, I think. This Jayne with a y has all the lines. Sally is being very quiet. 'What do you think, Sal?'

'Well…'

'I think it's too soon,' buts in Bridie, reddening at her boldness. 'What if John decides he's had enough of the grass on the other side of the fence and wants to come back to you?'

'That's not very likely,' says Carol.

'And anyway she wouldn't have him back,' I say.

'Marriage is for life,' says Bridie.

'John doesn't seem to think so,' I say, emptying my glass. This is a very good Sauvignon Blanc. It's going down a treat.

'I just think you shouldn't be hasty.' Bridie is looking suspiciously at Sebastos. 'And...I don't mean to be rude but - isn't this one a little young?'

'That's just what I'm thinking,' says Sally.

'Age is just a number,' I proclaim, which of course is as corny as hell but many a truth is spoken in cliché. 'What's the age gap between John and Shona anyway?'

'Twenty five years,' pipes up Carol without hesitation. We all digest this reality in sympathetic silence.

'I think you should go for it,' I say, 'YOLO.' (It's something the kids taught me.)

'YOLO?' Bridie frowns at me.

'You Only Love Once. LIVE! I mean You Only LIVE Once. Shit, talk about a Freudian slip.'

'I've already set up my profile,' says Carol, turning the screen and tapping a few keys, 'Jules helped me, let's see if I can remember how to-'

'Jules?' Sally's jaw drops. 'What on earth did you let *her* in on it for? Oh Carol, you should have asked me first.'

'Jules has been a great support to me,' says Carol.

'Really?' I'm sceptical. Jules is alright, but at the end of the day she's the paid help. She shouldn't be masquerading as Carol's friend. I'm with Sally on this one.

'She doesn't clean for John anymore,' says Carol, 'not since Shona made such a fool of me that night at Sally's.'

'She made a fool of herself,' says Sally, 'not you.'

Carol shrugs. She's still trying to work something out on the computer. 'All I'm saying is, she's stood by me.'

'So have we!' I say, indignant, 'and what's more we don't charge by the hour!'

'Let's not make judgements about Jules' motivation,' says Bridie, 'I'm sure she means well.'

'Isn't the road to hell paved with good intentions?' I ask.

'Ah, here it is.' Carol turns the screen and we all look. It's a good picture of her, I'll give her that. 'Jules took it,' says Carol, 'right here in the kitchen, just using my phone.'

'I didn't know you could play the piano,' says Sally, reading the hobbies and interests.

'I can't really. I mean, I used to play at school. Jules and I were struggling to come up with anything to say about me, I mean, there isn't much....'

I'm flabbergasted. 'Shit Carol. Your self-esteem is in your *boots*. We need to re-write this, it's crap. 'Wine club'? 'Cats'? This is hardly going to set Sebastos on fire. You sound like a dull old lady.'

Carol looks at me and I see her face crumple, literally, as she starts to cry. Fuck. I've gone too far. I jump up and put my arms around her, apologising, while she sobs that I'm right, she's just a dull old lady that no man is ever going to want, and we all disagree with her, vehemently, talking over each other in our frantic efforts to make the bad stuff go away.

It all calms down after a bit. We re-take our seats, Carol does a bit of deep breathing and I drain my glass.

'If you insist on going through with this you may as well do it properly,' I say.

I turn the laptop towards me and click 'edit profile.' 'Do you really belong to a wine club?' I ask her.

'Well, John does. I used to go with him sometimes.'

'Scrub that then. This is about you, not John.' I delete 'wine club'. ' And cats? Really?' I raise my eyebrows at her. I have a feeling that her cat died recently, wasn't he run over? I don't want to set her off again but this has got to be done right.

'I really do like cats,' says Carol.

'There's nothing wrong with that,' puts in Bridie.

'But you don't have one anymore,' says Sally, reading my mind, 'it looks a bit odd to say you like cats when you don't even have one. You could just say 'animal lover'.

'Some animal lovers are complete whackos,' I say, deleting 'cats.'

And so it continues. We quiz Carol about her passions and vices (sadly too few) and end up having a good laugh. Eventually, this is what we have:

Name: Carol

Age: 51

From: Kingsmead, Cambridgeshire.

Status: Divorced

Hobbies: I have a wide circle of friends and I like nothing more than meeting up with them for a chat over a few glasses of wine or a pot of tea, depending on the time of day! I also enjoy walking in the countryside, going to the theatre and singing, in the bath or with a piano accompaniment, not usually both! I am a member of a local amateur dramatics group where I help behind the scenes.

Interests: I love animals but I'm no activist, just a lady who's used to having a cat or dog in the house.

Sadly my beloved Ginger Tom was killed on the road and no doubt there's a kitten or a puppy out there that will melt my heart and find its way in to my home.

What I am looking for in a partner: Loyalty, laughs and a long term relationship.

I know it's not that great, but I for one am feeling a tad pissed so may have to edit it tomoz. We had a laugh trying to find more things beginning with 'L' to continue the illiteration….alliteration? Alliteration, hahaha! Another Freudian slip, I am illiterate because I can't spell alliteration.

Carol has made a lasagne and I try to eat some but it's a bit stodgy for me so I wash it down with some of her red wine, which is incredibly good, she has 'crates of it in the cellar', she's SO POSH I tell her and it's so bloody good to see her laugh. Bridie tells me I'm 'incorrigible' and I tell her I'm not a piece of fucking cardboard. This lasagne is like cardboard though, the lasagne is 'incorrigible', not me, I say.

Sally is off early. Something about her dog needing pills and that hopeless husband of hers Bertie not being able to deal with it. It's a rubbish excuse to leave a party. I try to persuade her to stay, it's only a fucking dog, it won't kill it to have its pills in the morning, but she doesn't look very happy with this truth, oops, me and my big mouth. BUT SO MANY PEOPLE CAN'T HANDLE THE TRUTH.

'He's in pain,' she says.

'Who? Bertie?'

Bridie giggles. She's so adorable. She's like one of her own children. I LOVE HER.

'No,' says Sally, who seems to have left her sense of humour somewhere, 'Kasper. The dog. I have to give him pain killers every four hours.' So they all start talking about what's wrong with the fucking dog and it's boring as shit.

'Tell Bertie to take it round to Jezza, he'll give it the pills,' I say, but no-one seems to be listening to me. Bridie says something about Jeremy being a doctor not a vet, but I remember this film where there was a vet serving in the first world war and he had to do operations on people, it's absolutely true, but I can't remember the name of the film.

'I thought we were going to watch *Spy*?' I remind them all, breaking up the dog conversation.

'It's too late now,' says Carol, 'we'll watch it another time.'

Lightweights.

'Haven't you got to be at work tomorrow?' asks Sally, getting up and putting on her sensible anorak. The lining is decorated with lots of little sausage dogs. I tell her my first appointment isn't until ten. She could do with having her eyebrows waxed. I think I may have said that out loud. When I've topped up my wine glass I notice Sally putting the bottle away in the cupboard. Boo. Misery guts.

I tell Carol she should definitely meet up with Fat Boat Man and Sebastos the Greek. I will sit behind a big newspaper in the corner of the restaurant and keep an eye out for her, I say. She says don't you dare. But Bridie is worried about Carol's safety. You have no idea who they are, she says, they could be rapists. Carol says there are plenty of guidelines on the website on how to keep yourself safe, and there's something about the way she says it, about wanting to keep herself safe while she's going out to meet these strangers because her husband has left her, it just cuts me up, it's so unbearably sad, and I start crying and I go over to her and hug her and tell her I love her. She laughs. She's trying to be brave and it's just the saddest thing.

I quote Anthony Perkins, from *Psycho*, '"We're all caught in our own private traps."' but she has no idea what I'm talking about. '"Sometimes we deliberately step into those traps…"' What's the name of the woman in *Psycho*? They don't know.

Bridie says I'm a nutcase and I couldn't agree more.

I need a wee. There's a loo downstairs somewhere but it's pokey and I like Carol's bathroom. It's an effort to get up the stairs. It's very quiet. This house feels abandoned. Like Carol. The stair carpet has been well hoovered by Jules. There are some pictures on the wall, nothing interesting, but I wonder if she's kept all the family photos out? There used to be a big one in the hall, a black and white professional photo, all of them looking happy and proud. It was in a gold frame. Is it still there? Does she want to look at the traitor's face every day? I'll look out for it on my way down.

I go in the wrong room. A very tidy, white bedroom. I can hear Bridie talking downstairs but this house is too quiet, like it's not breathing anymore. The next door I try is the bathroom. I lock the door behind me. The sight of the loo makes me feel nauseous. Association. I struggle with my tights and underwear, sit on the loo, relax, take some breaths, look around me. Everything in here is trying too hard to be tasteful. John Lewis meets The White Company. Except for the gold taps. They remind of John's gold tooth.

My tights and knickers have got all tangled up. I pull them off. I'll sort them out in a bit. It smells of soap in here. It's nice. Peaceful. The towels are all neatly folded and very thick and fluffy. Like the loo roll, embossed, expensive. I wash my hands with the creamy liquid soap and make the mistake of looking in the mirror. Who is that haggard, red-eyed woman with the mad hair? I run my wet fingers under my eyes. Why has my make-up smudged?

I have no idea what the time is, I left my watch at home. I go down the stairs, noticing how soft the carpet feels on my feet. I wouldn't want to live here. It's too empty. A hollow house.

They stop talking when I come back into the kitchen. There are mugs of coffee on the table, including one in front of my seat. I tell them I'm not quite ready for coffee yet and I help myself to more wine, I remember which cupboard Sally put it in. Where is Sally? They say she's gone home but I don't remember her leaving, or saying goodbye. How rude. Carol offers me a custard cream, she knows they're my favourite. I have several, one after the other, I love them. We talk about Carol's date. She tells me not to refer to him as 'Fat Boat Man'. Did I call him that? What's his name? Douglas, she says. He's not Scottish is he? Bridie says she loves the Scottish accent. What's wrong with Scottish, demands Carol. She's a bit tetchy but I suppose that's to be expected. Bridie wants to leave, I can tell. Everyone always wants to leave just when things are getting interesting. I want to ask Carol how many dates she would have to go on with Fat Boat Man, I mean Douglas, before she has sex with him. It's like being a teenager again. If I wasn't so happily married I think I would be quite jealous of all the excitement and anticipation Carol has in store, she could date a different man every week! I can't wait to hear all about them. 'When will we three meet again?' Like the witches. I'm standing in the hall now, I have no idea why, but Bridie has got hold of my arm and is steering me towards the front door. Where's my bag? Carol hands it to me and I hug her, really squeeze her, because she is being so incredibly brave, and I'm so happy for her, that she's trying to make a new life for herself, and she laughs again, wriggling out of my ardent embraces. I get a bit emotional sometimes.

I think I must have dropped off in the car.

Bridie is shaking me. We're outside my house. My lovely home. Simon. I want to crawl into bed beside him and cuddle him. Bridie asks me if I'm alright, she wants to show me to the front door. Of course I'm alright. How do you open this fucking car door?

I wave goodbye from the doorstep but it makes me lose my balance. I stop myself from falling just in time by grabbing hold of the door knob. Shit. Somehow I've hurt my arm.

Simon is waiting up for me. I natter away at him while he helps me undress. I tell him all about Fat Boat Man and Sebastos the Greek, but the only thing he says to me is, 'Where are your knickers and tights?' I must have left them in Carol's bathroom. There's no need for that po-face of his, what's the big fucking deal, she's my friend. It's funny when you think about it. I try to get him to laugh but he won't even smile.

Misery guts.

I love falling asleep next to him.

I love that feeling of giving way, of everything shutting down.

The completeness of oblivion.

7. Sarah

Confrontations

I'm on my way to a pub in Cambridge to meet Jack. I have decided to tell him that he may be the father of my child.

I found this place online, The Lamb and Flag, the sort of pub that's been there forever, built centuries ago around the generations of old men drinking at the bar. It's in a part of the city I would never normally go to, and neither would anyone else that I know, which is why I chose it.

I push open the door and take in the smell of beer and lavatory cleaner, wondering at the turn my life has taken and how I've managed to end up here, pregnant, joyful and afraid.

I ask the landlord for a bottle of sparkling water. The bar props stare openly. I'm a break in their routine. I say yes to ice and a dried up slice of lemon but no to a lunch menu.

I take a table by the window. There are cardboard beer mats, warped and stained, on the heavily lacquered surface, and a small vase of dusty, plastic daisies. I check my phone. No message from Jack. I'm ten minutes early.

I can hide my bump if I want to, if I sit in a certain way and wear the right kind of clothes. Apparently the baby is small for my dates but the doctors aren't concerned. Gary wants me to wear more fitted clothes, Lycra, tight dresses, to announce to the world that I'm carrying his child. He's over the moon. Totally ecstatic. I expected him to be pleased but I'm surprised by the level of his excitement and euphoria. I told him in bed, the day after I found out, and just after we'd had sex. I didn't tell him straight away because I needed time to decide what I was going to do. Naturally he thinks the baby is his, and there's a fifty-fifty chance it might be. After a few weeks of pretending that everything was ok and that Gary was definitely the father, I realised I couldn't do it. I have to know. I haven't yet decided what I'll do if it turns out that it's Jack's. I'll cross that bridge when/if I come to it – but I have to know.

The plastic hanging baskets outside the window are swaying in the breeze. It's a nice day. Summer is finally here. I feel the baby turn, a leg, or an arm, poking out then pulling back in. I can't help but smile. The love I have for this baby is a powerful force that has completely taken me over. It's stronger than anything, my sex drive, my commitment to my marriage, my love of my job, my fear about its paternity, they are nothing compared to my fierce protectiveness towards this growing life inside me. I would give everything away if I had to, everything and everyone, in order to keep my baby safe.

I look up when the door opens. An elderly, scruffy woman with Nike trainers on her feet limps in pushing a walking frame. The landlord greets by her name, Brenda, and asks her how she's doing. 'Oh, you know,' she says, 'living the dream.' The landlord pours her a pint.

A familiar figure is crossing the road, I see him through the window and my heart gives a little kick. Jack – he looks so young. He's wearing navy jeans and a faded red tee shirt. He's carrying an over-stuffed rucksack and his feet look enormous in grey and white converses. He reminds me of a big puppy, except of course, that he's sexy. Yes, even now, I still get that feeling when I look at him. He's walking like he hasn't a care in the world, but I know he'll be anxious, wondering why I've asked him to meet me here.

I smile and wave as he looks around for me, framed by the doorway. The others are taking all this in and probably jumping to the right conclusions.

I half stand to kiss him on the cheek. He smells gorgeous. He looks like he's recently had a haircut but his cheeks are rough with thin stubble. For a second I remember it clearly, that time in the shed, the feel of him, his self-conscious need, his wonder and his fear, he was so easy to read and so delightful. At the time I was slightly disappointed though, he felt too young after all, not quite ready to give me what I wanted. Maybe it would be better the second time...but there never would be a second time. I watch him at the bar getting himself a pint.

You might need that drink, Jack, when you hear what I have to say to you.

When he gets back to the table and sits down opposite me I tell him he looks well. He's says he got a 2:1 and I say well done, that's great, and we talk for a bit about his graduation ceremony (Minty got drunk and cried all the time, no surprise there) and his train journey down here (expensive because he's lost his student rail card). He drinks his beer too fast. He hasn't paid me any compliments or asked about me beyond the necessary 'how are you?' and I wonder if he no longer finds me attractive, he must surely have noticed I've put on weight. I picture him with his pretty young girlfriend, her young limbs around his body, her smooth skin, her firmness. His life has nothing to do with me, and yet we may be irrevocably connected forever.

We get to the point where the small talk has completed its purpose.

'Jack...there's something I have to tell you.' I have rehearsed this. Jack is staring at me, his foot is tapping against the table.

'What?'

'I'm pregnant.'

He looks away, out of the window, then back at me. 'I thought you said you couldn't have children?' His cheeks have flushed. The foot tapping has upped its tempo.

'That's what I thought, what I genuinely thought, I had IVF...'

'Why are you telling me this?'

Oh my. Work it out, Sherlock.

'There's a chance you may be the father.'

'Jesus. Shit...'

For a minute he looks as if he's going to get up and leave, but of course he doesn't. Where can he hide?

'Thanks, Jack, I guess that's the reaction I expected.'

'What do you want me to say? "Yay! That's great news!"?' He actually looks as if he's breaking out in a sweat. I need to put him out of his misery.

'Stop worrying, if it turns out you're the father I'm not coming after you for anything,' and then, rather cruelly, 'you have nothing I want.'

'Then why are you telling me?' He's relieved already. Little bastard. But totally understandable. I must be fair.

'Because I need you to have a DNA test, so I can be sure.'

'But it's bound to be mine! Of course it is! Gary must have been firing blanks which is why it never happened with you and him....Shit.'

It's irritating beyond belief that he's suddenly an expert on why Gary and I couldn't conceive, despite all the time and money we've thrown at it, all the doctors, the tests and the scans, it seems after all that, young Jack Morgan has all answers. The arrogance of youth.

'Our infertility was unexplained. We had all the tests and everything appeared normal. It could still be Gary's child.'

'Can't you work it out? The dates and shit?'

I sigh. 'Not possible. The only sure way is a DNA test. It's quick and simple, I'll pay for it and it can be done in confidence. No-one need ever know.'

'No-one would blame me, you know. Everyone would say it's your fault for leading me on.'

I wonder how many women and girls have heard that over the centuries. I thought the modern man was different. I thought the days were long gone when women were left holding the babies while fathers did everything they could to wriggle out of any responsibility.

I lean over the table and speak closely to his face.

'Your dick. Your sperm.'

I see him swallow. He looks around to check we're not being overheard. It's certainly gone very quiet at the bar.

'It takes two to tango,' he retaliates, summoning up some puerile courage.

'You're dead right,' I counter, 'and I'm accepting responsibility for my part. I'm keeping this baby and I want to know who the father is. All I'm asking is that you do your bit in helping me to find out.'

We stare at each other for a while. He looks down into his pint. I notice that his hands are trembling.

'Look, Jack,' I adopt a gentler tone, 'I understand that this is a bit of a shock...'

He snorts. 'No kidding.'

'But you have nothing to worry about. Honestly. I can sort everything out regarding the test, and if it turns out you're the father I give you my word I won't ask you for anything, ever.'

'What? You'd palm it off as Gary's?'

The word 'it' offends me, but under the circumstances I let it go.

'I don't know. I haven't worked that out yet. I'll see what the test reveals.'

He downs the rest of his beer. I offer him another one but he shakes his head. He looks young and scared.

'Will you do if for me, Jack?'

He takes a short breath, then nods, says ok, asks what he has to do, and quickly I tell him, making it all sound as straightforward as possible so that he won't change his mind. I'm so relieved. This is the first hurdle over with.

'Have you told anyone?' he asks, 'about us, I mean?'

I smile. 'No. And I was going to ask you to keep all this to yourself. I don't think Kingsmead is ready for this sort of scandal, do you?'

'Mum and Dad would go mental…'

'Gary wouldn't be exactly thrilled.'

We are silent in a small moment of conspiratorial comradeship. Then I ask him where he's headed and he says he's getting a train home. I tell him I'm going back to Kingsmead too, why don't I give him a lift? He hesitates, I persuade him. 'We're friends aren't we?' I see him relax a bit.

We talk for a while about easy stuff, job prospects and upcoming holidays, he says he's going to Paris for the weekend with some friends, and a bit about his new girlfriend, Tabitha. I think he's about to show me a picture then thinks better of it.

I flash forward in my mind to years from now, when this baby is eighteen and might want to break into Jack's life just when he's settled with a wife and family. And where will I be then?

It depends. It all depends on the result of this test.

It's awkward in the car. We're too close, too trapped. I regret offering him a lift and I'm sure he regrets accepting it.

I'm in the middle of a bend on the A10 going fifty miles an hour when suddenly, like a gasp, I come face to face with a large van overtaking a tractor on the other side of the road. I slam on the brakes and experience a second of complete clarity, when I know I'm going to hit it, that there is no way to avoid it, and that I have no idea of what the next few seconds are going to hold for us. The impact is massive. I hear the screech of tyres, then the bone shattering bang, followed by other sounds I wouldn't expect, hissing, metal scraping, engines whining, and smoke filling the cabin.

I'm breathing. I am alive, but something is wrong, I don't know what it is.

My baby. My baby.

The air bags are slowly deflating, bringing the outside world into vision. Through the smoke I see parts of the van, body work, some lettering, everything smashed, crumpled like paper. I see the figure of a person, a man, running towards us. He is talking to me, shouting through the window.

My baby. My baby. My baby.

I can move my hands. I put them over my bump. I can feel something pressing into my side. Something sharp.

The man is talking into his phone. I see other figures. I hear shouting, and a baby crying.

I close my eyes. My hands holding on to my belly.

I dare not look at Jack.

Later, when I see Gary, the tears flow quickly, as if they've been waiting for him to arrive. I am lying in a hospital bed, curtains drawn around me, I'm still wearing my dress but my tights and shoes have been taken off me. They've already checked me over, and the baby. When I heard the heart beat I wept with relief. I've some bad bruising on my legs, a broken rib and two broken fingers on my left hand, but I don't care, the baby is alive, the placenta is apparently still intact, and that's all that matters.

Gary holds my hand, strokes my face and wipes away my tears.

'It's ok, it's ok…' he says, trembling, as if he's freezing cold. Gary puts his head down in my hands. His shoulders are shaking with his sobs. We've been married for eight years but I've never seen him cry. The thickness and the curls of his hair are so familiar to me.

'I was terrified,' he says, kissing my fingers, being careful not to hurt me, handling me as gently as he ever has done, like I'm made of glass. 'I thought…Oh God. I can't live without you, Sarah. Nothing else matters, just you and me, and the baby. I can't believe how much I've lost sight of that.' He looks up at me. 'Nothing else matters. I love you.' His eyes are so green, so lovely, and so full of everything that we both desperately want to say. I tell him I love him, and my secret mocks me from the wings. 'I'm going to be different,' he says.

'Why different? I don't want you to be different…'

'There's something I haven't told you,' he says. Those green eyes are steady, fixed on me. My heart begins to thump uncomfortably, my broken rib is hurting. I stare at him, waiting for him to go on.

The curtain is pulled back and a nurse appears, wanting to take my blood pressure again. Gary and I pull apart. While the nurse is fussing with equipment Gary says he'll move out to make more room. The nurse asks me if I want painkillers and I say yes. She says the doctor will be round in half an hour or so. My blood pressure is a little high but nothing to worry about. She listens to the baby's heart beat and makes notes. She reassures me that everything seems to be fine. 'You've got a tough little cookie in there.' She packs up her kit and says she'll be back soon with the pills, pulling the curtain aside to let Gary back in. His shoulders are tense, he looks ten years older. He pulls up a chair, sits down, takes a short breath.

'The business is fucked, Sarah.'

The business. It's about the business. I don't know what I was afraid of but given the enormity of my own secret and everything that's just happened I thought it would be something far worse. He says it's been in trouble for months, he didn't want to worry me, he thought he'd be able to sort it out. He said he's spoken to Simon about it and taken some other advice, there's nothing to be done, there's no money and too much debt.

'It's been killing me,' he says, 'the stress. I was going to tell you, but then when you said you were pregnant I just couldn't.'

'We could take the money from our Virgin account if you need it to prop it up…'

He shakes his head. 'It would be throwing good money after bad. I've thought of everything. I had an idea for personalised boots but borrowing more money was going to be difficult. I can pay my debts over time, but it leaves us with nothing. Simon has been amazing, a really good friend. I was going to suggest that we have him and Minty over for dinner to say thank you for all the time he's put in, but obviously now…Jack's his priority. Oh God, that poor kid…'

My heart skips a beat. 'Jack's ok, isn't he? They said it was just a broken leg?'

'Didn't you know? They discovered internal injuries, he's in theatre now. It doesn't look good. Didn't they tell you?'

Oh God. Jack. Gorgeous, young, beautiful Jack. Minty and Simon's golden boy. It's all my fault. I start to hyperventilate.

Gary calls the nurse. My wind pipe is tightening, my heart constricting, I want to sit up but the nurse is pushing me down, putting an oxygen mask over my mouth, Oh God, Jack. What have I done to you?

I have no sense of time. It surprises me when I realise it's getting dark outside. I've been sleeping on and off, a heavy, drug induced sleep. Gary has gone home to shower and fetch some things for me. I long to go home. I long for my bath and my own bed. The lighting in here is sickly, a sort of iodine glow. My pillows smell like an industrial laundry, the sheets are scratchy, it's too hot. I'm on a ward with three other women, I know nothing about them and I'm not interested. Two of them are quiet, the other is demanding. She has an accent I can't place.

I can't stop thinking about Jack. One of the nurses, Becky, who is young and kind, promised me she'd keep me informed of any change to his condition. He's out of theatre, she told me, but still in ICU. He's young and strong, she said, it helps.

I told Gary that I'd happened to see Jack in Cambridge as I was on my way home from a meeting, he was walking to the train station, I said, so I offered him a lift. He'd been visiting a friend there en route from Edinburgh, someone who owed him money or something, you know what students are like…

It was too much information. It sounded suspicious. I'm a good liar normally. I wonder if Gary has passed that explanation on to Simon and Minty? I wonder if they blame me for the accident? I wonder if they've done the 'what ifs'? There were plenty of witnesses, Gary said, the police have statements and it clearly wasn't my fault. Even so, I know what Minty is like. She can be fierce. And I have a new understanding of the power of maternal protectiveness.

Gary has put my phone on the bedside table where I can reach it. I pick it up, wincing with the pain in my rib. It's loaded with messages of concern. I read a few, feeling woozy, not really taking them in. I think about texting Jack, then dismiss the idea. He won't be reading messages for some time yet, and someone else might read it. Too risky.

I lie back and think about those last moments in the car, the awkward conversation, the closeness of him, the lovely smell of him, the sense that he was looking forward to getting away from me, that he was regretting accepting a lift.

How ironic. We had no idea then how much we would both regret that car journey. Life-changing decisions are often made in oblivious seconds.

He has to pull through. I can't contemplate any other outcome. I won't accept anything less than a full recovery. If he dies, and this is his baby, how can I keep that from Minty and Simon? It would be cruel to deny them the existence of Jack's child.

He's not going to die.

Oh God. My head hurts. Will there come a time when everything is ok? The other day I read some advice from a 'lifestyle coach' in a magazine. It said, 'Will what you are worrying about today matter in five years, or even one year, from now? If not, then let it go.'

What I'm worrying about today is possibly going to matter for the rest of my life. I can never let it go.

Twenty four hours have passed since the crash, and my pain has changed. I can pinpoint my broken rib, my broken fingers, my bruised legs, and I ache all over. The doctor said that's the come down from all the adrenaline that's been raging through me. I'm still worried about the baby, and the painkillers. Should I be taking drugs? He says everything I want to hear and I'm reassured. I think he's German, his accent is like Karl's. It seems like another world when I was all fired up thinking about sex with Karl. I feel fat, bruised, clammy, in desperate need of a bath. I can't imagine ever wanting sex again.

I keep asking after Jack. No news.

One of the nurses helps me up to the loo. I'm a bit shaky, but it's good to get on my feet. When I pull the thick, paper towels out of the dispenser I feel the baby give a violent kick. I gasp, holding on to the sink, but I cry with joy. I so badly want to go home.

I get back in to my hot, uncomfortable bed. Becky, the kind young nurse, appears, my heart flips and I scan her face for clues about Jack before she speaks. She says he's conscious and he's communicating with his parents.

Communicating? How? That sounds bad. I'm thinking blinks, grunts, finger movements. Oh God.

She says that's all she's been told. She isn't looking at me now and I wonder what she knows, if they've been gossiping about me, but I'm being paranoid, how could she know anything? She's checking my notes, tucking in my sheet, tidying me up. She takes away my water jug to refill it.

When she's gone I think about Jack and the DNA test. I wonder if he'll ever be well enough to have one. He is going to get better of course. He has to.

Gary arrives and finds me in a state.

'Get me out of here,' I beg him, 'I can't stand it. It's driving me mad.'

He prises my hands from their vicious grip on the sheets, opens out my fingers, carefully strokes them. The two that are broken are bruised, swollen and throbbing.

'Hey, ssh, ssh, it's ok…'

'It's really not ok, I can't stand it in here, it's so hot and claustrophobic…'

'The nurse said the doctor wants to see you again before you're discharged remember?'

'I keep asking when he's going to see me and they just keep fobbing me off.' I'm tearful, almost hysterical. Gary looks alarmed, this is most unlike me.

An elderly lady in a floral dress and brown sandals pushes a tea trolley into the ward. While the noisy woman in the opposite bed is choosing biscuits I ask Gary if he's heard anything about Jack.

'I spoke to Simon last night…'

'And?'

'He's really worried about him…obviously…he's lost his spleen…'

'Oh God…'

'But it's not as bad as they thought.'

'He's going to be alright isn't he?'

For a second Gary's expression is quizzical. He knows me very well. I feel my cheeks burn.

'He's out of danger.'

'Thank God…'

'Hopefully they're transferring him to the regular ward today.'

'That's such good news. And what about Simon and Minty? I feel bad for not messaging her, I just didn't know what to say, not until I knew how he was. I'm sure she'll blame me in some way. Have you spoken to her?'

'Not yet.'

The elderly lady rattles over to us and offers tea. We decline politely. She offers biscuits, magazines, flap-jack…we decline again. She scuttles off disappointedly to the next bed.

'I've got to get out of here,' I say.

'I know. Stop worrying. It's not good for you.' He's still giving me that quizzical look. 'Poor you…' he leans forward to hug me, awkwardly avoiding my bump and my broken rib. The familiar smell of him and his gentle touch soothe me.

'Will you go and see what you can find out?' I ask, stroking his lovely curly hair, 'if the doctor sees me today I could be in my own bed tonight.'

'Our bed you mean. I'll see what I can do.' He stands up, then grins. 'Don't go anywhere.'

I have a text from Minty. I daren't open it. She must know by now that the accident wasn't my fault but even so, I can't help but be a little afraid of her. And what if Jack confesses everything in his weakened state? What if he's told her about the baby? About us? He's so young. How is he going to deal with all this? Shit. What a mess.

After ten minutes Gary comes back looking pleased with himself. I hide my phone under the sheet.

'The doctor's on his way,' he said, 'I just spoke to him. You should be able to come home this afternoon.'

I start to cry again. Everything just feels so weird.

'It's the shock,' says Gary.

When we finally get home at about seven in the evening Gary becomes obsessed with looking after me. It's nice, but worrying. It's unlike him to be so frantic. It gives me the jitters. After running me a bath, which I lie in for half an hour (bliss), he sits me in front of the TV like an old woman in a care home, makes me camomile tea, clatters about in the kitchen until delicious smells make me hungry.

I'm so tired.

I still haven't read Minty's text. I'm afraid to.

He's made a vegetarian curry. He is a great cook.

'Not too spicy,' he says, handing me a good sized serving topped with fresh coriander and a dollop of natural yoghurt, 'we don't want to give Baby a tummy ache.'

Gary's picked that up from the midwives, using 'Baby' and 'Mum' as proper names. He looks tired, he's trying too hard. Poor Gary. And I can't believe his business is going under and he's kept it all to himself for so long. But then, look at the secret I've kept inside of me. It's ironic really. We always thought we had the most honest relationship of anyone we know. We were too pleased with ourselves. He talks about it again but only briefly, guiltily, as if he's ashamed. My mind has gone to mush and he knows. So we stare at mindless TV for a while and go to bed early, but I can't sleep.

In the middle of night I open Minty's text.

8. Jules

Reality, Risks and Revenge

On Mondays I do the Morgans. The Morgan's house is my favourite. Araminta keeps things nice. She's an alcoholic, but she likes the house kept nice. She hides her drink in the picnic basket in the garage. Nothing gets by me.

I found condoms in Jack's laundry basket last week; they must have fallen out of a pocket. Jack and his friends are planning a weekend in Amsterdam, but he's told Araminta and Simon that they're going to Paris. I know because I've seen the Facebook page, he left it open in his room. It's called 'Smoke Weed and Fuck Bitches'. Everyone thinks these posh boys are so nice and proper. I know the truth. Jack never notices me, except when I get in his way round the house.

Jenny has had her belly button pierced and Simon and Araminta don't know about that either. I heard her talking to her friend on the phone. It got infected and she had to go to Dr Gray for antibiotics. She kept them in the drawer beside her bed and I thought for a minute she was on the pill. She's very pretty and no doubt will break someone's heart one day. I like Jenny. She's always happy to chat with me. She asks me about my cat, which is eighteen years old, and my family.

Just after Christmas Simon threw the broken bits of an antique vase, a family heirloom, in the black wheelie bin, and Araminta still hasn't noticed the vase is missing. Simon's alright. Very patient. Not many men would put up with a wife like Araminta. She needs help, she'll kill herself with the drink.

The Morgan's house is on Elm Road, the smartest road in Kingsmead. All the houses on Elm Road are big and pricey. The Huths' house, next door to the Morgans, is the smallest, but I'll talk about them later. It has a nice front door, old fashioned, solid wood, which leads into a hall with stairs off. I don't know how old the house is but it's nice and modern inside. Classy. Araminta likes her towels changing every day, I put them in the tumble drier to keep them soft, even if it's a nice day and they could dry just as easily on the line. Araminta doesn't like things dried on the line. And the sheets on their bed are those really pricey ones, thick white cotton.

There's always a lovely smell in the Morgans' house. Araminta's perfume, or the fancy oils she puts in the bath, or something exotic cooking, or scented candles. Araminta has candles everywhere, I think they're a fire hazard. Simon is always checking the batteries in the smoke alarms.

There's a photo on Araminta's dressing table, a black and white one, in a silver frame. It's of the baby girl she had that died before it was born. Joy, they called her. Personally, I wouldn't want a photo of my dead baby on my dressing table. She was born dead on 13th August seven years ago, and on that day every year Araminta switches off her phone, shuts herself in her room with two bottles of wine and stays there all day. She always makes sure I'm working for her that day, and tells me not to let *anyone* in to see her. I protect her from the outside world. Every year on that day Bridie Gray calls round with flowers and a sad face, and every year I have to tell her that 'Mrs Morgan is indisposed to receive any visitors,' like they do on Downton Abbey, and I take the flowers and she goes away again.

I had to do the same for Carol when her rat of a husband left her. I was doing my regular clean at her house when her

117

neighbour rang the doorbell. She looked behind me over my shoulder into the house, wanting to have a good look at The Victim. I sent her away and Carol was really pleased with me. I believe in loyalty.

It happened to me you see. My first husband had an affair with a woman who lived on our street, she was married too, with children. We got divorced after that. I still hate him, and her. Two marriages broken, and for what? Because they got a bit tired of what was on offer at home? Because they couldn't keep their pants on? It's disgusting. They're not together now. What goes around comes around. I feel sorry for Carol, she's a good woman, and she still loves that dirty rat of a husband of hers, I can see it in her eyes when she talks about him. I think she's well shot of him, personally.

Carol's house doesn't get much sun because of the trees, but now it feels gloomier than ever, with Carol mooching about in it on her own. It's too big for her, my house would fit in it three times, but she doesn't want to move. 'Too many memories,' she says, which is exactly my point. Memories of a life with a man who was a liar and a cheat. I wouldn't stay there if it was me. It spooks me sometimes, the shadows of the trees on the walls, the wind whistling down the chimney. Each to their own.

I'll let you in to a secret. It was me who cut up that tramp Shona's clothes. When the rat asked me if I would go and work for him in his new place (Shona calls it their 'Love Palace') I said No at first. Not on your nelly, I thought, I'm not working for the enemy. Then I thought it might be a way to get some revenge for Carol. Keep your enemies close, that's what they say. So I changed my mind, and I took Carol's key (she still has one to the big house, they were doing it up together)and I had another one cut - she's so pumped with drugs she didn't notice it go missing for a day - and I left it a few weeks, just so they wouldn't suspect, and I went into Shona's dressing room the day of Sally's party when I knew Shona was out shopping in Cambridge, and I took all her best dresses, proper designer ones, all paid for by the rat, dirty money, and I cut them into ribbons. I thought of my ex-husband and the slut he ran off with, and it felt good. I left them in a pile on their bed, which is enormous. I think of them having sex in that bed and it makes me sick to my stomach. Filthy whore she is.

She blamed Carol, the stupid bitch. She came crashing into Sally's house in front of everyone, accusing her, and I felt like beating her to a pulp. As if Carol would ever do a thing like that! The rat persuaded Shona to let it drop, I heard them talking about it afterwards. He's got so much money the clothes don't matter to him. She still thinks it was Carol but I think the rat is suspicious of me. I left no trace of me. I messed up a few other things in the house just for good measure. When I think about it now it still gives me a thrill that I got away with it.

Carol has joined a dating agency but not many people know about that. She doesn't want the rat to find out, which is mad. I helped her to set up her profile, she's not very good like that. I filled in all the forms and took the photo. She's got her first date coming up, with a man who owns a yacht.

On Tuesdays I do the Gray's. Bridie could use me more often but she doesn't want to spend the money. They have six children under twelve. She's a Catholic, which explains that one, but still, you'd think, wouldn't you, that a doctor would know better. Their eldest two are twins, Peter and Maggie, then there's Patrick, Beatrice, Theresa and baby Martha. They're all named after saints, so she told me. I never knew there was a saint called Beatrice, that was news to me.

I babysit for them sometimes. The house is a mess, but they seem happy enough. Bridie is a saint herself, that's for sure, those children run her ragged. Dr Gray does his best, but he's a man after all, so we shouldn't expect too much of him. My boy, Dillon, is the same age as Peter, but they don't get on. Peter is loud and sporty. Dillon is an only child so he's not used to all that noise. He's sensitive. Bridie understands but not everyone can see that. When Dillon got into trouble with the police last summer I tried to explain how he just gets led into things. He's frightened of being left out. It comes from being an only child, I'm sure it does. So if the toughest boy in the school says Jump, Dillon will say How High. Or in this case, Why Don't You Go And Slash The Tyres On Mr King's Car, then Dillon won't think twice about it. I explained all that to the police, but they wouldn't listen. He was guilty, they said, the CCTV caught him, and that was that.

Of course I couldn't tell them that Dillon was really doing it for me. He knew how mad I was with Mr King, the headmaster of Kingsmead, but I would never tell him to go and do something like that. It was the other lad that put him up to it, put the idea in his head. You have to be careful if you want to get your own back on someone. You have to bide your time. Which is what I'm doing now.

You see, Mr King wouldn't take my boy into that posh school, he's not good enough for them, my Dillon. Carol told me about the Scholarships they have, or Bursaries they call them I think. They give boys like Dillon, who are bright but can't afford the fees, a chance to get a place in the school. Carol showed me how to apply. She said Dillon had as good a chance as anyone, and Dillon went round telling everyone he was going to Kingsmead. His teachers were very helpful and everyone said he stood a good chance. He went and did the exam, it was easy, he said, and I bought him the new Fifa Play Station game because I was so proud of him. I said he'd probably end up the first in my family ever to go to a University. He was the little star of our house for a while and he lapped it up, all the attention.

When we got the letter I read it quickly and afterwards I couldn't speak for a while, I was that angry. It said they were 'unable to offer Dillon a place'. I was working at the school that day and all, it was real hard, going into Mr King's office and cleaning his desk, hoovering everywhere, knowing he'd turned Dillon away. It's good job I didn't see him. I don't think I would have been able to stop myself from giving him a piece of my mind for getting Dillon's hopes up then turning him down without any say so why.

Yes, it's a good job I didn't do that. Revenge is a dish best served cold, that's what they say. I have something on him, Mr King, that will ruin his career. The scandal will drive him out of town. I just need proof that's all. I'm biding my time. It will come. He'll slip up like everyone does sooner or later, and then I'll seize my chance. You wait.

Enough about Mr King.

I said I'd tell about the Huths. I do them on a Friday. He teaches German, he's German himself, and she teaches art. What a pair, do they love themselves? How much! They have rude pictures in their bedroom, they call it art, and there's all sorts of weird underwear and funny kit in her wardrobe and I know why. It's because they go in for wife-swapping, you know, foursomes. I know it for sure, I have proof, but I don't say anything when I hear the gossip. I like to keep things to myself. I know it's true because I've seen the messages on Petula's phone. I've seen some from Gary Simpson, which were filthy, and also some from his wife, Sarah. One of them said *What did you do to Gary?! He's a wreck!*

I work for them too, Gary and Sarah Simpson. I do them on Thursdays. Odd couple. Fitness fanatics. House like a morgue. And she's sex-mad. I found a pornographic DVD in the cupboard under the TV. I played it, just for a few minutes. It showed a woman having sex with three men, all at the same time. She was half-dressed in some kind of waitress uniform and was making such a noise I had to put it on mute. It was shocking, what those men were doing to her, the way they spoke to her. I watched it for a while, wondering if that was what it was like with Sarah, Gary and Karl. It made me feel strange. What does Petula do while the other three are at it? I carefully put the DVD back where I found it. I haven't looked at it again, but I know it's there and it gives me the shivers. Those images have stayed with me.

Gary and Sarah had been trying for a baby for years before she finally fell in the spring. It nearly ruined their marriage I reckon, all the trying and the failing. That, and all the goings on with the Huths. What goes around comes around, that's what they say.

I'll tell you something else too. Sarah doesn't know who the father of her baby is. I saw the browsing history on her phone, it was all about paternity tests, DNA and everything like that. I don't think Karl knows yet, that the baby might be his. It will all come out in the wash as they say, and when it does, they will only have themselves to blame.

What goes around comes around.

So all in all I know a fair bit about the women of Kingsmead, and the men. They meet in coffee shops and pubs to compete with each other. They talk about their children, and other people's children, and gossip about people they don't know.

They talk about little things as if they're big. They don't seem to know how much money they have or the price of anything. I could tell Araminta that she owes me for two weeks work and she would just pay up. Sally gives me M&S vouchers for Christmas, fifty pounds worth, she says she has lots of them from her credit card company and she keeps forgetting to use them. I don't forget. I spend them on Christmas puddings, mince pies and socks and pants for Dillon and Doug. It goes a long way.

Doug can't work anymore because of his back. He used to work in the Tesco warehouse but he can't lift, and he can't drive the forklift without a break every ten minutes because of the pain. Tesco tried to find him other work but it was no good. He sits at home and watches Bargain Hunt, Antiques Road Show and Flog It, then he goes to car boot sales at the weekend with his mate Steve, looking for something he can sell for a fortune. The house is full of his rubbish. The best money he ever made was on an old Rolex watch. It looked like a piece of junk to me, but apparently it was a rare one. He made two hundred pounds on that and spent most of it in The Cross Keys.

I live in one of the council houses on Fern Road. They back on to fields which stink when the farmer is muck spreading. Doug has lived in our house for thirty years. His first wife died there. I haven't told Dillon that. It would make him freak out. As I said, he's sensitive.

Doug used to keep the garden neat before his back problems, but now I do everything. Dillon mows the lawn for me in the summer, but I do everything else.

I keep the secrets of Kingsmead. I don't tell a soul what I know. Not even Doug. For the first time ever though I'm going to blow the whistle on someone, because it's 'in the public interest'. Mr King is a liar and a fraud. I'm just biding my time. I want to get it right. I need concrete proof, and good timing.

I don't drive, I get around on my trusty bike, and Doug sold his little car when he could no longer drive because of the back pain. Steve drives him to the car boot in his van, and he walks to the pub. The doctor told him it's good to keep active.

I work hard and keep myself to myself. I like what I do. Every time I go into someone's house it's like a new chapter in a book. I never know what I'm going to find out next. Computers and smart phones are great ways of working a person out. I don't have one myself. I tell everyone it's all double-dutch to me, that way they don't suspect me. I have a Nokia, a 'dumb phone', and everyone knows it because I make sure they do, I leave it lying around. They laugh behind my back at the Nokia ring tone. They think I have no idea about social media or the internet. But I went on a computer course and I know everything I need to know about browsing history, searching emails, opening folders and photos, getting into Messenger. The hardest part was getting the passwords, I had to observe very carefully when their backs were turned. I'd be hoovering behind them while they punch in their passcodes and they have no idea I'm taking it all in, watching their fingers skip across the keys, committing it to memory.

Today I'm back early because I should be at the Simpson's, but Sarah is back from hospital and Gary is looking after her, so he sent me home. Jack is in a bad way, he said, but not at death's door. I think it's odd that he was in Sarah's car. Very odd indeed. I will have to investigate that one. I'll be able to get into Jack's phone or laptop when he gets out of hospital.

I get a thrill, thinking about that. It's such a kick. They all think I'm stupid.

But I know everything.

9. Carol

Surprises, Disguises, Tears and Trinkets

I go through the revolving door of Browns' Brasserie in Cambridge feeling slightly sick. I'm so nervous I can hardly walk. I haven't taken any of the pills Dr Grey gave me for two days now, I've been trying to wean myself off them, but now I regret it. Real feelings like these are still too much for me.

I could have backed out of this date many times, but Minty has been very forceful and insisted on escorting me as far the agreed venue. She persuaded me it was going to 'fun', even if it's a disaster. We can have a laugh about it afterwards, she said. But who will the laughter be aimed at? I wonder if she's really got my best interests at heart, of if she's just bored and flying on my coat tails for a vicarious thrill.

We came in on the Park and Ride, she's going to go off shopping, buy yet more things for Jack, she's been spoiling him rotten since he came out of hospital, which is understandable, it's been a horrible time, and then she's going to come and rescue me, I mean fetch me, at three. Oh dear. What am I doing, I must be mad. I told Minty that I hope I don't see anyone I know in Browns'. She replied she hopes I do. It will let everyone know you're getting on with your life, she said, that you're not letting your traitorous husband get the better of you, which is what Jennifer Aniston did when Brad left her for Angelina, she made sure she was photographed out on the town looking fabulous. Apparently. Everyone loved her for it. I reminded her, as if I needed to, that I am no Angelina, and John is certainly no Brad Pitt.

And I don't feel fabulous. Minty and Sally came over last night to supervise my wardrobe choices. Really, Minty behaves like a teenager sometimes. Sally is more sensible but I get the feeling she's very uncomfortable about all this dating lark and her reticence is not helpful to me.

I feel as nervous as a rabbit right now and if I could run away I would, with my little white tail in the air, but I suspect that Minty is hiding somewhere, watching me, to make sure I don't do just that.

My therapist, who's called Hamble, like the doll on Play School, says that I am in control of my own life. I am the mistress of my thoughts, feelings and actions, she says. I have techniques to follow when things feel like they're getting out of hand, techniques to remind me that I'm in charge. I have a mantra to repeat when I feel like things are getting on top of me, and breathing exercises. Sometimes they work and sometimes they don't, but I keep trying. Breathe. Channel your fear. Centre yourself. Breathe.

I scan the restaurant for my date, hoping that maybe he has chickened out and didn't come after all, then I see him, very similar to his photographs only a little greyer and fatter, standing up behind his table to wave at me. I smile as graciously as I can muster and go over to him, hoping not to trip in my kitten heels which I've only ever worn once in my life, to a wedding.

We shake hands, then awkwardly, he leans in to give me a brief kiss on the cheek. I accept as if I do this all the time. We make all the usual enquiries, health, journey time, weather, relief that neither of us have been stood up, a light laugh, and we sit, and I put my bag on the floor and pull in my chair. He's half way down a pint of beer. He asks what I'd like to drink and I can't decide, mainly because I don't

127

care. Anything will do, because all I can think about is how embarrassing this all is.

He looks around for a waitress. His cheeks and nose are red, sunburn maybe, or rosacea, it's difficult to tell.

'Have you been here before?' he asks, then laughs at himself. 'Do you come here often?'

'We used to come here a lot when the children were young, they like the chips.'

It's alright to mention children isn't it? We know all this stuff already, it's been dealt with, got out of the way, divorce, children, job, interests, lifestyle, habitat. The basic building blocks of a profile. We are both divorced (tick) and we both have grown up children (tick).

'There's one in Bath,' he says. Douglas lives in Bath and works for a soft drinks company. It occurred to me that there is much about him to do with water.

'Did you have a nice time in Mallorca?' I ask, remembering the photos of him on his latest nautical adventure.

'Fantastic,' he says, with a steady gaze which I suspect is suggestive, but of what I have no idea.

A young waitress with bad skin comes to take our order. My eldest son had acne and I immediately identify and sympathise with any fellow sufferer.

'Hello Amelia,' I say, reading her name badge, 'may I please have a glass of Prosecco?'

'A bottle!' barks Douglas heartily and so loudly that I jump.

'I think a glass....'

'A bottle! Bring us a bottle,' he says, 'and two glasses. We're celebrating.'

Thankfully Amelia doesn't ask what we're celebrating although I can't help wondering what he would reply. What could he possibly mean? Perhaps he's one of those people who always manages to find a reason to have a bottle of wine in the middle of the day, as if everything and anything is worth celebrating. As Arsene Wenger once said, 'If your team play well, you deserve it, and if they play badly, you need it.' John is an Arsenal fan. We used to go to some of the games. A long time ago. I wonder if he takes Shona now?

'And I'll have the Caesar Salad,' I tell Amelia, who is committing all this to memory without a notepad. 'Are you a student?' I ask, wanting to be friendly. She tells me she's at Anglia Ruskin but doesn't elaborate.

'I'll have the steak,' says Douglas, 'rare. With extra chips.' He gives me a wink, as if we have an understanding.

When Amelia has gone Douglas leans back in his chair and appraises me as if he's considering a purchase. It's most disconcerting and I fiddle with my napkin, not knowing where to look. He is wearing an expensive-looking blue and white striped shirt which is stretched over his enormous belly, like a stuffed pillow case. He has a gold signet ring on his right hand, matched in gaudiness by its neighbour, a large, shiny watch. My mother told me never to judge a book by its cover, or a sausage by its overcoat.

'So,' he says, taking two large swigs of his beer and licking his lips, 'here we are.'

I smile. 'Have you been on many...I mean, have you met many ladies through *Classy Connections*?'

'Some of them definitely weren't ladies,' he says, grinning, waiting for me to laugh.

'You're my first,' I tell him.

'I can tell.'

'Oh dear. Can you?'

'It's obvious.'

'How?' I oblige him out of genuine curiosity.

He shrugs. 'It's obvious,' he says again, unhelpfully.

'Whereabouts in Mallorca were you?' I ask, after a short and awkward pause.

'Palma mostly, we docked the boat there. Have you ever been to Mallorca?'

My mind drifts.

Yes, many times, with John soon after we were married, we stayed in a small hotel in Deia, and spent most of the time lying down, on sun loungers, in bed, on a tiny beach near Llucalcari which we walked to along the cliff tops, and the sun beat down on us as if it approved of our pure, unfettered love for each other, and then we went back there with babies and toddlers, pushing the buggy around the cobbled streets of Soller and Valldemossa, and spending hours on the beach under parasols, making sandcastles, paddling, splashing, catching the sun, eating out with glowing skin and sand between our toes, we ate pizza, tapas, grilled locally caught fish, we drank rose in the day time and we loved the island so much we went back year after year.

'Yes, I've been a few times,' I tell him, but I don't think he wants to talk about me, because for the next ten minutes he's telling me all about his boat and swiping through photo after photo on his phone, which I look at with feigned interest. I've never liked boats. They're just floating caravans if you ask me, which thankfully, he doesn't. One of the pictures is of him with his arm around an attractive brunette in a navy swimsuit and big sunglasses.

'Ooops!' he swipes it away and I sit back, knowing that I won't ever have to see this man again, so nothing matters really. 'That one didn't work out,' he says, as if by way of some sort of apology, as if I care. He taps the phone. 'Delete,' he says, smiling, like he's done something really nice for me.

Amelia comes back with our drinks. She shows us the bottle then opens it and pours it carefully into our glasses. Douglas is smiling at me. He looks…how can I put this? He looks pleased with himself and confident, as if he does this all the time and is sure of a good outcome. He's behaving as if he's about to go to a party. I am only three feet away from him but it could be a mile for all the connection I have. I wish I'd never come. It was a mistake. But I'm stuck here for at least an hour and a half with this odious man, I'm not the sort of woman who can think up a plausible excuse to leave, or risk offending him by telling the truth.

When Amelia has gone he proposes a toast.

'To good times.'

I raise my glass.

'So,' he says, 'you do a bit of amateur dramatics? Fancy yourself as a bit of an actress?'

'I just help with the costumes and publicity…'

'My daughter went to stage school,' he gets out his phone and I anticipate more photos, 'you know Hollyoaks?'

'I think so…'

'She was in that for a bit last year, do you recognise her?' He holds up his phone and I see a photo of a young woman in a tiny dress and thick make-up, staring out at me with a vacant expression, like a doll in a window.

'I don't really watch it, sorry. She's very beautiful.'

He shows me another. This time she's in a bikini on a boat, his presumably, and something about the way he looks at my reaction makes me squirm.

'She's hot, don't you think?' Then he laughs. 'I shouldn't talk about her that way. But I'm sure you understand. We're all proud of our kids, right?'

'Is she working at the moment?'

'She's between jobs,' he says, still scrolling through his phone, 'she's does a bit of modelling to keep her busy.' Then he talks for a good ten minutes about the famous people that she's met and the small roles that she's had on Casualty and Eastenders. He gossips about them as if I know who he's talking about, but I have never heard of these people. Clearly he thinks he is impressing me. I smile and chant my mantra in my head.

When Amelia returns with our food I am so pleased to see her I could cry.

'What are you studying at Anglia Ruskin?' I ask her desperately, then realise how odd this looks. I am showing more interest in the waitress than I am in my date.

'Film Studies,' she says, 'can I get you anything else? Ketchup? Mayonnaise?'

'Ketchup,' says Douglas, 'and lots of it.'

I thank Amelia, hoping to compensate for his bad manners, but I really don't think she cares.

There is a big station clock high up on the wall and I wonder if it's stopped because the big hand moves so slowly. Douglas eats enthusiastically but this doesn't stop him from talking. He mentions his ex-wife briefly in passing and I see his eyes go glassy and cold.

'I hated all women for a while,' he says, taking a swig of prosecco and looking at me with brazen reproach, 'she's a first class bitch, my ex. But after a while I decided I wasn't going to let her ruin my life. Did you take your husband to the cleaners?' This sounds like an accusation. I stare at him in disbelief. 'Sorry,' he says, looking anything but, 'I still get mad sometimes when I think about what she did.'

I don't want to know what she did exactly, but he tells me anyway. She worked for him in his plumbing business (water again) and was syphoning off money while carrying on with his best friend, who was also his accountant. My head spins with it all, his bitterness and hurt are too familiar to me, too much like all the poison I've been carrying around inside me these last few years. I'm dizzy. When I can stand it no longer I tell him I have to go to the ladies and I get up, hoping I don't look unsteady on my feet. I don't want to look as though I'm drunk.

You hear stories don't you, of people escaping horrendous dates by climbing out of lavatory windows? The only window in here is so small you wouldn't fit a cat through it. I lean against the wall and do my breathing exercises, recite my mantra, think of Hamble's reassuring voice. I send Minty a message, *Help, this is torture, please come as soon as you can*, then I wash my hands, check my appearance (shocking) and make my way reluctantly back to the table.

I have a chance to look at him before he notices me. His bravado has been put away in my absence and I see pathos in its place. He has finished his steak and is picking his teeth. As I approach he runs his hands over his thin hair and readjusts his belt. I don't think he hates his ex-wife like he claims to. I think he is still in love with her. Just as I am with John. I would like to have this honest conversation with him, it would be far more interesting and fruitful than talking about B-list celebrities and boats, but it's not going to happen. He's built a wall around that part of his past and it's not for me to knock it down. When I get back to the table I ask if his children know he's looking for a new partner.

'Of course,' he says, 'they're all for it. Although my youngest was a bit put out at first. He was a student at university when I first started dating and he grumbled that I was getting more action than he was! Ha ha ha!'

Am I supposed to think that's funny?

'I can't bring myself to tell my daughter,' I tell him, 'she took our marriage break up very badly.'

'How old did you say she is?'

'Nineteen.'

'Old enough to understand.' He refills our glasses. 'What about your sons?'

'Jonty, he's twenty-four, is fine with it, as long as I'm careful…'

'And avoid all the rapists and serial killers, you mean? They might be disguised as respectable men who play golf and have a yacht in Mallorca.' This is accompanied by a grin.

'He looks out for me that's all,' I say. Oh my. This is dreadful.

For the first time I feel tension between us and I'm relieved. At least I won't have to fob him off. Him disliking me is the perfect outcome.

'And Dan, the middle one, isn't a talker. I've no idea how he feels about anything really.' I feel sad, thinking about Dan.

Douglas has lost interest I can tell. We force our way through some pretty banal, excruciating conversation about meaningless stuff until Minty rescues me, half an hour earlier than planned. I have never been so pleased to see her. She is laden with rope-handled shopping bags and looks fresh and lively. Douglas perks up immediately on her arrival. For a moment I worry that Minty is going to settle down and join us for a drink (she never passes up that opportunity) but she's registered my pleading eyes.

'Sorry to be a bit early,' she says, 'but I've just had a call from work and I need to get back, and as I'm giving Carol a lift…'

'What a shame,' says Douglas, his eyes scanning Minty's cleavage, 'you could have joined us for a glass of prosecco.'

'That would have been lovely.' Minty's smile is wide and dazzling. How does she do it?

Douglas insists on paying the bill which mortifies me after all the uncharitable thoughts I've had. We exchange goodbyes but it's obvious we won't be seeing each other again. As I step out into the street I feel like a bird released from a cage.

We laugh uncontrollably like teenage girls all the way to the Park and Ride bus stop. I have tears in my eyes and I'm not sure where they're coming from.

'We mustn't be unkind,' I say, my diaphragm clenching with another spasm of laughter. Minty is clutching my arm as we walk, her bags poking our thighs.

'It was your face!' she says, wiping her eyes and setting me off further, 'I've never seen anything so funny in all my life, you looked absolutely desperate! So, so funny.'

'I'm sure there's someone lovely out there for him,' I say, trying to calm myself and failing, collapsing into a bundle of laughter again because Minty won't stop.

'Why was he so *RED*?' she squeaks, 'he looked like he was about to *BURST*!' But I can't answer, I can't speak through the laughter, and the pain in my tummy from it is lovely, the loveliest pain I have felt in a long time.

When I get back home John's car is in the drive. My breath catches at the sight of it. An immaculate, brand new, pale blue Jaguar which he bought after our divorce. I have never been in it. I suppose the leather upholstered passenger seat is moulded to the comely shape of Shona. John is sitting in the driver's seat, I can see the shape of his shoulders and the profile of his face, in shadow. I can't get used to the feeling that he is so familiar to me and yet so estranged. He is someone I knew in another life and now I can't quite place.

He looks up from his phone when he sees me. I carry on walking towards the door as he gets out of the car. He has a key of course, but he never enters the house without my permission. It's part of our 'agreement' and is both absolutely bizarre and completely acceptable at the same time.

'Hi,' he says.

'Hello. Are you coming in?' It's more a request for information than an invitation.

'If that's ok. I tried to call but I think your phone's switched off.'

'I've been out for lunch.' I put my key in the lock and open the door.

'Anywhere nice?'

'Browns.'

I feel my heart quicken.

'Was it busy?'

'Not really. Would you like some tea?' I am wondering if Jonty has told him about my date.

'Thank you.'

John likes Earl Grey with only a splash of milk and a teaspoon of sugar. As I move about the kitchen he talks about Pippa, who is drinking too much he says.

'All students drink too much.'

'I don't care about all students, I only care about Pippa. Don't you?'

'Please don't give me a lecture on caring about my family. You're the one who walked away remember.' My hands are trembling. *Stay calm, Carol, stay calm.*

'Just because our marriage broke down it doesn't mean I've stopped caring about my children.'

'Our marriage didn't break down, YOU walked out.' I throw the teaspoon in the sink and the noise it makes is far too loud.

He sighs, as if I'm the problem. 'I didn't come here to talk about this.'

'If you came here to talk about Pippa's drinking you can tell her yourself, she'll be home in a couple of weeks.'

'That's not it either. Although I do think it wouldn't hurt for you to have a word with her. You know how she is with me at the moment.'

Yes, I do, she hates what you've done.

I put the cup of tea on the table and he picks it up. Handing it to him directly would be far too intimate.

'Why are you here then?'

'Shona's pregnant.'

The floor falls away. Oh my God. I want to sit but I resist the temptation.

'Well, congratulations, thanks for coming to share the good news. Champagne?' I make as if I'm going to get glasses. If actions can be performed sarcastically I hope that's what I'm doing. My legs have gone to jelly.

'I didn't want you to hear it from someone else.'

'Oh, how kind.' My voice is thick with bitterness. It sticks to the roof of my mouth and my tongue like toxic paste. I can almost taste it. 'How very kind. Thank you, John, thank you for thinking of me, for coming to tell me in person. You bastard.'

I glare at him, aware that I am alight with fury, but what finally undoes me is that he is looking at me with something like tenderness. I can't bear it.

His phone rings. He doesn't look at it.

'You'd better get that,' I say, 'she'll be wondering where you are.'

'She knows where I am.'

'You lied to me but you won't lie to her?' The pain is like a dart.

'I didn't lie to you, Carol, I withheld, it's not the same.'

'Sounds like you've been talking a lawyer. Bullshit.'

He picks up his tea and drinks it quickly, as if he's about to leave. But I haven't finished here.

'When's it due?'

'Christmas.'

'How lovely.'

'I should go.' He finishes the tea in one go and puts the cup on the table, like he always used to, when he lived here. He never knew how the dishwasher worked, never put anything in the sink. 'Thanks for the tea.'

He heads for the door.

'When will you tell the children?'

'I don't know. I wanted to tell you first.'

'A little brother or sister. Wow. I'm sure they'll be thrilled.'

I know what he's thinking. When did I become such a sarcastic cow? I was never like this. It's the woman I've become. Hamble tells me I'm in control of all my emotions. She says I don't need pills. Do I believe that?

As John passes me I catch his familiar scent.

I don't answer him when he says goodbye and I don't watch as he pulls his big, shiny car out of the drive, but I can hear the engine for a long time as it fades, or I think I can. I'm probably imagining it.

I ache all over. I take the pills Dr Gray gave me out of my bag and swallow five of them with water.

I can't stay in this house.

I look at the time and realise the shops will still be open. I will walk into town. It's a nice afternoon, the sun is still out, it's warm.

My kitten heels make an unfamiliar sound as I walk, as if my feet belong to someone else. I have walked down this street a thousand times, but I don't feel a part of it anymore. My toes hurt. The horse chestnut trees on the green whisper gently as I pass. A group of young boys are playing football, their shouts are like the calls of seagulls, synonymous with summer and holidays, freedom, happiness.

There's a shop in Kingsmead, just off the High Street, that sells trinkets and handbags, scarves and little gifts, pretty stationery, greeting cards, china cups with slogans on, that sort of thing. It's aimed at people like me, middle-aged ladies with too much money and too much time who are looking for a comforting treat to soothe the sadness of our inevitable decline. It feeds our denial.

The woman who owns it wears the things she sells. She is draped in scarves and silver jewellery. Her dyed blonde hair is stiff with lacquer, her skin pasted with make-up, her nails glossy and dangerous. She has named the shop after herself – *Kirsty*.

A little bell rings when I enter. It smells of lavender. Kirsty is talking loudly to a customer about scented candles, working hard on a sale. She looks up briefly and greets me with passing interest, like a lioness assessing prey. Fresh meat.

I know exactly what I am going to do. I haven't done it since I was at university, and I got away with it then. I feel a rush of adrenaline and I greet it like an old friend who's come to rescue me. My heart is thumping hard now, my blood is hot in my veins, I'm alive again, the pain has gone, all the humiliation, the fear, the sense of loss, all are washed away in the flood of endorphins created by fear.

I scan the goods in front of me. The two ladies are talking but their voices are meaningless sounds. I see a purse encrusted with diamante stones. Too big. I see some small books with pretty covers, books meant for presents, love quotes, funny sayings, jokes about marriage. One has a picture of Dolly Parton on the front cover. It's pink and yellow, retro looking. It's nice. I pick it up and put it in my bag in a single, swift movement, the adrenaline is so potent I feel as though every one of my internal organs is dancing.

'Excuse me!' The ground falls away. I freeze. 'I saw you put that in your bag!'

Kirsty has abandoned her customer and is standing in front of me. Her eyes are small and dark, framed with black eyeliner. I can do nothing but stare. I know my mouth is open and I've stopped breathing but I am powerless, rooted to spot, as if by not moving I can freeze this dreadful moment and make it go no further.

The customer, who has until now had her back to me, turns around.

'Carol!'

I pull my eyes away from the terrifying Kirsty and see that it's Bridie, looking flushed and upset as if she's the culprit herself.

'You know her?' barks Kirsty at her, then without waiting for a reply she turns back to me, holds out her hand and moves her fingers in a 'give it' gesture. 'Hand it over,' she says.

I look at her horrible face and I hate her. I take the book out of my bag and put it back on the table. My heart is racing uncontrollably and I wonder if the pills I took will kill me.

A part of me wishes for it. I could just drop down dead right here and now, and it would all be over.

'I knocked it into my bag by accident,' I say, pronouncing each word very carefully.

'Do you think I'm stupid or what?'

Oh God. It's too awful. I'm in the middle of some dreadful reality show. My life is truly over. Bridie comes over and links her arm through mine. I am so grateful to her I want to cry.

'Carol would never, *ever*, steal anything. I can vouch for her character. If she says it was an accident, then I am sure that it was.'

'I saw her!' Kirsty is screeching. I have been in this shop a few times before, Christmas shopping, or looking for a birthday present, or just browsing the pretty things, and I always thought Kirsty was just a harmless, ageing bimbo. I hadn't realised how internally ugly she is. I stare at her with new fascination, feeling a little emboldened by Bridie's support, and, perhaps, the pills, if they're kicking in.

'Maybe you were mistaken,' insists Bridie, bravely I think, because I don't think it's in her nature to be confrontational or to get involved in other people's messy business. The door opens and two teenage girls come in. They look around cautiously, the atmosphere in here is thick and they can obviously feel it. They huddle together over the scarves, stifling nervous giggles behind their hands.

'I wasn't mistaken,' says Kirsty, quietly now, which only makes her appear more menacing. She steps up close to me and whispers in my ear. I can smell her horrible perfume. 'It's a good job for you that I'm such a nice person,' she says, 'I won't call the police this time, but if I ever see you in my shop again, you'll totally regret ever pissing me off. Now get out.'

Bridie says 'Thank you, thank you,' as if she's the one who's been let off the hook, and steers me out into the street.

You think you know someone, and then they can surprise you.

You think you know yourself, and then one day you don't.

10. Bridie

Sarcasm, Stealing and Pots of Tea

Carol is sitting on the grubby sofa in my kitchen, stroking Wes' ears, looking far, far away. Poor Carol. I feel so sorry for her. I don't quite know what to do with her. I couldn't let her go home on her own after that awful scene with Kirsty.

I pour the boiling water from the kettle into the tea pot. Wes is whimpering with pleasure and looking at me with reproach, as if to say, '*you* never stroke me like this!' It's early in the afternoon, the first day of the school summer holidays, Peter and Patrick are in the garden, Martha is having a nap, Theresa and Beatrice are at friends' houses and Maggie is in Norfolk with my sister and her family, they have a cottage there near the sea. I know that Jeremy will be home soon and I look at the clock anxiously. Jules has just gone. She was babysitting for me while I popped into town to buy a birthday present for Minty, and that's when I saw Carol in Kirsty's shop, being accused of shoplifting. It's all just too awful!

I hand Carol a mug of tea and she looks up at me with a sad smile, the sort that people give at funerals.

'Tea puts everything right, doesn't it?' she says, taking the mug, and then she starts crying. Oh, poor, poor Carol, I could cry myself! I lean down to give her a hug. I can feel her little sobs shaking her shoulders. She's too thin. Wes gives a jealous whine and I shove him away with my foot. Peter comes running in, takes one look at Carol and me and goes straight back out again.

'You're very kind,' sniffs Carol.

I pull up a chair so I'm closer to her.

'Don't let that Kirsty get to you,' I tell her, 'I don't know why I go in that shop, she's not a very nice person.'

Carol smiles. 'I think you're right,' she says, 'but on the other hand she let me off. She could have called the police and then I'd have been in an even worse mess than I am already.'

'It would have been her word against yours.'

'She saw me. And I'm not a very good liar, Bridie.'

This throws me. 'But it *was* an accident, wasn't it?'

'No. I did it. I put that stupid book in my bag.'

I'm shocked. I would never have thought it. Patrick comes in and stares at Carol. Peter has obviously told him that there's some kind of drama going on and he's come to check it out for himself. I shoo him back into the garden.

Carol is looking quite serene now. I wonder if she's still taking those pills?

'But - I don't understand. Why did you do it?' I don't want to sound like I'm passing judgement on her, but I'm completely baffled. 'John hasn't left you short of money has he?'

Carol sighs and rests her head on the back of the chair. 'No, it's nothing like that. It's nothing to do with money. I don't know why I do it.'

'You mean you've done it before?' This gets worse and worse!

'Only once. A long time ago. Bridie, my darling, don't look so terrified. It's not important. I won't ever do it again.'

'I'm sorry. I just don't understand…'

'Neither do I. It's probably some sort of psychological problem I have. This tea is lovely by the way, what is it?'

'I don't know, I can't remember, just regular builders', Yorkshire probably. Do you want a top up?'

As I fetch the tea pot I hear Martha grizzling through the baby alarm. She'll be alright for a bit. I pour more tea into Carol's mug. I'm in shock. Carol, a shoplifter! It's like one of those ridiculous dreams you have that you laugh about in the morning.

'I'm worried about you,' I tell her, handing her the mug.

'Well, don't be.' There is a pause, filled by the sweet sound of Peter and Patrick playing outside. I think we are both just resting our minds for a bit, enjoying their innocence. Martha's grizzling picks up momentum. 'Do you want to fetch her?' Carol asks.

'No, she'll be ok for a bit.'

'John came over today.' Carol is looking past me, as if she's talking to herself. Martha cranks the grizzling up a notch. 'He said…' She hesitates, as if she's deciding whether or not to carry on.

'What?' I prompt her, but Martha is properly crying now. I apologise to Carol, tell her I'll be right back, and run upstairs to take Martha out of her cot. I love the warm, sleepy feel of her. I squeeze her to me, breathing her in.

Back downstairs Carol hasn't moved. She smiles at us as we come in. 'She's so adorable,' she says. She looks a bit spaced out. I give Martha a cup of milk and we watch her as she drinks. Carol has apologised to me so many times for the crash, but I know she's thinking about it again now. I had nightmares afterwards. I still don't think I'm fully over it. But I don't blame Carol. It was an accident. And no-one was hurt. Thank God. Carol's being punished enough anyway, with her husband leaving her so publicly and parading that woman around the town, and now this business in Kirsty's shop, it's just too awful. Poor Carol. It's no wonder she's in such a state.

'Did Minty tell you about my date?' she asks.

'No! How was it?'

'Dreadful.'

My hopes that we were going to change the subject to something a bit happier are dashed to the floor. 'Oh, no, that's a shame. How dreadful? In what way?'

'As dreadful as it could possibly be. I'm sure he'll be a lot of fun for someone else, with his boat and his...*joie de vivre*. But he's not for me.'

'I don't think anyone will be 'for you' right now, Carol. It's too soon.'

'I'm meeting with Sebastos next week. He looks much more interesting.'

I can't imagine having to go on a date. It's like trying to imagine what it's like to walk on the moon. There will only ever be one man for me. If I ever lost Jeremy (God forbid) I would be a lonely widow for the rest of my life. The thought of having dates with strange men is just truly awful and totally terrifying. And as for sharing a bed with someone else...it's unthinkable! I look at the clock, wishing Jeremy would hurry up and come home.

I put Martha in her playpen where she starts throwing Duplo bricks around.

'I love your house,' says Carol.

'But it's such a mess compared to yours!' I say, pleased. I love my house too. I know how lucky I am.

'It's homely. It's a proper family house. Like mine used to be.'

I can hear Jeremy's car on the drive. Carol finishes her tea and says she should go. She stands up a little unsteadily.

'Are you sure you're alright? Just stay for a while and have a chat with Jeremy.'

My wonderful husband walks in. To me he is like an angel come straight down from Heaven. He greets Carol, gives me a kiss and picks up Martha, who has spread out her arms in joy at seeing him. We exchange a bit of chit-chat, I think Carol doesn't want to give Jeremy the chance to ask too many questions about her health, which he wouldn't do anyway, he always keeps his work and home life separate. Martha is tugging at his ear lobes.

When Carol has gone, with a promise to call me if she needs me, I can't get the words out quick enough. Jeremy helps himself to tea from the pot, which has gone cold but he drinks tea in pretty much any sort of state, and I tell him about Carol and the shoplifting, and the horrible date she went on and Jeremy listens as he always does, but expresses no real interest or surprise. Martha starts howling because Wes has stolen her biscuit and when she's been settled again and the dog has been shooed out into the garden in disgrace, I tell Jeremy what Carol said about her having a psychological problem that makes her want to steal things from shops, then Peter walks in.

'Did Carol steal something from a shop?' he asks, wide eyed.

'No, it was all a terrible misunderstanding,' I tell him, 'and look at the state of your shoes! What on earth have you been doing out there?'

'We found some coins, look.' He holds out a muddy hand.

'Pennies,' I tell him.

'I'm going to get in the shower,' says Jeremy, putting Martha back in her play pen. I follow him to the door.

'Is there such a thing though?' I ask him at the bottom of the stairs, quietly so that Peter won't hear.

'As what?'

'A psychological thing that makes you want to steal things.'

'Yes, there is, but hopefully this was just a one off.'

'She's done it before.'

'Really?'

'She told me.'

'Oh. Well.' He starts to climb the stairs and I take the hint. He's tired and doesn't want to talk about patients anymore.

I go back to all the things I have to do, tidying up, scrubbing potatoes, washing out pans. It's Minty's birthday tomorrow, a big one, the half century, and there's a group of us going to The Olive Tree for a meal on Saturday, and I can't wait. I don't get out much. I know already what I'm going to wear, a little red dress by Ted Baker which I bought in the Age UK shop for ten pounds. I'm making a cake which the staff at The Olive Tree have agreed to cut up and serve on the night, and I've bought helium balloons and fortune cookies for the table. I'm hoping Carol won't back out, it will do her good.

Later, as I'm just about to serve up roasted lemon chicken with new potatoes (from Simon's allotment, absolutely delicious) Minty turns up. She apologises for interrupting our meal, but when Minty's in full flow nothing will stop her. We make a place for her at the table and Simon offers her some elderflower juice but she's knows we don't usually have wine and has brought her own bottle, a ready chilled Sauvignon Blanc which she produces from her bag. The children look at her in admiration and I catch Jeremy's eye. He fetches her a wine glass and tells Peter not to be silly when he asks if he can have a glass.

'In France they let the children drink wine with water,' he says.

'We're not in France,' I point out.

'Cindy's mother is an alcyholic,' says Beatrice.

'You mean alco-holic,' corrects Peter.

'That's enough,' says Jeremy.

'Are you an alcoholic?' asks Beatrice, looking at Minty.

'Beatrice, that's enough!' barks Jeremy.

I stroke Beatrice's hair because she looks upset.

'What's an alcoholic?' asks Theresa.

'Oh God!' laughs Minty, 'Kids! Aren't they great?'

'You said it was alright to ask you questions,' says Peter, 'you said we could always ask you anything we like…'

'That's true,' says Jeremy, 'but it's not always an appropriate time. We have a guest.'

'Don't mind me,' says Minty, 'fire away.'

I say in a rush, 'An alcoholic is someone who drinks too much, so much that they ruin their lives and put their health at risk.' Theresa, looking terrified, pushes away her glass of elderflower juice. 'No, darling, not juice, alcohol, grown up drink. Now let's talk about something else.'

'Yes, let's,' says Minty, crossing her legs and leaning in closer, 'although what I want to talk about may not be suitable in front of the children either.'

'Then perhaps we should discuss whatever it is at another time?' suggests poor Jeremy.

'Or you could talk in French,' says Patrick, trying to be helpful as always, 'Mummy and Daddy talk to each other in French when they don't want us to know what they're talking about,' he explains to Minty, 'like surprise presents and stuff.'

'Well, that's a great idea,' says Minty, 'except that my French is shit.'

The children giggle. Even Martha starts banging excitedly on the table.

'Bad word, children,' says Jeremy.

'Sorry,' says Minty, 'or should I say, pardon my French!' I wonder if she already had a drink before she got here and if she intends to drive home. No doubt her big 4x4 is parked right in the way on our drive. 'I just spoke to Carol,' she says.

'Carol was crying,' puts in Patrick, 'Peter saw her.'

'Why was Carol crying?' asks Beatrice. She hates anyone to be upset. It can be a drain watching the Disney movies.

'Because she'd had a bit of a shock,' says Minty, refilling her glass, 'but don't you worry, she's going to be absolutely fine. What I want to know is this,' she fixes her questioning eyes on Jeremy. 'Should she see a doctor? I mean, in your professional opinion, under the circumstances.'

'I don't know the circumstances,' says Jeremy, spearing a potato.

'What Carol needs is the love of her family and friends,' I say.

'Yes, yes,' says Minty, 'all of that, but after what happened today I'm worried about her. It smacks of losing control. Don't you think, Jeremy?'

Jeremy doesn't answer straight away. Nervously I add another potato to Martha's tray and tell Theresa not to eat with her fingers.

'If Carol comes to see me at the surgery I will give her my professional advice.'

'So do you think…'

'Minty, please, I don't think this is an appropriate conversation, now or at any time, but particularly in front of the children.'

'We don't mind,' says Patrick. He's such a sweetie.

It's time to change the subject I think. 'What is Simon getting you for your birthday?'

'Don't mention birthdays.' Minty puts a melodramatic hand to her forehead.

'It's my birthday soon,' says Theresa, 'in November.'

'That's not soon you idiot,' says Peter, 'that's ages away.'

And so it goes on. Minty gets steadily drunk, Jeremy is very quiet, Martha continuously throws bits of potato and chicken on the floor for Wes (her best friend at meal times), and the children chatter and squabble and fill the room with their joyful innocence.

Minty's not in a hurry to leave. Simon is out with friends apparently, Jack is back working part-time at The Olive Tree and Jenny is in Ibiza. Minty doesn't like an empty house. She was going to call on Carol but Carol said she wanted to be alone.

While I clear the table and start getting the little ones ready for bed Minty tries to draw Jeremy out on his professional opinion again. She's done the whole bottle and I sense Jeremy is losing patience with her. He offers to take her home and she accepts without protest. It's gone eleven by the time they leave. He drives her home in her car and says he'll walk back, it takes 15 minutes from Minty's if you get a move on. Jeremy won't mind. He likes walking and he likes time to himself.

I wait up for him, which is hard because I'm so tired. I'm a lark, Jeremy's an owl, it works well for us.

He comes quietly into our bedroom.

'Everything ok?'

'Sorry my love, did I wake you?'

'No. I was waiting for you.'

I watch him undress in the dim light.

'Minty was totally drunk,' he says, rather unnecessarily.

'I know. Nothing new in that.'

'She doesn't see the irony. She kept on about Carol needing professional help when it's her that's out of control.'

'Do you think so? I know she drinks a bit too much sometimes...'

'She's got a problem.' Jeremy throws his trousers over the back of the chair. 'But she's in denial. She's not admitting it to herself.'

I am quiet, thinking about this. I can't imagine Minty ever giving up the booze, or even cutting back. Her drinking is part of what makes her who she is, loud, funny, affectionate, unpredictable. Jeremy is making it sound like something altogether much darker and he's worrying me.

He goes into the ensuite bathroom.

'Do you think we should say anything to her?' I ask.

He doesn't answer straight away. He's cleaning his teeth. He comes back into the bedroom and finishes undressing.

'In theory, yes.'

'But in practice?'

'It's very difficult to help someone who doesn't want to be helped.'

'As her doctor though, what would you advise?'

'Therapy. Rehab. AA.'

I sit up on my elbows.

'Really? Are you serious?' But I know he is, and I could cry. Why couldn't I see that Minty had a problem? What sort of friend am I after all?

He gets into bed. He's cold, we snuggle up.

After a few moments of thoughtful silence he says, 'There's something else though.'

'What?'

'Shona came to see me a few weeks back and told me that she's pregnant.'

'Really? With John Dixon's baby?'

'Well, yes, that's the assumption.'

'Oh my.' I am wide awake. 'Poor Carol. Does she know?'

'I have no idea.'

'Oh my.' I don't know what else to say. It was bad enough for Carol that her husband of twenty-five years dumps her for a younger woman, but this...having a baby, at his age, starting all over again, a new family when his first one is grown up, it's...it's just wrong. Poor Carol.

'Something's wrong though...' says Jeremy.

'You're telling me! It's awful...'

'No, I mean with Shona. I examined her today and... it didn't feel right. If her dates are right the fundus is in completely the wrong position. I'm sending her for an early scan.'

'What do you think is wrong?'

'I don't think she's pregnant. I think it may be a tumour.'

'Oh God...'

'I know.'

'Have you told her that?'

'No. She didn't ask. She thinks it's a routine test.'

I hold him tight. The house is very still. Moonlight is shining through the cracks in the curtains. An owl hoots. I think of Shona, not yet thirty, out there right now holding on to something inside her that she thinks is a baby, and Minty, out for the count in her enormous bed, alcohol pumping through her lovely veins, and Carol, who's like a boat cut adrift with no land in sight.

Nothing is as it seems.

It's a long time before I can sleep.

11. Minty

Cougars, Curses and Cake

Today I am fifty fucking years old. *Fifty.*

You know when you hear stories on the news about people being killed in car crashes or fires or found in the bottom of rivers and they say, Joe Bloggs died, aged 35, or 40, or even 49...? Well, I think to myself, that's tragic, far too young to die! But when they say it was Joe Bloggs, aged 50, you think, Oh well, knocking on a bit. Sad but hey, not a bad innings.

Fifty.

By the time I get used to the idea I'll be fifty-five. Shit.

I wanted to close the salon today, give myself a day off, but it's so busy right now, there are loads of weddings and hen nights going on, and all the good ladies of Kingsmead getting 'beach ready' for their holidays in the Algarve or their villas in Mallorca, I'm booked up all day.

So I find myself here, with a slight headache (had one too many round at Bridie's last night) giving the lovely Petula Huth another intimate waxing. She really is quite adorable, I could fancy her myself if I wasn't totally hetero, and if I wasn't married to my lovely Simon of course.

'How's Jack?' she asks.

'Getting better every day, thanks,' I tell her, carefully applying the hot wax to her remarkably dainty labia, but then, she is only thirty three. Grrr! 'The plaster came off last week and he even did a whole shift at The Olive Tree last night.'

'Really? Wow. That's amazing. I guess because he's so young and fit…'

I strip off the wax and she winces. I know Jack's gorgeous, women are bound to love him, but I'm not having cougars like Petula trying to get their claws into him.

'He's still limping, and his ribs ache in the morning, but other than that...' I apply more hot wax.

'Has he got a girlfriend?'

'Yes. So hands off.'

She laughs. It's a pretty, girly laugh that shows perfect teeth. I strip off the wax and it shuts her up again.

Beyond the screen I can hear Krystel, my lovely Goth on reception, taking a call, another booking for Friday, it's going to be mental, I've told her not to book anything after five on Saturday, because we've got a table booked at The Olive Tree, there's a crowd of us going for my birthday. Bridie has organised it, which probably means they'll be lots of hideous balloons and cakes with the big Five-0 on.

'So what did Simon get you for your birthday then?' asks Petula.

I smile, feeling rather smug, and show her my yellow sapphire and diamond ring. It gets a satisfying and suitable reaction. Then I have to tell her to hold still while I get to the tricky bit.

'I bet Sarah felt really bad,' she says, breathing out again after a particularly brutal strip.

'About the accident?'

'She was driving wasn't she?'

'Uh-huh. Wasn't her fault though.'

'Even so. If I'd been driving with your Jack in the car and he ended up in intensive care...Jeez. I'd feel bad.'

'She's got her own worries.' I dip the spatula in the hot wax.

'She's alright isn't she? The baby I mean?'

'As far as I know.'

I don't want to tell Petula this because I don't know her well enough (despite our current intimate situation), but for some reason Sarah is avoiding me. I haven't spoken to her since before the accident. Obviously, in the immediate aftermath, I didn't leave Jack's side, but when I started to really believe that he was going to be ok, I texted her. She didn't reply. I've sent her lots of messages and tried to call her. Nothing back. Carol has seen her, and so has Bridie, and they say she's not well, too thin and feeling sick, etc. etc. but I don't know, it's weird. I tried to wheedle some info out of Jezza last night when he drove me home, but he never tells me anything. What's the good of having a GP as a friend if he won't give you little hints now and then as to what's going on? When I first mentioned it to Bridie she asked me what I'd said in the text, that first time in the hospital, and I told her. It said, 'I know everything. Jack told me. I'm not mad with you.'

Bridie said maybe Sarah just can't face me, because she was driving when the accident happened and Jack....well, it was very serious for a while. Shit. I still shake when I think about it. I do forgive her though. I don't hold her responsible, I heard all the details from Jack and the police and it clearly wasn't her fault. She was doing Jack a favour, giving him a lift home, it was nice of her, she didn't mean for it to happen (*Gandalf didn't mean for a lot things to happen*– Frodo, Lord of the Rings) and I just wanted her to know that I'd heard all the witness reports and didn't bear a grudge, I mean, shit, it could have been worse, and she was pregnant and everything, so I knew she'd be freaking out about that too.

Anyway, there's nothing more I can do, and to be honest, she was never a close friend, just the second wife of Simon's best mate, it's no great loss to me. It's probably her hormones raging, sending her a bit bonkers. Bridie did invite her and Gary to my birthday bash on Saturday but apparently they're going to Norfolk. I'm surprised they want to spend their money on hotels right now, what with Simon's business going under and everything. Poor Sarah, no wonder she's going a bit round the twist. It just goes to show, they're not quite as in control of life as they thought they were.

While Petula's getting dressed she tells me they've got Michelle and Tony King coming over next week for dinner.

'Sucking up to the boss?' I ask, because Tony is the head of Kingsmead School and both Petula and Karl are teachers there.

'They're a lovely couple,' she says with a small, reproachful smile, 'and no amount of sucking up to them would make any difference to our careers anyway. He's as a straight as anything. I bet he's never done anything wrong thing in his entire life. Or Michelle, come to that. They're pretty much perfect.'

'Oh, you never can tell,' I say, taking the paper sheet off the couch and throwing it in the bin, 'all kinds of things go on behind closed doors.' She doesn't answer. Personally I think Michelle is a smug, snooty cow, but I won't tell Petula that.

I leave her to dress.

Krystel takes the payment and Petula thanks me and wishes me a happy birthday, tells me that I look forty not fifty (huh), says she hopes we have a good night on Saturday. She leaves as my next client arrives. No time even for a coffee to keep me going. I think of my hip flask in the cupboard out the back of the shop and anticipate it keenly, feel its warmth even before the rim has touched my lips. *Later.*

In the middle of the afternoon Krystel tells me that Kirsty, the woman who has the gift shop two doors down, has cancelled her eyebrow shape. Something to do with a delivery of jewellery that hasn't arrived so she has to stay in the shop. Anyway, it's good news, I don't feel like being nice to Kirsty since she was such a bitch to Carol the other day, but it's not good for business to take sides. It also gives me time to nip out for a sandwich in Kate's Tea Room, catch up on my messages and pick up something for supper from the deli. It's amazing what you can pack into thirty minutes if you have to. And to think how easy it is for me sometimes to lie in bed all morning, wasting hours. That's the thing with me. I'm an all or nothing kind of a person.

I go and fetch the hip flask and slip it into my bag with the thrill of a secret lover.

The tea room is busy, it always is. I choose a brie and cranberry sandwich on granary bread and take it to a table in the window. I like to look out, see what's going on, which isn't much usually. There are three fat ladies on the table next to me, talking excitedly, bangles jangling, perfume wafting, flesh filling out their pastel coloured clothes, handbags and carrier bags occupying the fourth chair and their foot space. They all go quiet while they read the menus with close attention. Important stuff clearly. Then the one with pink lipstick says she's going to treat herself to a slice of strawberry cheesecake. The one with black hair that looks like a wig says, go for it, she's having scones with strawberry jam, butter and clotted cream. The one with tiny feet in white plimsolls says she's having chocolate cake with cream, because she intends to enjoy life while she can. Black Wig and Pink Lips agree, as if she's spoken a wise truth. Mind you, says Tiny Feet, that's what Caroline said, and *look what happened to her*. They all fall respectfully silent for a moment. I desperately want to ask, what the fuck happened to Caroline?

I drink from my hip flask without anyone noticing (it looks like a sports drink bottle) and I finish my sandwich and latte while doing stuff on my phone and keeping an eye on the time. In the corner of my eye I see someone come in, and when I look up I realise it's Sarah. She hasn't seen me, and I watch her for a while. She's wearing white jeans and a loose, pale green shirt. She's far too thin, her bump is the size and shape of a football. She pushes her big sunglasses on top of her head and goes to the only table left, at the back of the room, and puts her shopping bags on the floor beside her. She crosses her legs and reads the menu closely.

I go back to my phone for a bit, deciding how to deal with this, and then I call the waitress for my bill. At the sound of my voice Sarah looks up. I give her a little wave but she has frozen at the sight of me, the menu suspended in front of her in her bony hands. I squeeze through the tables, past the three fat ladies, until I'm standing right in front of her.

'Hello, Sarah! How are you?' I move to kiss her but she flinches as if I'm going to slap her. What is wrong with this woman? 'I haven't seen you for ages, not since before the accident. How have you been? How's that baby coming along? You've only got a few more weeks haven't you? September it's due, isn't it?' It's a bit irritating that I'm the one doing all the enquiring. Isn't she going to ask after Jack? But my mouth as usual is running away with me in this bizarre awkwardness between us.

She finds her voice at last.

'Yes,' she says, in barely more than a whisper, 'It's due September the fifteenth.'

I smile and nod. 'Did you get my messages?' I know it's mean to ask her that, because of course she did, and for some

159

reason she's been avoiding me, but I can't help myself. I can't stand bullshit and I like to cut to the chase.

Any little amount of colour she had in her cheeks drains away. 'We need to talk,' she says.

'What?'

'Won't you sit down?'

What the fuck is this about?

I shrug. 'Ok.'

I pull out the chair and Sarah continues to look at me as if she's afraid of me, but I see something else - pity. I need to get to the bottom of this. I look at my watch and realise I'm going to be late for my next client but fuck it, this feels like it's important. One of us is losing our mind here and I need to make sure it's not me. I can't afford to go any madder than I already am. The coffee machine gurgles and the fat ladies tuck into their cakes, oblivious to everything else.

'What's up?' I ask.

Sarah purses her lips together, then takes a deep breath.

'This is difficult,' she says. I wait. Losing patience. 'How *is* Jack?'

She puts the emphasis on the word 'is', as if we have already been talking about Jack, as if he's the subject here.

'He's doing ok. He was at work last night. He's not fully recovered but, yeah, he's doing ok.'

'I hope he's told you that I won't ask for anything.'

She's lost me. 'What do you mean?'

Her eyebrows furrow. 'If it turns out that the baby is his? I won't expect anything from him, ever, that's a promise. I may even want to carry on as if Simon's the father, keep it all under wraps. I don't know yet. I really don't know...' Her lip trembles. She looks down into her tea cup. I stare at her as if she's just fallen from the sky. Everything else around me disappears. Is this a dream? A nightmare? 'I've written you so many emails and never sent them,' she says, appealing to me now, her eyes big and watery, 'when I got your text, that first one from the hospital, you know? Saying that you knew all about it and you forgave me, I panicked, I didn't know what to do, I've been hiding away and praying that Gary doesn't find out, that neither you nor Simon will tell him, not yet, not until I know for sure.' She looks me in the eye. She's shaking. 'Thank you,' she says, 'for not causing a scene. For keeping it to yourself. I appreciate it. I'm still trying to work it all out.'

I stare. 'You're not the only one.'

She gives me a weak, grateful smile as if I'm being funny.

'Has Jack talked about it? We didn't have much of a chance really, because of the accident, and he's not answering my calls. It seems we're all trying to avoid each other.' She smiles a crooked smile, sniffs, looks for a tissue in her bag, finds one.

'Sarah, what the fuck are you talking about?'

She stops mid-blow and stares at me, a chilly horror visibly draining her as she realises what's happened. I have just about been able to register that she is telling me that Jack is possibly the father of her baby, but as yet the reality hasn't penetrated. I need her to spell it out.

'I thought you knew…Oh God. You didn't know? You said in that text you knew everything…Oh God. You didn't know?'

My phone is buzzing. It's Krystel, trying to find me. ' Are you telling me that you slept with my son and now you think he may have fathered your child?' My fury is a monster I can barely contain.

She swallows. Then tries pathetically to gather herself together.

'He's not your little boy anymore,' she says.

'You fucking bitch…'

I see the shutters come down in an instant, like those in front of bank tellers during a hold-up. Her face is a mask. Anything I may have seen there earlier, fear, pity, regret, has all gone. She gathers up her bags and makes to leave.

'I'm sorry for the misunderstanding,' she mutters, pushing her way past.

I let her go. I'm speechless.

My phone buzzes again. The fat ladies are laughing at something in a magazine. It's too hot in here. I have to get out. I'm about to step out in to the street when the waitress stops me. I haven't paid my bill. She's embarrassed and blushing furiously. I recognise her, she was at school with Jack. I pay cash, leaving her a big tip, wondering if she knows about Jack and Sarah.

Jack and Sarah. Christ. This can't be happening.

The daylight is harsh. I feel outside of myself.

Krystel is relieved to see me. My next client, a typical yummy mummy, is sitting with a cup of tea, looking amenable but expecting an apology for my lateness.

'I'm so sorry. Family crisis. Come on through.'

I amaze myself. I chat to her as if nothing is wrong. We talk about holidays while I roll the exfoliating cream over her face, she's going to Italy she says, Tuscany, her parents have a house there, it's very romantic, but it will be busy at this time year, and very hot. I cleanse and polish, moisturise and massage, and all the time I am like a normal woman having a normal day, chatting about the summer and the children and how time flies, don't they grow up fast?

I let Krystel go at five but I work until six.

On the way home I rehearse what I am going to say to Simon. I have known Simon nearly all my adult life, but I have truly no idea how he is going to react to this news. It's the most peculiar feeling. Almost as if I'm going to meet him for the first time.

But Jack - he will hate me for knowing. He will accuse me of interfering if I try and offer him advice. He will shut himself away from me just as we were beginning to get close again.

That fucking slut Sarah.

I could kill her.

My phone rings as I walk through the door. It's Carol. I'm on another planet right now and don't want to talk to anyone except Simon, but Carol's going through a tough time. She needs a friend to keep an eye on her.

'Carol, you ok?' I walk into my kitchen and dump my bag on the table.

'Yes, fine.'

'You're not backing out of Saturday night are you?'

'No, of course not.'

'Good, because I won't let you.'

'I'm looking forward to it.'

'So what's up?'

'You mean apart from my husband impregnating a trollop half his age…'

'Euch….don't use that word.' I open the dishwasher and start unloading. I'd heard about Shona being pregnant. Shit. Seems like it's a growing trend around here, cradle snatching.

'Don't use which word? Impregnating? Or trollop?' she asks.

'Stop it.'

'I phoned to tell you I've got a date with Sebastos.'

163

'Fantastic! When?'

'A week on Thursday. Will you come with me again?'

'You bet. I'll just need to check my diary, see if there's anything I can't move.' I can hear Simon coming down the stairs from his office. My heart starts thumping at the prospect of telling him about Jack and Sarah. He comes over and kisses me on the cheek.

'I've actually spoken to him on the phone, he sounds pleasant enough,' Carol is saying, while Simon takes over unloading the dishwasher.

I laugh. 'Pleasant enough…! You're hilarious Carol. Listen, I have to go, I'm sorry, I've just got in. Can I call you tomorrow?'

'Yes please, if you have time. Give my love to Simon.'

When the call is ended I tell Simon I have something to tell him. My voice is shaking.

He looks at me quizzically, a tea cup in one hand, its saucer in the other.

'You might want to put those down first,' I tell him.

He does. Then stands leaning against the work top, arms folded.

'I've just spoken to Sarah. And I've discovered at last why she's been avoiding me.' He says nothing, just raises an eyebrow in question. I'm a drama queen, he knows that, so this could be something big, or it could be nothing at all. 'Shit, Simon, there's no easy way to tell you.' I put my hands over my cheeks to cool them down. 'It seems..that there's a chance that Jack …Jack could be the father of Sarah's baby.'

'You what?'

'I know.'

'Sarah who?' He looks totally confused.

'Sarah Simpson! Gary and Sarah, pregnant Sarah! How many pregnant Sarahs do we know?'

'But...' He looks like someone's tripped him up, an invisible person, an unexplained phenomena. I tell him about the chance meeting in Kate's Tea Room, about how Sarah misunderstood the text I sent her in the hospital and about her saying she wouldn't ask anything of Jack if it turns out to be...Oh God. It's too unreal. Simon is gawping at me in disbelief.

I ask him when Jack will be home from his shift. He doesn't know. He gets out his phone and starts texting. As his fingers move clumsily over the phone I see his expression change. By the time he's finished the text he looks furious.

'What did you tell him?' I ask.

'Just told him to get home as soon as he can.'

'Can you believe it?' I'm dying for a drink. Maybe under the circumstances....

'Was it a one off? Or have they been seeing each other? Shit. It's unbelievable.'

'I don't know exactly. She ran off before I had the chance to ask her any questions.'

'Stupid, stupid idiot.' He is gripping the smooth edge of the granite work top behind him and his knuckles have turned white. Despite my own rage and disbelief I don't want Simon to overreact and say or do anything rash. This could be permanently damaging to our relationship with our son and I don't want us all to fall apart over this. Besides, he's still recovering from the accident, he still needs us.

'Let's not be too hard on him. What's done is done. It's too late now. There's no undoing it.'

'And what the hell was she thinking of? After all the crap Gary has been going through with the business going under,

165

there was I thinking how supportive she was being, and how great it was that she was pregnant. Shit! And Jack! He's twenty two years old!' He shakes his head. 'I can't believe it.'

And neither can I, not really, even though I know it to be true. Why would Sarah make this up? And Jack isn't exactly the talkative type. How are we supposed to know what goes on if he doesn't tell us anything?

The baby's due in September. I do the maths.

'It must have happened while he was home for Christmas.' I think back, what were we doing? What was he like, back then? New Year's Eve was mental, I know that. I can remember much more about my crushing hangover than I can about… Jack was angry with me. We fell out. He lectured me on my drinking. He worked long shifts at The Olive Tree.

Simon is still in shock. 'How could she?' he says.

'It takes two to tango.'

The dishwasher is open, its contents half unloaded. The room is full of sunshine. Here we are, on a normal summer's day, trying to absorb this new information, together and yet still separate.

'It's not what I imagined becoming grandparents would be like,' I tell him.

'This is no joking matter.'

'I promise you, I'm not joking.' Fuck, I need a drink so badly. I sigh, a short, angry noise, and drop my head in my hands. He reads my mind. I hear him go to the cupboard and get out the glasses. The tension eases already, even in anticipation.

Everything will be ok in the end. If it's not ok, it's not the end.

I listen to him mixing vodka and tonic. I hear the fizz, the plonk and chink of ice, the screw cap going back on, and finally, the glass being placed on the table in front of me.

166

'Thank you.' I could down it in one, but I restrain myself. I've been managing to convince him for months that I've cut down, I don't want to re-arouse his suspicion and undo it all. 'So. What now?'

A text comes through from Jack. Simon reads it out. 'Leaving in ten.'

I drink my vodka, impatient for it to kick in, not showing it though. I'm good at that now.

'Sarah said there's a possibility that Gary is the father.'

'Does Gary know about Jack? He's never said anything to me. All I've had from him is how great it is that she's pregnant at last.'

'No, he doesn't know. She doesn't want him to. Not yet. I think she wants to find out for sure first, before she decides what to do.'

'I don't how Gary will deal with this if he finds out. He's in a bad way about the creditors on his back. Shit. Poor guy. Why can't she just go ahead with the test? DNA from Jack might prove it's not his.'

'Maybe you have to wait until the baby is born, I don't know.'

Simon takes out his phone and starts Googling. 'Let's face it, after all those years of trying for a baby, how likely is it to be Gary's?' He shakes his head again. Poor Simon. He's hating all this. All he ever wants is a quiet life. A quiet life, a quiet wife, and children he can be proud of. He reads out what he finds on the internet. Taking DNA samples from a foetus carries a small risk of miscarriage. Presumably that's why she's waiting until the baby is born. Simon blames her entirely. He seems to think Jack is an innocent victim.

'She should have had a termination,' he says, with uncharacteristic viciousness.

'That's not an easy decision, particularly when you've been longing for a baby.'

'She should have thought of that before she seduced a boy into her bed.'

I remember Sarah saying, 'he's not your little boy anymore.' But he is. He always will be. We've both finished our drinks long before we here Jack's VW Polo pull up on the drive.

'Stay calm,' I say, but I can see how tense Simon is, his shoulders tight into his neck, his eyebrows low and his mouth pinched.

The door slams. Jack comes in, filling the room with his youth and his sheer size. Six foot two and still growing. I see him then as Sarah might have.

He looks at us both warily.

'What's up?' he says.

Oh Jack. My baby. What have you done?

12. Sarah

Wild Horses

I can't get hold of Jack to warn him. He's not picking up. I left a voicemail but I don't know if he'll get it in time. It's not that I care about what Minty says to him, he can stand up to her, he's got no respect for her. I only care that this doesn't get out. It's vital that Gary doesn't hear about this. I've come this far, I don't want Minty or Jack, or Simon for that matter, ruining everything when I'm so close to finding out the truth.

If Gary is the father, then all is well, and we can carry on as normal, as if all of this never happened. No-one will be hurt and Gary will be none the wiser. If he's not the father, then I want the freedom to decide what I am going to do, and I may decide not to tell Gary, ever. I could bring the baby up as his. It won't be the first time in history that a child has grown up thinking the man who raised him is his father.

Minty needs to back off and leave me to sort out my own problems. I don't know how she can pass judgement and stick her oar in other people's business. She needs to look to herself and her own family, God knows there are enough issues there. The trouble is, all this time that I thought Minty and Simon were keeping my secret for me, it was really just that they didn't know. It was too good to be true, of course it was, that they should take it so well and stay quiet. But now Minty knows for sure. And if Minty knows, it probably means Simon knows, and Simon is a good friend of Gary's. If it turns out that Jack is the father and Jack tells his parents… will Simon keep his mouth shut? Would he be able to, when Gary talks proudly to him about 'his' baby and Simon knows he's really talking about his and Minty's grandchild? I thought Minty was protecting us all with her silence, and now I'm full of doubt. She looked livid.

Oh God.

I want to leave this place, kick the dust of Kingsmead off my heels. Cut the risk that rumours will spread and ruin me. It all goes round and round in my head, making me feel ill.

I am lying in the bath thinking about all this while Gary is packing for our weekend in Norfolk. I can't wait to get away. I need to escape this town. I wish I could escape it forever. I will talk to him tomorrow night over dinner, tell him that I want us to move. Now that his business has folded there's nothing to keep us here. I want to live in a city again, away from small town gossips. You can't fart in Kingsmead without someone making something of it.

I feel so fat, even though the mid-wife tells me I'm too thin. My belly is hard and round, lying here like this it looks enormous, like a camel hump. I can't wait for it to be born, to get my body back, to have the paternity test done, to move on with our new life. I'm yearning for it. I yearn for order and control.

I suppose it was naïve of me to think that I could avoid bumping into Minty. When I saw her standing there in front of me in Kate's Tea Rooms I thought I would faint. God, the irony that it was me who spilled the beans! Me and my big, panicking mouth.

Gary has turned the music up. When he's finished packing he'll go out for a run. I envy him that. I miss the running so much. I CAN'T WAIT FOR THIS BABY TO BE OUT OF ME.

I made a salmon and asparagus flan earlier which we will have with new potatoes from Simon's allotment. Simon, my husband's best friend, possibly the grandfather of my child.

I'm tired. I want tomorrow to come. Tomorrow is one more day nearer to my baby, and answers.

We arrive at the hotel in time for lunch. I love the food here and I'm hungry. It's sunny, but there's a breeze coming in off the estuary, it's perfect. Children are hanging crab lines off the quay, Mums and Dads join in, grandparents watch with dogs on leads. There's always a muddy Labrador somewhere in this place, and the dress code is shorts and posh wellies, which remind us of the business we've lost. It's Kingsmead by the sea really.

'Perhaps we should have gone further away.' I'm worried we'll bump into someone we know.

'But you said you didn't want to spend hours in the car,' says Gary, which is true. He checks us in, the girl on reception is dumpy and officious to the point of rudeness but Gary doesn't seem to notice. He asks for a Guardian in the morning, books a table for dinner, then we go to our room, it's one we've had before. It has a sea view. The bed is huge, the pillows plump and white, there's a smell of new carpet and soap. I open the window. Gary hangs up his shirts in the old, mahogany wardrobe and the feeling that I don't ever want to go back to Kingsmead is overpowering.

He comes to stand behind me, puts his hands on my hips.

'Do you remember when I had you from behind against this window seat?'

'I do. I was sure someone was going to look up from the quayside and see us.'

'I know. That's what made it so sexy.' He kisses me on the neck, turns me round, kisses me again on the mouth. 'I can't wait to fuck you properly,' he murmurs.

I kiss him back, feeling his arousal, remembering how it used to be, before we had secrets.

Sex is too uncomfortable now, Gary has stopped expecting it. I undo his trousers and start to massage his expectant cock, standing there by the window with the sound of seagulls and happy families drifting through on the breeze. After just a few minutes his semen covers my hand and spills onto my dress as he comes, trembling, growling, gripping hold of my hip with one hand and the back of the chair with the other. I love watching him come.

He kisses me all over my face and asks if I'm ok because he knows he gripped me hard. His concern for me could make me cry.

I take a shower then smother myself in body oil, put on the hotel's fluffy dressing gown and lie on the luxurious bed to watch the Antiques Road Show while Gary takes a bath. I scroll through my phone. I started my maternity leave last week but still I get the emails wanting my attention. I delete a few, flag a few, open one or two and read them quickly, without enthusiasm. One catches my eye though. It's from someone called The Snitch and it's titled, 'Your husband is a cheat!!!' Probably junk, but some instinct makes me open it.

Immediately I recognise it as a private Facebook conversation, cut and pasted into the email, and at the same time I recognise Gary's profile picture. My heart thumps as I read it, someone called Tilly Grant, her picture shows a young woman with long dark hair, pouting, with bony shoulders and full breasts, a fuck-me photo. I read on, frantically. I hear Gary turn on the hot tap again in the bathroom, oblivious.

Tilly: noooo I've always liked older men!!!!

Gary: I'm not that old!

Tilly: old enough to know what you're doing….

Gary: definitely ;)

Tilly: do you want to know what I like?

Gary: Tell me

Tilly: you might be shocked!!!

Gary: I doubt it…

I don't want to repeat what she says. Or how Gary replies. He loses himself.

Tilly: meet me tomorrow I'm gagging for you

Gary: where, when?

Tilly: my mate's flat, on Cromwell Road

I'm hyper ventilating. I put the phone down, try and control myself. I feel a Braxton Hicks contraction tighten my belly. I take deep, quiet, secret breaths. Fiona Bruce on the telly is moved by some wartime memorabilia. I pick up my phone again. I re-read the email. I check the date. The day before yesterday. What was I doing the day before yesterday? I was in Kate's Tea Rooms, spilling my secret to Minty. My face is hot. The heat spreads over my body. I undo my dressing gown. A dog barks. Children call out. Seagulls squawk. Breathe. Breathe. Breathe.

I delete the email.

I'm shaking. I stroke my belly with a trembling hand, soothing my baby. I listen to the splashing sounds coming from the bathroom and I want to scream *WAS SHE GOOD? WAS SHE FUCKING GOOD, THIS TILLY? WHO THE FUCK IS SHE? DID YOU FUCK HER? DID YOU USE YOUR FINGERS AND YOUR FUCKING TONGUE LIKE SHE ASKED YOU TO, YOU LYING CHEATING BASTARD? YOU SAID NO SECRETS! YOU SAID NO LIES!*

But the tears are pouring down my cheeks because of course, I can't say any of this. Yes, we said no lies, it was the deal. We could meet Karl and Petula for sex, we would do it together, but no lies, no secret relationships, no fucking behind closed doors. Everything open, everything honest, we thought we were so clever, so cool.

And then I had Jack. And I got pregnant. And you…I wipe my face with my hand.

Gary steps out of the bath. He looks handsome, naked, he's drying his hair. I've seen him have sex with another woman, but that's the point, I saw him. With Tilly I can only imagine, and it tears me apart. It's mad. It doesn't make sense.

He asks me if I'm ok. I smile and tell him yes, I'm fine. Something has changed in these last few minutes and he's noticed it. We dress quietly, exchanging only a few banal words. And then we go downstairs for dinner.

They give us a table by the window. Some of the families are still out on the quay, the tide is going out, the boats are low in the water, we can see for miles, right out to the horizon. We order a bottle of sparkling water while we read the menu. I was hungry before, but I've lost my appetite.

He asks me again if I'm ok. I so want to tell him. I want to tell him everything about Jack and about the email, I want to tell him that I know about Tilly. I want him to make everything alright, but how can he? How can either of us? We have created this mess between us. Somehow I've got to find a way out.

When we have given the waiter our food order Gary leans across the table and takes my hands in his.

'Sarah, there's something I have to tell you.'

I stare at him. He won't make eye contact. This is something big. This must about Tilly. He's going to confess. If it's anything else I don't think our marriage would take it.

'Please don't freak out,' he says.

'What have you done?'

There's the briefest of pauses while he appears to gather strength.

'I was set up. A honey trap. And I fell for it.'

'A honey trap? Who set you up?'

'Can I just say, nothing happened. I fell for it but nothing happened.'

'I don't understand…'

The waiter comes with a bread basket and a pair of tongs, offering us a selection. I pull my hands away from Gary's. When we are alone again I glare at him expectantly.

'You know I owe some people a lot of money,' he says, 'because of the business going under, and there's this one guy who's particularly unhappy about it. He's been threatening me, just nasty emails, nothing specific, and then he went quiet, I thought he'd given up.'

'What's this got to do with a…honey trap?'

'Wait, listen, I'll explain. I thought this guy had given up, I was relieved, it's been hell, Sarah, I can't tell you.' He shakes his head. 'Then I get this message on Facebook, from this girl calling herself Tilly, she said she knew me, she said we'd met at some conference, I didn't remember her but I made out that I did, and she started coming on to me, I mean really properly coming on to me, and I just..fell for it. I arranged to meet her.' He steals an anxious look at me. I want to tell him I know, but I keep quiet. I dare not make yet another mistake. I so want to play this right and regain control of what's left of our marriage and our future. 'But she didn't show up. And then I got this email,' he picks up his phone, unlocks it, searches for the email and hands it to me. I read it quickly. *You think you can walk away owing me 10k and get away with it. I'm sending this to your wife. That will teach you…* etc. etc. there's more, but I've seen enough. I hand him his phone back.

'So Tilly doesn't even exist?'

'Apparently not. It's irrelevant.'

'Do you know who this man is?'

'Yes. I do. But there's nothing I can do, if that's what you're thinking. He's hasn't broken the law.'

'You're talking to a lawyer.'

'I know. I'm sorry. I mean I'm sorry for all this.' He waves his phone. 'I had to tell you before you got the email. You haven't have you?'

I lie without thinking about it. 'No.'

'If you get it promise me you won't open it. Just delete it. It will only make you upset. I'm sorry, Sarah. I love you. Please believe me.'

Then he says he would never have gone along with it if he hadn't been feeling so shit, what with the business folding, and *US*, he says.

'Us?'

'We're not the same, are we Sarah? It's not how it used to be between us, and it's not anything to do with the baby, I couldn't be happier about that, it's what we both longed for isn't it? It's something else. I don't know…'

I feel the tears prick my eyes. He takes my hand again but has to release it when the waiter comes back with our starters. He says 'bon appetit' and leaves with a flourish. The restaurant is full. No-one is taking any notice of us. No-one knows what we're going through.

I tell him I love him. He looks over whelmed. He asks me if I can forgive him, and I say yes, I forgive him. I'm angry and disappointed, but I forgive him, and he has to promise me that from now on there will be no more lies, no more secrets. He agrees and it should make me happy but I feel like a hypocritical piece of shit. His eyes are loving me, bathing me with gratitude. I tell him I have something to tell him too, and I wonder, just for a second, what he would say if I told him the truth about me and this baby. I crave normality; I crave our old life, before the Huths, when it was just about me and him. But if I tell him about Jack it can never be unsaid, and it's not just our future that depends on this, it's the future of our baby and what he grows up knowing about his father, whoever he may be. I have to steer this troubled ship carefully.

'I want to leave Kingsmead,' I tell him, 'I want to move away. Start again somewhere else.' My voice is breaking. It's a relief to share even this with him.

His expression lifts, like a child opening a present. 'I can't believe it!' he says, 'that's exactly what I've been thinking!'

'Really?'

'Yes, really! I hate Kingsmead now, losing the business has nearly killed me and to be honest I don't like bumping into the Huths all over the place either.'

'I know what you mean.'

'But I thought you liked it, I thought you'd object if I suggested moving away.'

'We haven't been talking to each other enough,' I say, 'we were too busy chasing thrills and worrying about money and not spending enough time actually looking to ourselves and our relationship with each other.'

'But at least you were playing the straight game, you didn't go behind my back.'

He says it like an apology, a statement of fact, but there's a hint of a question in there.

'I told you, it doesn't matter now, and you didn't do anything anyway. I don't want to talk about that anymore. We need to talk about the future, not the past.'

The lies, the deceit, why does it all come so easily to me? I long for escape, for freedom from all this.

I say we should eat, his soup will be going cold. I have dressed crab, fresh and delicious. I know what I can and can't eat while I'm pregnant, and this is a treat. I think Gary is finding it hard to believe that I have forgiven him so easily. If he knew the truth about me, he would understand. I won't, can't, accept now that the baby is Jack's. I want so badly for it to be Gary's, if only I knew, I can't stand the waiting. Jack has already had the DNA test, so now I just have to wait for the baby to be born before I will know. It has to be Gary's, it has to be, then we can run away and get on with our family life and Gary will never know how I betrayed him and Jack will be completely out of my life forever. I long for this so much that I can hardly swallow my food.

Then Gary says he's been talking to his parents in Canada. His father is Canadian, his mother English, Gary was born in Montreal but they came over here when he was a boy and stayed here until he was twenty one. They live now back in Montreal.

'They want us to go out there,' he says.

'We will, of course, when the baby's born.'

Gary's eyes are shining with excitement. 'No, I mean to live. Permanently.'

I hadn't thought of it. Canada…it's certainly far enough away from Kingsmead. We visit Gary's parents every other year, and in between they come to the UK to catch up with us and all the other friends and relatives they left behind. It's nice, Montreal, Gary loves it, and I enjoy our visits. Living there has always just been a remote idea, something we might think about in the future. Suddenly it's here, in front of us, a real possibility, right now.

'Can we do that? Can we just up and go, just like that? Where would we live?'

'Mum and Dad have enough room, until we find a place of our own.'

'We can't afford it…'

'We can, I've worked it all out.' And he tells me. He's been thinking about this for some time, he says. His father has many contacts out there, and they're certainly in a position to help tide us over, they have plenty of money and are happy to spend it on their children. Gary's sister is already out there, she works in the Montreal hospital as a midwife. It couldn't be better. She might even deliver our baby.

Our baby. It has to be. It just has to.

We talk and talk. The waiters bring the main course, Gary has a pudding, we take coffee in the drawing room, we're as excited as children on Christmas Eve, and the idea of our escape builds and builds until it's no longer a mere possibility. We have no doubts now about what we intend to do. Our excitement is feverish, we're high on it.

We go to bed but cannot sleep, entangled together, re-united.

We have booked two nights here but I want to get back to Kingsmead and start getting our affairs in order, packing everything up. I'm not kidding. Now that I know I have a way out of my life I'm lunging towards it like a drowning man towards the shore.

Gary reins me in. We've paid a lot for this weekend, it's a lovely hotel, it won't do us any harm, he says, to stay here another day, think about our future. I worry he's changing his mind. He laughs and says, no way. Wild horses wouldn't stop him now, he says.

Wild Horses. I find the Rolling Stones track on my phone and we listen to it. It makes me cry. I tell him I love him so much.

We walk on the beach, as far as Cley, and have tea and cake there. It's too far for me to walk back, my hips are aching, the baby feels like a ball of lead, I shouldn't have walked so far but I miss not being able to exercise to the limit. We make enquiries in a second hand book shop about the local bus service and catch one back. We hold hands all the time. When we are silent we're thinking about Canada. When we talk it's our only topic of conversation.

Back in the room we take a siesta, falling asleep on the bed to the sound of seagulls, children calling, voices, dogs barking, cars coming and going. Sunlight fills the room. It's the most peaceful I have felt in a long time.

On the morning of our last day we treat ourselves to a full English breakfast. The baby was moving a lot in the night, and now it seems he's sleeping it off. Even when I give him a poke he doesn't respond. The midwife said they can sleep for hours. It always worries me though.

I say 'he' because I have a hunch it's a boy. I don't know for sure and I won't know until we meet face to face for the first time. It's a perfect dream, like going to Canada, and one day it will happen. The anticipation of all that lies ahead is exquisite.

We pack up our things and take a stroll along the quay before heading back for home. *Home.* Already that feels like the wrong word. Gary forbade me from making any phone calls or sending emails about the move while we were in Norfolk. He says it was our 'on your marks, get set' weekend, and as soon as we're back in Kingsmead it will be 'Go'.

The house feels strange. As if it knows. Gary makes a phone call to Bertie Hambleton, telling him to put it on the market. I call several removal and shipping companies for quotes, as well as the local auction house to take what we don't want. I call the garage where we bought the cars and make arrangements for them to take them back. It's not a fantastic deal but we need shot of them. I drive to the office and tell Hannah, my partner, that I'm leaving. She's shocked and asks too many questions. We discuss the preliminary details of my opting out of the partnership and selling my share in the business, I want everything drawn up ASAP. I ask her if, for a fee, she will be my representative here while everything is tied up with the house and cars, I give her keys and codes, names of all the people involved in packing and shipping the stuff out. When I leave I can tell she's annoyed. I guess she thought we were more than just business partners and that she should have known that such a momentous move was on the cards. But how could she? I didn't even know it myself.

We Skype Gary's parents. They're over the moon. We couldn't have predicted how thrilled they would be. They feel sad for my mother though, for her 'loss' that we're leaving the country, and I remind them that I see my mother once a year on my birthday. No great loss then. (It was a greater loss when my father died eight years ago, but there's nothing anyone can do about that.) This visibly pleases them. They know they are top in-laws and will be top grandparents too.

I bat away the thought of them loving Jack's baby over the years as if it's their own flesh and blood. I won't allow it head space.

I manage to get an appointment with Jeremy because the airline needs signed evidence that I'm fit to fly, and thank God, he can provide it for me. He can't hide his surprise. He asks how long we have been planning this move and when I say two days he stares at me as if he thinks I'm mad. When I leave the surgery I can't stop smiling.

We pack four large suitcases to take with us, clothes, boots and shoes, a few small items from the house, photos, pictures, our favourite bed linen, but there is much I'm happy to leave behind.

Finally, we book the flights, and that's when I know for sure that this is happening. Two tickets from London to Montreal, one way. Gary insists on splashing out on Business Class because of my pregnancy and naturally I don't object.

We fly in two days, at six o'clock in the morning from Heathrow.

Goodbye forever, Kingsmead.

It's been shit.

13. Carol

Floating

There are few places as depressing as the Wisteria Lodge Care Home. How it can call itself a 'home' is beyond me, and there's precious little evidence of any true 'care' going on. Jilly Cooper calls them Scare Homes and that's about right. I abandoned my mother to this institution three years ago and it pains me every time I think of her, and every time I leave her.

John didn't want her living with us when the dementia got so bad that she could no longer live alone safely. We argued about it, but I gave way. If I'm honest I was afraid of the responsibility and worried that I would come to be afraid of her too. Perhaps John was right, perhaps I wouldn't have been 'strong' enough to deal with it. That was the word he used. He uses it a lot. He admires strength, whatever that is, and clearly I'm devoid of it.

John pays the fees for Wisteria Lodge and it's not cheap. It's considered one of the best in the area. The house is in a scenic spot by the river Cam, so it makes for lovely pictures in the brochure, lots of weeping willows, ducks, daffodils, that sort of thing, and fake, posed photos of young, kindly nurses laughing with residents who don't look old enough to be there.

John chose it because the manageress had good legs and flirted with him. No, that's not fair. It seemed like the best of a bad bunch and I insisted that she was no longer than half an hour away in the car, which eliminated the other 'homes'.

Of course, I can't help thinking, now that John has left, that maybe I could bring Mum home and take care of her myself. I would need help of course, lots of it, but there are plenty of organisations that provide that sort of service. I'm thinking about this as I walk through the front door, which is framed by the abundant, eponymous wisteria. It's Friday, the sun is shining, it's the middle of the afternoon, a perfect day on which to be happy, but sadness descends over me as soon as I step over the threshold. The air is fetid, the smell is always the same, sickly air fresheners and school dinners. The colour scheme is pale pink, light green and cream. There is a photo on the table in the foyer of the latest resident who has 'passed away peacefully' and will be 'greatly missed'. It looks like an award. Congratulations Edith Mary Toogood, 1923-2017, on reaching your goal. Her captured image smiles with benign resignation. One day it will be my mother's face in that frame.

Linda on reception greets me as she usually does, as if she's having a bad day and if it wasn't for her the whole place would fall apart. She has pink stripes in her blonde hair and a nose piercing. On her desk there are photos of her plump, laughing toddlers and when she talks about them it's difficult to get away. I'm sure she's a very good receptionist, efficient, reliable, all that sort of thing, but the residents are invisible to her. If any one of them wanders out for advice, and they do, frequently, she barely looks at them and her answer, if she gives one, is usually monosyllabic. She's completely different with the visitors, people like me, family members or friends bringing flowers and fruit as if they've come to see someone who's ill. She would talk at me for ages if I let her. I made that mistake when Mum first came here. Now I just say a quick hello, sign in and walk down the corridor towards Mum's room, my heart dropping in stages with every step.

She has a view of the garden now, I had her moved as soon as the room became free because her first room overlooked the car park where the Wisteria Lodge mini bus was usually parked. She sits for most of the day in her armchair looking out of the window and I never cease to wonder what is going through her scrambled mind. I tried to make her room feel familiar. She has furniture from home, a mahogany chest of drawers, a Victorian mirror that belonged to my grandmother, lots and lots of photos in frames and some plants that she used to like taking care of. They look a bit neglected now, even though I water them. It's probably too hot in here.

'Hello, Mum.' I make sure she knows I'm here before I touch her, she's easily startled. She turns her head to look at me with vacant eyes and smiles. I kiss her on the cheek. She smells of damp wool and I notice there is a wet tea stain on her cardigan. 'What's all this?' I pull two tissues out of the box by her bed and dab at the wet patch. She stares at me, still smiling. That's good. I like it when she smiles. Sometimes she just sits there looking unbearably sad and I hate that.

I talk to her about this and that, the children, the beautiful weather, and she appears to take it all in, but then, inevitably, 'How's Michael?'

She often thinks I'm her other daughter, my younger sister, Rosie. Rosie and Michael divorced ten years ago but Mum forgot that in 2013. I don't look a bit like Rosie, who lives in a pub in Edinburgh now with her new man and hardly ever visits, I don't know why Mum thinks I'm her, and does she wonder what's become of the real me, the elder daughter, Carol? Does she think I never call to see her? I used to correct her at first but she would get upset by the confusion, so then I went along with it for a while, I'd tell her that Michael was very well and sends his love, but now I just ignore her inquiries and that seems to work alright for both of us. It's funny that she asks after Michael and never after me. It makes you wonder what lurks in the depths of people's minds, unseen.

After a few minutes of this one way conversation I go to make some tea. The kitchen is across the other side of the room that they call The Lounge. The enormous TV blares out in one corner, watched half-heartedly by the regular TV addicts, planted in their chairs around the edges of the room like misplaced furniture.

I say hello to them all, some of them answer me, and always, always, two or three of them will put in a request, 'could you please pass me my hand-bag?' or 'excuse me dear, I need an extra cushion, would you be so kind…?' or 'I'd love a cup of tea if you're making one,' and I look over at the window of the staff room and see, without fail, three or four members of staff chatting around the desk, doing nothing important it seems to me.

I've thought about saying something to the manageress in the short skirt about this, but what? However nicely it's put I'll be telling them that they're useless at their job. And I never complained to John for fear that he would go in and 'have a word' and I'm afraid to ruffle feathers here. If they take a dislike to me they might take it out on Mum. Perhaps I'm being unfair, paranoid, but who knows? You hear such terrible stories.

So it's twenty minutes by the time I finally get back to Mum with two cups of tea. I sit opposite her, and we both look out of the window. The birds are singing. You can just see the road through the hedge at the bottom of the garden and the flash of colour as the cars go by.

'Have you had your tea?' she asks me.

'Not yet.'

'You look too thin. Why don't you have some cake?' She looks around for it, annoyed, as if someone has taken it or eaten it all.

I often wonder what she would say if I told her everything, if I sat here and just poured it all out. 'John has left me for a younger woman and now she's pregnant. Since finding out about the baby Pippa is refusing to have anything to do with him. That will be very hard for John, she was always Daddy's little girl. She'll come round eventually. Or will she? It's not unheard of for families to be torn apart irrevocably by divorce. The boys are bit more pragmatic. Men are, aren't they? Women get so emotional over everything. By the way, I've joined a dating agency. Imagine! Me, going out on dates! The first one was pretty dreadful, but I'm looking forward to meeting Sebastos. He's Greek but he lives not far from here and works at Addenbrooke's. He's only thirty five. Is that too young? Dad was ten years older than you and you were both as happy as anything before the drink took hold of him. Anyway, we'll see. It's nice to go out for lunch if nothing else.'

I don't say any of this of course. Mum never asks after John, I don't think she ever liked him much. Before we got engaged she said she thought he was 'fly'. It was funny at the time. She was always polite to him, always gracious, even when he…we…stuck her in this place.

I stay for three quarters an hour. I read articles out of the paper, and when I laugh at something she smiles. I carry on with some of her knitting, long ago abandoned by her but she likes it in the room, she always says she's going to finish it later. She watches me knitting as if in a trance.

One of the carers comes by to say hello. She raises her voice when she talks to Mum and addresses me as if the two of us are complicit in something that Mum doesn't know about. I've seen her many times before. She's called Janine and she's engaged to a soldier. She wears a lot of make-up and her uniform is too tight. She's not the brightest, but she means well. I ask her if Helen is on duty and she tells me no, she's on a training day. Mum lets out a little laugh.

'A training day,' she says, and I could hug her. Sometimes, for a second, she's just like she used to be.

Helen is my favourite, she's lovely. She doesn't move the residents around as if they're sacks of potatoes and she gets genuinely upset by all their daily concerns and worries. It's as if every one of them is her own mother or father. When she talks to Mum they hold hands and Mum won't take her eyes off her. Helen is an angel. If it wasn't for her I think I would take Mum away from this place.

Janine goes off to raise her voice at someone else, and after a while I pick up my bag, kiss Mum goodbye and leave. She waves.

'Take some of that cake with you,' she says.

I hate this place.

It's Saturday night and I'm going out. I'm getting myself in the mood. I've put on a Beyoncé CD and turned up the volume (I think it's an old one of Pippa's) and I have put five dresses on the bed for me to choose from. It's only The Olive Tree, nothing too special, but we're celebrating Minty's birthday so I want to make an effort.

In the end I go for an old faithful, a blue dress from Monsoon. I'm surprised to find it's too big for me now, I must have lost weight. Maybe Mum was right. I need to eat more cake.

Bridie is driving tonight, she and Jeremy are giving me, Minty and Simon a lift. She picks me up last, Minty is already half cut (no surprise there) and I squeeze in the back between her and Jeremy. It's a seven seater and Simon has been relegated to the rear. Everyone is dressed up and trying to be jolly, but I get the feeling that it's only Minty who's really feeling it. I think Minty could have a great party all by herself.

At the restaurant we see Tony King, the headmaster of Kingsmead, with his wife, Michelle. I'm embarrassed to see her because she was there that night at Sally's when Shona came barging in shouting her mouth off at me in front of everyone. I cringe at the memory. But she is so perfectly well behaved, so friendly and gracious. It's a gift she has. When she talks to me she makes me feel like a respectable woman again. While we are all gathered at the bar choosing aperitifs, she asks me about my nephew, Liam, he's the eldest child of John's sister, a bit of a handful actually, and he's been accepted into Kingsmead school, which I have to say was a bit surprising. He's a rogue, and definitely not the brightest crayon in the box. Michelle is quite interested in him and is asking lots of questions about his background, which I try to answer honestly without being unkind to Liam and his family. I have a vague recollection of him sitting the Kingsmead entrance exam back in January, but what with everything else going on in my life, not to mention being drugged to the eyeballs half the time, I haven't really given him much thought. Apparently he started at the school early, in the summer term (I had no idea) after some 'difficulties' at his other school, and I get the impression that Michelle is a little disappointed that I can't tell her more about him. I ask her how he's getting on, and she smiles and says she thinks he's finding it a 'bit hard to settle in'. I don't have much time to wonder what that means exactly, because we are ushered to our table then. Someone has handed me a large vodka and tonic while I was talking to Michelle and it's delicious.

The Huths turn up with a crowd of Germans, family probably, and I watch Petula chatting to Michelle. Michelle has her serious look on her face, as if Petula is telling her something of vital importance, but Petula, as usual, is bubbly and pretty in a sweet little dress. She doesn't look much older than Pippa. I wonder how she does it.

Bridie tells me Sarah and Gary are in Norfolk, so they couldn't come. I say to Minty, who is sitting next to me, that I haven't seen Sarah for a while and Minty makes a face as if she's sucking a lemon. Perhaps they've fallen out over something but I can't imagine what. I ask her when Sarah's baby is due and she says she doesn't want to talk about her. I ask her what's up and she says she can't say, but maybe one day she'll tell me. What on earth could that be about I wonder?

Bridie and I exchange news about our children. I ask her if she's heard about Shona and John expecting a baby and she says yes (news travels fast in this place) and looks awkward. I tell her how difficult it's been for Pippa to accept the news. It will be especially hard, I say, if the baby is a girl and Pippa feels like she is sharing her Daddy with another little princess. Bridie tells me not to worry, we can't see what the future holds. She has become quite flustered and I wonder if I've said something to upset her. I seem to be continually putting my foot in it tonight. Sometimes I have the feeling that I have no idea what's going on. Perhaps it's the drugs, although I'm on such a tiny dose now. After my melt-down in Kirsty's shop Jeremy advised me to stay on a low dose for a bit longer. He's across the table from me talking to Simon about rugby.

Minty's sister, Charlotte, is here with her husband. He's an actor and has a big part on Doctors, one of the waitresses wants an autograph, 'for my Mum' she says, which causes some amusement. Sally and Bertie are here too, and because I'm on my own the seating plan is awkward. I think I am the only person who notices this. Do I wish that John was here with me? I really can't answer that. Too much has happened. Too much has changed.

Minty tells everyone that I've got a 'date with a gorgeous Greek toy boy.' If she were anyone else I would be annoyed, but, I don't know what it is about Minty, she just gets away with it. Then she begs me to tell them all about 'Fat Boat Man' as she will keep calling him. It's embarrassing, but we have a laugh. I wonder if that poor man's ears are burning. I've even forgotten his name.

The food here is very good. Jack is on duty tonight, he looks pale, it's not long since he was out of plaster. I remember him well as a little boy. So good looking. Shy though, much more like Simon than Minty in temperament I think. I don't think he has ever given them a day's worry in his life. Apart from when he was in intensive care just a few weeks ago but that wasn't his fault. It wasn't Sarah's fault either by all accounts. Maybe Minty blames her for that though. Maybe that's why she doesn't want to talk about her and looked so put out when I mentioned her.

Everyone drinks too much, myself included, even Sally is letting her hair down a bit. Bertie has gone very red in the face. Jeremy orders another pint of organic beer and Minty tells him to be careful, alcohol loosens the tongue, she says, and Jeremy must have half the town's secrets to hold. Poor Jeremy. It's true though. He probably knows everything about us all.

Petula and Karl are leaving with their gang of Germans and they come over to say goodbye. They really are a very good looking couple. Araminta is flirting with him and whispers something in his ear which makes him laugh. Simon is pretending not to notice.

We linger over puddings and coffee and we're the last people to leave the restaurant. Jack went home early. Minty says they've been good to him here since the accident, letting him go early, keeping an eye on him. It helps that the managers are gay, she says, too loudly, they adore him. Why wouldn't they, I ask her, he's adorable. She agrees. Too bloody adorable, she says, some people can't keep their hands off him. There is a flash of anger in her eyes and I wonder if it's just the drink talking or if there is really something going on that she hasn't told me.

Poor Bridie is very patient, it takes us all a long time to gather ourselves up after paying the bill, she waits in the car for us like a long-suffering taxi driver and takes us all home. I feel woozy with all the food and booze and the buzz of the evening. It's been fun. I give Minty a hug and tell her she's a good friend. She looks completely out of it. I don't think she'll remember it in the morning.

My bed is big and cold.

A week later Minty and I are on our way to Browns' again, this time for my date with Sebastos. As my nerves kick in again I become convinced that this is another waste of time. Sebastos is far too young and good looking for me, I have no idea why he has agreed to meet me. Minty tells me not to 'put myself down'. She says it's a shame though that I didn't lie about my age, and because I'm so tense I snap at her.

'I've just come out of a relationship that was full of lies. I'm not going to go straight into another one.'

'Ok, ok, pipe down, this is supposed to be fun, lighten up.'

'Easy for you to say, with your devoted husband and perfect children. You're not the one having to suffer this humiliation.'

'Who says my husband is devoted and my children are perfect?' She sounds quite cross, I've no idea why.

'Well, they are, aren't they? There's no way on this earth that Simon would ever leave you.'

'It wasn't your fault that John walked out, Carol.'

I wasn't thinking of blame. Of course I have asked myself if there was anything I could have done to prevent it, but I can't make myself young again can I? He wanted a younger woman. Obviously. What could I have done? And yet, maybe if I'd been a bit more interesting and lively...

'I'll drop you off here then,' says Minty, 'and remember, smile, look happy, be your lovely self.' She pulls over, indicator clicking, and a car hoots in irritation. 'Dickhead,' says Minty, then turns to me as I undo my seat belt, feeling sick again, like a child being dropped off at a horrible school. 'Give me a hug.' We embrace, she wishes me luck, I get out and wave her off.

He's not here.

I'm at the table and have ordered a sparkling water. There are two menus on the table. I pick one up and scan it, not feeling hungry. He's only five minutes late, stop fretting. And Cambridge is always so busy and can be a nightmare to park.

'Carol?'

He is standing in front of me, tall, dark, good-looking, gorgeous actually, like someone out of a film. It's ridiculous. I feel a hundred years old.

'Sebastos, how nice to meet you.'

We shake hands. He's too lovely to kiss, it would be presumptuous, like kissing a god.

'It's so nice to meet you too,' he says, with a lovely accent, and he sits down opposite me. He's looking at me so intensely I wonder if there's something wrong.

'You look just like your picture,' I tell him, but really I want to say his picture doesn't do him justice.

'You don't,' he says, still staring at me.

My cheeks flush. 'Sorry, I must be a disappointment. The picture flatters me I know, it was taken by a friend in a dim light...'

'No, no, you don't understand. I mean that you're more beautiful than your photo.'

It's so silly, I know, but I fall for it completely. 'Oh, I don't know about that,' I say, stupidly, all coy and girly.

'It's true,' he says, and then he smiles, and his face is transformed, he is so heartbreakingly good-looking.

I open my mouth to speak but the waitress comes. Fortunately it's a different one to last time. I'll get myself a reputation if I keep coming here meeting different men. We order white wine and two main courses, I randomly pick the first thing on the menu and by the time the waitress has gone away again I've already forgotten what it is.

'Sebastos, I hope you'll forgive me if I ask you a personal question when we've only just met, but..'

'Fire away!'

It sounds like he's recently learnt that expression and is trying it out. I smile, trying to ignore the maternal instinct which has suddenly and alarmingly come out to join another one which I haven't felt for a long time.

'You are a very lovely looking young man...'

'Not so young! I'm thirty seven years old!'

'I thought you were thirty five?'

He shrugs, with a cheeky grin. 'A small lie,' he says. 'Are you going to tell me that I'm too young to be here, with you?'

'Well, yes, it did cross my mind, but to be honest I'm surprised you need a dating agency, you don't look like someone who would have any trouble finding a date.'

'Well, let me tell you,' he says, but the waitress comes back with the wine and we're silent while she opens it and pours it into two glasses. When she has gone I take a grateful sip.

'You were saying?'

'Let me tell you, Carol, I'm very shy.'

'Really?'

'Yes, really. I left my friends and family in Greece, I came here because I got a good job at the hospital here. I work long hours. It is hard to go out and meet people when you are shy and your job takes up so much time.'

'You're an optometrist aren't you?

'Yes. I look into people's eyes.' He grins. It's so silly. I'm loving every minute.

'Well, I'm surprised that you're so shy. You seem very confident to me.'

'Don't judge a sausage by its coat.'

'No, indeed.' How very sweet he seems. If he doesn't ever want to see me again at least I will have passed a very pleasant couple of hours in the company of a gorgeous young man who appears to think I'm delightful. He is looking at me as if I've fallen from heaven. It's been many years since John looked at me like that.

He asks me about my family. I still hate the word 'divorce'. It's a word that doesn't feel like it belongs to me. I suppose I will get used to it eventually. I talk about the children and he listens very attentively. He has the most beautiful green eyes, they're very distracting. He says he was engaged to be

195

married once, but his fiancé broke it off saying that she had cold feet and wanted to travel. He later found out that she was in a relationship with his best friend. He has a younger sister, he shows me a photo of a very beautiful young woman, the female version of him, and a brother who is disabled and lives at home with his parents.

We talk continuously, without any awkward silences, which is surprising because really we have little in common. I like the theatre and music, going for walks, I hate animal cruelty and I've no real interest in travel. He on the other hand seems to have travelled half the world, he's mad about football, he's never been to the theatre in his life and I haven't heard of any of the music artists he listens to.

The food arrives, he even eats beautifully, cutting his steak up into little portions with cutlery held like surgical instruments by hands that should be playing the piano. I'm surprised when I get a text from Minty asking if I need rescuing. The time is going by so quickly.

I excuse myself and go to the ladies to refresh my lipstick and reply to Minty. My reflection looks back at me in the mirror, it's a younger version of myself. Foolish woman! But how nice it has been, to sit opposite a man who listens to every word I say and watches me as I talk with eyes that seem to know everything about me, it reminds me of that beautiful song by Roberta Flack…"I felt as if he knew me, in all my dark despair…" Oh, Carol, pull yourself together! I text Minty and tell her to take her time. She immediately sends back lots of thumbs up and winky smilies. Honestly. If the children could see me now.

We linger over coffee. He's taken the whole day off, he says. He knows I gave my job up years ago, I told him all about that, how I then went to work part-time for John as his business grew, and now I just fill my time as I please. He thinks I'm lucky to have all the money I need. Money doesn't buy happiness I tell him, feeling very wise and emotional after all the wine I've drunk, twice as much as him I'm sure.

'Some of us are in the gutter looking at the stars,' he says. How very sweet.

Minty turns up at the appointed time and makes a bee line for our table. I introduce them, feeling rather pleased with myself, and watch as Minty falls under his spell. Sebastos asks if she wants to join us for a drink, but…I may be imagining this…I think he's just being polite. He gives me a private look as if to say, 'it was nicer when we were alone' and I feel as if I could just float up and away, like a helium balloon, and get stuck on the ceiling.

Minty is beside herself with excitement as we drive home, it's as if we've just announced our engagement. She can't stop talking about him.

'And you're seeing him again so soon!' she says, 'he's obviously dead keen.'

'I don't know,' I say, but my skin is burning, I feel like I've just stepped out of a sauna.

'Oh, stop being so bloody cautious Carol, he's gorgeous and he wants to see you again, what's wrong with you?'

'I just can't believe it that's all. It all seems so unlikely. What on earth does he see in me?' It's not a rhetorical question.

'Grrrr! What am I going to do with you! You're beautiful and clever, you're…'

'Mind that cyclist!'

'…and you're so graceful, and dignified, you're like… you're like Kristen Scott Thomas…'

I laugh.

'…or Audrey Hepburn…'

'Stop it. For goodness' sake.'

'And he's a young man who knows a classy older woman when he sees one.'

'I'll disappoint him in the end. Perhaps I remind him of his mother.'

'God, I hope not. His mother is probably a sun-roasted prune in a headscarf.'

'That's rude. And possiby racist. How dare you talk about my future mother-in-law like that.'

We giggle like teenagers. As we make our way home I have the strangest feeling, as if I'm going to a party that I've been looking forward to for a long time.

I didn't hear the text come through on my phone, I didn't even notice it was there until I was about to go to bed. I was glad to be alone when I opened it. It was from John.

Not pregnant. Turns out it's cancer. Stage four. I thought you might like to know.

14. Jules

A Dish Served Cold

I'm outside the Simpson's house and I can hardly believe my eyes. There's a Hambleton's Estate Agents' For Sale Board planted like a new tree on the front lawn. Something else is odd. I can't put my finger on it.

I turn my key in the door. As soon as it opens I know. They've gone. There are letters on the mat and it feels chilly, even though it's a warm July day. I can't believe it. They've gone. And I never knew. I didn't see this coming. I feel shaky all over because they fooled me. They didn't tell me a thing. They've just upped and left.

All the furniture has stickers on. *Swift Sales.* That's the auction house in town. Doug and Steve are always there, poking about for lost treasure. The rugs are rolled up. The cushions bagged.

I wander from the hall to the sitting room, taking it all in, then into the kitchen. It's like a ghost house. All the kitchen cupboards are empty. The fridge and freezer too, which are switched off. Dead. Lightless. Silent. It's like they've been robbed.

I go upstairs. It's so quiet. All the doors are open, and I can see straight away that all the clothes have gone from her dressing room, the bed is stripped, but there is still some linen in the airing cupboard. The bathroom is empty. All her fancy soaps and lotions gone. There is still half a loo roll though. I go for a pee. There's a spider in the bath.

Downstairs I fish out my old Nokia phone and dial Sally's number. If Bertie is selling this house they will know what's happened. My stomach tightens at the thought of having to ask someone else about something I should have known myself. I know everything.

'Hello, Jules, is everything alright?'

She's probably worried I'm cancelling my shift at her house. She relies on me. They all do. Or that's what I thought.

'Well, I don't know, I'm at the Simpson's house.'

'Oh…shoot. I forgot to tell you, I'm so sorry, they've moved away.'

'I can see that. I just turned up to work.'

'Oh, well, that's absolutely fine, Jules, you go ahead and do the place, it needs sorting out before we start the viewings.'

None of the ladies of Kingsmead can say the word 'clean'. They ask me to 'do' the kitchen or bedroom or whatever, or 'sort' something out. And they don't call me their 'cleaner'. They introduce me as their 'godsend' or their 'sanity saver' or something like that. I don't know why. It's like 'clean' is a dirty word, which is funny, if you think about it.

'Why didn't they tell me?' I sound cross, like a parent, but Sally is nice. I may only be the cleaner but none of them want to upset me. They need me. They really do.

'It all happened so quickly, nobody knew, she only told Hannah, her business partner, and even that was last minute. It's come as a bit of a shock.'

I'd like to know more but don't want to ask. I'll find out eventually. And then I'll know more than everyone.

It gives me the spooks, cleaning the empty, half-stripped house. I'm getting out here as soon as I can.

I'm thinking a lot about Sarah and Gary as I cycle over to Kingsmead School to clean the headmaster's rooms. I wonder how long they've been planning it? Maybe months. You can't just up and leave like that, without making some sort of plan.

It makes me angry to think of this. How could I not have known? I know everything. I see Minty and Carol in Minty's car, they're laughing, and they don't see me.

They didn't see me either when I went along to observe Carol on her date. I got the bus into Cambridge. I saw them through the window, Carol and the man who owns a yacht. They seemed to be getting on ok, he looked alright, quite jolly and everything, but Carol never mentioned him again and I didn't like to ask. I stood outside the restaurant for about twenty minutes, pretending I was waiting for someone, and every now and then I pressed my face up to the window and watched them.

She's got another date, with a Greek, who is only thirty five, I know when it is. I read the emails. I'll go along to that one as well, just to keep an eye on her. You can never tell what sort of weirdos there are out there.

I put my bike in the rack and walk towards the part of the building where the headmaster's rooms are. School has broken up for the summer now, but I have one last clean to do. He still has meetings and such like, even in the holidays. The place has to look nice all the time. Parents spend all that money sending their kids to this school, they expect it to be spotless. I hate coming here now, since Mr King wrote and said they wouldn't take my Dillon. I only come because I'm waiting for my moment, and you never know when that will come. Like I said, best to keep your enemies close.

Mr King's swanky car is in his parking space, which means he's here somewhere. I prefer it when he's out of the way. I don't like having to be polite to him. I cross the hallway with its tiled floor and pictures of past headmasters on the wall. I keep my cleaning stuff in the kitchen off the secretary's room and reception room, where they greet all their smart guests and give them fresh coffee while they're waiting for His Lordship.

I get my stuff and go back to his office. The door is open and when I make myself known to him, he looks startled to see me. He has a worried look. He says he didn't realise I was coming in today and I remind him I come in every Tuesday, nothing's changed. I try to sound polite but I know it comes out sharp. His mobile rings. He goes out in to the hall to answer it and I start with polishing the book shelves. I can hear him talk, he sounds agitated, I tune in my ears, which are as sharp as anything. I could hear pins drop if I wanted, if I tune in properly, if I concentrate. I polish the shiny wood and hear him say that 'it's not convenient at the moment' and then there is a very long pause. For a minute I think he must have ended the call or gone out, but then I would have heard the door go.

'Alright. I'll see you now. In my office.'

My heart rate goes up a bit when I hear that. Whoever it is that Mr King was talking to on the phone is coming over right now, and this is a person who has upset him over something or other. I need to find out.

I hear the front door open and close. I stop polishing and peep out in to the hall. He's gone. I go back into the office and look out of the window and then I see him, under the tree that has such lovely pink blossom in the spring, smoking a cigarette. I think I'm the only person in the world who knows that Mr King smokes. Michelle doesn't even know. I heard her telling Sally at that party that he'd given up, and how proud she was of him, because it was so hard.

Too hard by the looks of it. He's puffing away like a man condemned. He doesn't smoke much though, I've seen the packet of Marlboro Lights in his drawer and I count them. He only has about one a week, and I know it's the same packet because it has a tear in it. I think he just smokes when's he's feeling under pressure. Like now. I can't wait to see who it is.

Then I remember that my voice recorder is in my bag, and if I'm quick I could get it and hide it in the office, record the whole thing, whatever it is. I rummage around, find it, set it to record mode, and look around for a hiding place. The big wooden book case, that will do. If I put it on the bottom shelf it won't be visible, and it will be close to his chair, just a couple of feet away. I rest it on top of a big book about Oliver Cromwell.

I hear him come back through the front door. I move to the window and start wiping down the sills. I can smell the cigarette on him, even though he's across the other side of the room. He says he's got a meeting in ten minutes and asks me to go and do what I can in the other rooms. I've never seen him look so agitated. His skin is shining, as if he's sweating. My curiosity is burning. I tell him I can do the reception room and I leave, taking all my things with me. He thanks me in a peculiar way, as if he's forgotten who I am or why I'm here.

This is going to be good.

I keep a look out. The reception room looks out over a small garden and the gateway into the car park, so I will see whoever it is arriving. I rearrange the magazines, polish the tables, plump up the cushions and run my feather duster over the lamps, my eyes constantly checking the view through window. Before the ten minutes is up I see a car I recognise cruise through the open gate into the car park.

It's the rat. John Dixon. Him who abandoned his wife and went off with a woman young enough to be his daughter. She's pregnant now. Poor Carol, and the children, how they must feel about a new baby coming into the family I can only imagine.

He pulls up far too fast, as if he's in a hurry, or a bad temper, or both. I can't see him now, but I can hear the car door slam, and his footsteps marching up to the door. He stalks right past the reception room and straight in the headmaster's office without invitation. The door slams. I hear voices, I strain to pick out the words, angry words, the rat is mad as hell about something. Mr King is quieter, not saying much. I feel the tension through the walls. I stand as still as a statue, my ears cocked. I hope the voice recorder works. This is a gem. I am so wound up I clean the room in double quick time, then start on the little kitchen. Mr King's voice is louder now. They're arguing about a deal they made. There's money involved. The rat is threatening him, but what with I can't tell.

Then there is silence. My cloth hovers over the coffee machine. For a horrible, stomach dropping second I wonder if one of them has seen my voice recorder, but then I hear the rat again, really bad language, and the door opens and I hear him marching back out again.

There's not a peep from Mr King as the rat starts up his car and roars out of the car park. It's deathly quiet now, after all that, so quiet I swear I can hear my own heart thumping I'm that wound up.

Silence from Mr King's room. What if the rat's killed him? What if I go in and find his body slumped over the desk with a dagger in his back? So I have some words with myself, 'you watch too much TV you do' I say in a whisper. Mr King's a big strong man, he used to play rugby, he's twice the size of the rat. But then my Doug always says it's not the size of the dog in the fight that counts, it's the size of the fight in the dog.

I venture out into the hall. Still silence. I walk very warily over to the door of his office and peep in. No dead body on the floor, no pool of blood. Mr King is sitting in his chair staring at the phone in his hand as if he's trying to work out what it is. His eyes are wide and wild. He looks dreadful. I ask if I can help. He looks up, surprised again to see me there. He says no, thank you, and then, the strangest thing, he asks me how my Dillon is getting on. My skin prickles at the sound of his name in this room, this place that rejected him. I tell him Dillon is just fine at the local school. Mr King nods in approval and says 'good, good'. It's a bit awkward then. I glance over at the bottom shelf of the bookcase, at the big book about Oliver Cromwell.

'Mr King,' I say, all meek and mild, 'talking of Dillon, I couldn't help noticing your book about Oliver Cromwell, and it so happens that Dillon is doing him in history. I wondered if he could borrow it, you know, just for a week or so. Unless it's a precious thing, then of course…'

'Which book? That one?' To my horror he starts to get up, as if to fetch it himself, but I get there first.

'Yes, this one here. Would that be alright? I'll bring it back myself, next week.'

'Of course. Take it.'

I cleverly manage to take the book and the voice recorder together, without him noticing anything funny. I slip the recorder in my pocket and tuck the book under my arm. I'm buzzing. Time to get out of here, but steady, Jules, steady, don't act weird, don't arouse suspicion.

'I'll just finish off in here then and I'll be off.'

But he says, no, leave it, he has some work to do he says, I can make up my hours next time, but I can tell he's not interested in my hours. Right now he has something much more important on his mind, something to do with the rat, John Dixon. I turn to leave and he says he's so glad that Dillon is getting on so well at this new school. He says, 'it's not for everyone you know, Kingsmead School. It's not always the best choice.' He tries to smile then but his face just goes all wonky.

'I never said he was doing so well,' I say, not able to help myself, 'I said he was doing just fine.'

He nods again. Then just before I leave he says, 'Jules, you didn't hear any of that conversation did you?'

'Certainly not,' I say, all cross and offended at the idea that I might have been eavesdropping. Mr King seems to recover himself a little. He straightens out his shoulders and tells me I can go, like he's dismissing one of his pupils.

I can't get out of there fast enough.

Outside I put the book in the basket of my bike and set off. My legs feel peculiar as I pedal. I don't have any more jobs today, so I go straight home, thinking about everything I've just seen and heard. I can't wait to listen to the recording because I know, I just know, that this time I will have all the evidence I need to ruin Mr King, just like he ruined my Dillon's chances of a posh education and a place at a university.

I stop at the lights. The town is busy today. I set off again, wobbling a bit, it seems to take forever to get back to Fern Road. The ice cream van is there again.

'You were only here yesterday, Gino!' I call out as I pass. I don't think his real name is Gino, but that's the name on his van so that's what everyone calls him. I bet his Italian accent is fake and all.

'I can't keep away from you,' he says with a wink. I roll my eyes and pedal on up the hill to my house, the last one on the

206

left. Steve's van is outside. He spends more time at our house than he does at his own.

I get off the bike and push it through the side gate. The kitchen door is open, letting in all the flies.

'I wish you wouldn't leave that door open,' I shout. I prop up my bike and go indoors. Steve greets me, cheery as ever, and Doug goes to flick on the kettle.

'What's up with you?' he asks me, suspiciously.

'Nothing. What are you talking about?'

'Your face is all red.'

'So would yours be if you had to cycle up that hill in this weather.'

'I wish I could, I do, I wish I could.'

I've heard all this before, about how he'd give everything he owns, which isn't much mind, to have his back pain taken away. Steve cuts in with an offer of a biscuit, one of my own I might add, and I take one from the tin.

'Bring the tea in, will you?' I ask him. I go into the lounge and fish the recorder out of my bag. I stand by the window, looking out on our little garden, which is as neat as a pin.

Rewind.

Play.

I listen.

Oh my.

Oh my.

This is priceless.

I can hear every word, clear as a bell.

Doug shuffles in with tea. I tell him to leave it on the table, shushing him.

'What's going on?'

'I'll tell you later,' I tell him, shooing him away.

I listen. I listen to the whole thing. From the moment John Dixon comes storming in to the office to when he threatens to expose Mr King for taking money in order to accept the rat's nephew in to the school, a boy who would never have got in the normal way.

A boy like Dillon. Except that Dillon is worth ten of him, and I'm not. I can just about pay my bills and that's it, no spare thousands lying around to bribe head teachers.

They're all lying, cheating snakes. I knew you see, I knew that John Dixon had paid Mr King to take his nephew into Kingsmead, even though he's nothing but trouble and failed the exam. It was a big sum of money. More than I've ever had in my life. Mr King thought it was easy money and that no-one would ever find out, but I see everything. I just needed proof. Then it got messy when the nephew started behaving so badly that Mr King had to suspend him. He had to. What else could he do? Everyone would have been suspicious if he'd let him get away with such behaviour, he was setting fire to things, starting fights, calling girls vicious names, walking out of lessons. Mr King should have known better than to take that boy. He was too greedy.

So now the rat is mad as hell that the nephew has been suspended, 'after everything I've done for this school,' he said, 'you'd better re-instate him pretty damn sharpish if you don't want your reputation shredded.'

Oh, don't you worry your nasty ratty head about that, John Dixon, I'm going to do your dirty work for you.

Priceless.

Revenge is sweet.

And so much better served cold.

15. Minty

Drowning

Today is the thirteenth of August.

It was eight years ago today I gave birth to my baby, Joy. It is her birthday, and yet it is also the anniversary of her death, although actually, she died the day before she was born. But you can't have an anniversary of a death before you're even born. It doesn't make sense. I knew she'd died before I had the scan which confirmed it. I just knew it. I kept telling them. The obstetrician told me he always tells his students to 'listen to the mothers', and when I saw him after the scan he said, you were right, and I said, I told you so, as if we were talking about something trivial. When things like this happen you don't behave in a normal way. I was mad then, and he knew it. I guess he'd seen it before.

I dread this day.

It creeps up every year like a dark, silent monster. I sense it approaching even when I'm not really thinking about it. It's as if the evil thing that made my baby die comes back to remind me. It hangs over my days, it breathes into my bones, and sometimes I fight it, and sometimes I don't. I respect it. The presence of the monster means that Joy is still in my heart and I haven't forgotten her.

Usually I take a bottle of wine, or two, and lock myself in my room. I can't face anyone. It's just me and the monster on that day. I'm its slave. Bridie always comes round and Jules sends her away. This year she caught me out, she came over three days early. The little minx.

'Why don't you come to Brancaster with us?' she said, 'we're going to my sister's holiday cottage for a few days.' She's a very good woman is Bridie. Possibly the purest, most angelic woman I know. A bit timid perhaps, a bit of a mouse, but GOOD.

'Simon's over in Birmingham all week,' I reminded her, assuming she meant the both of us.

'I know,' she said, 'that's the whole point. I don't want you left here on your own.'

We didn't have to mention why. Bridie always remembers this day.

Jenny and Jack both have summer jobs and are out nearly all the time. I'm on my own.

'Is Jezza ok with this?' I ask her, 'I don't want to butt in on your family holiday.' But I did. I really did. It has never occurred to me to actually try and do something to ease the pain. To go away somewhere different. To be with friends.

'He's fine,' she said, which wasn't hugely convincing but good enough for me.

So we have to take two cars. Bridie, the twins and I go in my car, following Jezza most of the way but losing him when he stopped to refuel. We arrive in Brancaster in time for tea. I find my secret stash of wine in my case while Jezza and Bridie are unpacking and the kids are running around, all over-excited. The cottage is a snug fit for all for us, but I have my own room, which is just big enough for a single bed and a small chest of drawers. I have to be careful not to bang my head on the sloping roof when I get out of bed. The view from my window is of a small, well- tended garden with a swing and an old fashioned shed. Over in the distance I can just see the sea.

Early this morning I took myself off for a walk. Wes looked at me pleadingly but I'm not great with dogs, knowing me I'd end up losing him or something, so I ignored his big eyed begging and left him shut in the kitchen. He'll get plenty of fresh air later.

The beach was almost empty, just a few dog walkers and runners. I think about Joy as a little girl, running along the sand, turning to me, shouting out for me to follow her down to the sea. It's odd how clearly I see how she might have been, when really she was never much more than a foetus. It's nothing specific, no definitive hair colour or body shape, no detailed features, but it's a strong image. It's *her*. Maybe that's how we'll see each other in the afterlife, if there is one. We will be spirits with just a suggestion of form, and yet we will recognise each other instantly, and know each other better than we ever have done here on earth.

Sometimes I can't wait to get to heaven.

I get messages from people who remember. Simon phones me when I get back and the silences mean more than the words. Nothing from Jenny and Jack. They always go to her grave and put flowers there. They never forget. They don't have to say anything to me. I used to think, 'they'll understand better when they have children of their own,' but now Sarah is pregnant and it might be Jack's, and he doesn't want to know. He's scared, angry and defiant. So I was wrong. I hadn't foreseen anything like this.

I wonder if Jezza knows about Sarah and Jack? I wonder if Sarah told him when she went for her check up? Maybe she asked him about the paternity test. There's no point in me asking him, he never lets on. His lips are sealed with super glue, stapled and stitched. Spoil sport. Bridie definitely doesn't know. She wouldn't be able to lie to me and she can't act. She's still happy for Sarah and Gary and their unexpected pregnancy, she says it's a miracle. No, she definitely doesn't know and I don't need to tell her. I don't need to tell anyone. If it turns out the baby is Gary's after all then we can move on.

But will she ever tell us? They've completely disappeared. Rumour has it they've gone to Canada where Gary's family are, but no-one knows for sure. Bertie has an email address and that's it, apparently.

We have to know about the baby. We have to. I'll wait until the end of September and if I haven't heard from her by then then I'll ask Sally to contact her for me.

Jack won't talk about it. Which is just as well. The whole thing is sickening.

Someone is calling their dog, a high pitch call like a classic Red Indian in an old Western. It brings me out of my thoughts and I remember what the day is. It's incredible. The thirteenth of August, and here I am walking on the beach and thinking about something other than Joy for at least five minutes. Now that, Bridie, really is a miracle.

When I get back everyone is getting ready for a day on the beach. Bridie is turning an entire sliced loaf into cheese and tomato sandwiches and Jezza is folding a pile of beach towels. They have one of those pull along cart things (it used to be mine) and already it's full of beach gear. I offer to help but no-one takes me up on it, so I go up to my room and pack a few things in a big bag. I look out the window, sipping neat vodka from a hip flask. I can hear the thump of children's feet running up and down the stairs, voices shouting, Wes barking, beside himself with excitement.

Above it all I hear the silence of Joy's voice.

The monster is creeping up behind me as we walk to the beach…

Bridie

I have to take over from Minty here. She's in hospital in Norwich, Jeremy is with her, and I can't stop crying. The children keep asking me if she's going to be alright and I don't know what to say. I don't believe in lying to children or giving them platitudes but what do I tell them? I said we should all say a prayer for Minty, and we did, but then Theresa started crying and I couldn't stand it. She wanted to know why Minty's guardian angel hadn't been looking out for Minty when she went into the sea.

The day started out ok. Minty went for a walk before we were up, she obviously wanted to be alone. It's always a very difficult day for her, the anniversary of Joy's stillbirth. It's the first time I have managed to persuade her not to spend it on her own, shut in her house, refusing visitors and any offers of comfort. I thought it would be good for her to be out with friends, by the sea, with all the fresh air and sunshine. I thought it would help her get through the day. I was wrong. It's all my fault for bringing her out here when she's in such mental turmoil. I messed up. Oh dear God, please let her be alright. Make her well again and I will say three Hail Marys every morning and every evening for the rest of my life.

When she got back from the walk she looked…if not happy, then at least not too sad. She offered to help with the picnic but I didn't want her to lift a finger, I told her that today was all about her and I was going to try and make sure she had a good one. Oh dear God. What's the time? Too soon to call Jeremy again and find out what's going on. I wanted to go with her to the hospital but he told me to stay back at the cottage with the children, and he was right of course, he's a doctor, he's much better equipped at keeping an eye on her there than I would be. I'm falling apart as it is. Oh, poor, poor Minty, what are we going to do with you?

This is what happened.

We packed up the cart and walked to the beach. Minty was quiet, but the children were making enough noise for everyone. The tide was out and there was lots of room on the beach even though there were families everywhere, it was such a lovely day. Jeremy put up the windcheater and the chairs, the children unpacked the buckets and spades and the football, and they played a little way off while I sat with Martha and tried to stop her from eating sand. Minty took a bottle of wine out of a cool bag she'd brought with her and poured some into a plastic goblet. I didn't say what I was thinking, that it was too early in the day to be drinking and we wouldn't be having the picnic for at least an hour yet. Minty won't be told. She does what she likes. I admire it in a way. And today is different. The thirteenth of August is the one day of the year when she can drink from morning til night as far as I'm concerned. Jeremy gave her one of his looks but she didn't notice and no doubt she wouldn't have given a hoot even if she had.

When Jeremy went off to play football with the children I asked Minty how she was feeling. She was wearing sunglasses and still wasn't saying much so it was hard to tell. She let out the most enormous sigh and I suppose that answered my question.

Martha was demanding my attention and I played with her noisily, hoping to distract Minty from whatever was going through her mind.

Then suddenly she said, 'I fancy a swim,' as if it was something she had never done before and she was feeling brave.

'Is that a good idea?' I said, thinking about the wine she'd drunk, and with nothing to eat all day.

'Why not?' She sounded cross as she stripped off so I shut up. I watched her with resignation. Now of course I wish I'd screamed at her, tied her ankles together, poured away the wine, buried her in the sand, I don't know, something, anything to stop her from going into the sea.

She wore a Breton stripe swimming costume with a little bow on the front. Jeremy would say that she's overweight but I think that Minty has a beautiful, voluptuous figure. Is she still wearing that costume now, in her hospital bed? Dear God, save her, please, please save her.

It was a long walk down to the sea. I kept her in sight until she was just a tiny speck in the distance.

That's what she feels like now. A tiny speck in the distance.

Oh why why why didn't I stop her?

Because Minty does what she likes, that's why.

I must stop crying, I'm frightening the children. Should I call Jeremy now? Maybe in another half an hour. No news is good news, isn't it?

The sea wasn't particularly rough, a few white horses but nothing to worry about. There were no warning flags. Only my own internal warnings but then I always have those, I fret about everything, I always think the worst, and usually the worst doesn't happen. I must remember that now, usually the worst doesn't happen. Minty is going to be alright. She has to be. Oh, it's all my fault!

She'd been gone for half an hour when Jeremy said he was going to take the children paddling. There's a strip of water half way down the beach that's a perfect paddling pool but because I was getting worried about Minty I persuaded him to go right down to the sea and look out for her. As the minutes ticked by I began to relax. Martha had nodded off, so I covered her with a towel and closed my eyes, imagining Jeremy and Minty splashing around with the children.

I jumped when I heard Peter and Maggie shouting for me, they were running towards me, distressed and out of breath, and as I tried to piece together all the breathless words I saw the lifeguard's beach buggy scramble into action, speeding towards the sea, and, God forgive me, I was relieved when Peter said that it was Minty who was in trouble. I was thinking of my own children. I couldn't help it. Dear God, I couldn't help it. And now Minty is lying there....I must stop crying, I must pull myself together. I must pray.

Minty

What the fuck is Jezza doing in my room?

Jesus, I feel like shit.

Wait…this isn't my room.

Where the fuck am I?

It looks like a hospital.

'Where is she?' I ask him. My throat is incredibly sore. What have they done to me? He looks at me with a puzzled expression. 'Where's my baby?' I ask.

He puts his hand on my forehead. It feels cool and strong. Those are nice, safe hands. I feel something give inside me, as if time is shifting.

'Do you remember going into the sea?' he says.

The room closes in. Fear rushes through me. I'm drowning.

Jezza holds me firmly by my shoulders and tells me it's ok, I'm safe.

'I wanted to die,' I tell him, and then I wonder why I said that. I search his face for disapproval, but there isn't any. 'I didn't mean that,' I say. There's an apology in there and he finds it.

'I know,' he says. 'Don't worry. You're going to be fine.'

A nurse comes in. They exchange a few words about my blood tests and I don't bother trying to listen or work it out. I trust Jezza. He's gold plated. It gives me a good feeling, having him here looking after me. No one is going to give me any crap as long as my friend the good hero Dr Jezza is fighting my corner. The nurse writes something on my notes and goes out again.

'How are you feeling?' Jezza asks.

'Like shit.'

'You gave us a bit of a scare.'

'Me too.'

He looks at me as if he's trying to make a diagnosis, trying to figure me out. I hope he succeeds, then he can tell me what the fuck is going on in my messed up head.

'Simon is on his way.'

This overwhelms me and I fail to hold back my tears. Between my choking sobs I manage to get out the words 'I'm sorry,' but he tells me to calm down, relax, take some deep breaths. My throat hurts, my stomach hurts, every muscle in my body aches.

How has your life ended up like this, Araminta Morgan? What the fuck happened?

Jezza gave me pills, wonderful pills that sent me to sleep. When I wake up it's dark and Simon has taken his place. I put out my hand and he holds me tight. The smell of him, the feel of him, the familiar, lovely warmth of him, I close my eyes, feeling the closest I have felt to peace in a long time. Of course, it doesn't last. It wouldn't, would it?

'First Jack,' he says, 'now you. This hospital thing is becoming a habit.' He smiles weakly.

'I'm so sorry…' I say.

He lets out a short, quick sigh, looks like he wants to say something, then changes his mind.

He plays with my fingers, thinking.

'You need help,' he says, with big serious eyes. I have a horrible urge to laugh. He sounds so like someone out of a dreadful movie. Dear Simon, bless him, I love him so much. 'I mean it,' he says, like he can read my mind. I squeeze his hand.

'When can we go home?'

Jezza pops his lovely head round the door. He pulls up a chair and sits down. It gives me a funny feeling. Like he's going to tell us something bad.

'I've got the results of some blood tests we took earlier,' he says.

'Don't tell me, one hundred per cent proof,' I say, trying to get a laugh, failing.

I know Simon listens to every word of what comes next, but I drift in and out of it, I can't help it, it's like reading a bad book, I skim over the words, just taking a few in here and there, something to do with my pancreas, and drinking, and cancer, possibly, in the future if I don't stop, and Simon is very attentive and asks questions but I want to tell them both to shut up, to talk about something else. I just want to go home, to be in my own bed, to see my children...

'Do you understand what I'm telling you?' Jezza asks me, as if he's testing me.

'When can I go home?'

They exchange a look. 'Tomorrow,' says Jezza, 'maybe.'

'I'm sorry for spoiling your holiday.'

'Don't worry about it. It's more important that you get well.'

They think I don't understand. They think I'm still in denial. But although I only picked out a few words of what Jezza said, I picked out the important ones. I know what's going on. I think I've known it for some time.

I just want to go home.

Jack and Jenny are waiting for me. Jenny comes out to the car and hugs me, her tears make my hair wet. Jack gives me a less heartfelt hug, but it's a hug nevertheless. The house is immaculate. They know that nothing would set me back quicker than a messy house. The fruit bowl is full. The candles are lit, despite the brightness of the day. It's so good to be home.

I want to go to the fridge and get myself a glass of wine. A physical pain darts through me when I realise I can't. I say nothing. They know. I'm looking through the wrong end of a telescope at my future without alcohol. Endless, meaningless days. I will fight. This is one monster I have no respect for. This one I will fight every day.

Bridie is sitting on the end of my big, squashy sofa with a mug of tea in her hand. We can hear Jenny playing with Martha in the garden. I'm having a bad day. I'm not drinking tea because I'd spill it, I'm shaking too much. Bridie is telling me how fantastically well I'm doing. It's all I can do not to tell her to fuck off out of my house. What does she know? But of course I don't. Birdie is one of life's angels.

We talk about my first AA meeting, which I thought would be depressing but actually was anything but. I haven't had a drink for twelve days. It feels like twelve years. Bridie likes it that at the AA meetings we recite the 'serenity prayer'. She smiles in approval when I mention it. It's her favourite prayer she says. She asks if I know the 'footprints' story? I say no, never heard of it, and she loves telling me, about how there's two sets of footprints in the sand when you walk with Jesus, and when there's only one it's not because he's abandoned you, it's because he's carrying you through your darkest days. I tell her Jesus would have to be built like Arnold Schwarzenegger to carry my great carcass along the beach. She doesn't tell me off for blasphemy. Like I said, Bridie's is one of life's angels.

Apparently I have to take this 'one day at a time'. I have to have 'achievable horizons'. The view through the telescope is still the wrong way round.

One hour at a time is more like it.

My friends visit me as if I'm sick, which I guess I am. Jezza is keeping an eye on me, or rather on my pancreas and liver and other vital organs. He's delighted with my progress and prospects, bless him, he and Simon look at me with glowing pride. It's like being the genius child of a gay couple.

I'm trying to keep the salon open but it's hard. I've employed someone to help me out so I only have to go in part time. I'm too shaky to be much good, so mostly I'm just supervising, keeping an eye on the place. Krystel has been a star.

Carol comes round and gives me all the latest news. She tells me that Mr King has resigned, the whole town is talking about it. They've moved out of the school house that came with the job and rumour has it they've gone to live in Cornwall. Apparently John Dixon, Carol's loathsome ex-husband, had paid him off to accept his nephew in to the school and the governors found out when someone blew the whistle. Details are sketchy. She also tells me, as we sit on my sofa drinking tea (I get through gallons of the stuff when the shakes aren't too bad, Earl Grey, Darjeeling, Rooibos, I have a cupboard full of it, just like I used to have a fridge full of wine) that Shona's bump is not a baby after all, but a malignant growth the size of a grapefruit. Stage four cancer. That someone so young should be staring death in the face makes my pulse race. To think that for years I've been killing myself with booze when Shona would give anything now to be able to live. Carol says she's got months at the most. I don't know what to say. I can hardly show sympathy, she's the bitch we all hate for stealing Carol's stupid husband, but even so. It's shit. I ask Carol how she feels about it, the fact that the woman who stole her husband is being killed by cancer. After a pause she says, 'Sad. Just really sad.' I don't push it and ask her what, specifically, she's sad about. There's so much. We change the subject and talk about Sebastos. Wow. The expression on her face changes in an instant. I want details, but she won't dish up.

'Have you slept with him?'

'I'm not saying.'

'You have! You've gone bright red!'

'It's ridiculous, he's far too young for me.'

But she wants reassurance, I can tell, so I give it, full on. I'm so happy for her. She's excited for the first time in years.

'Does John know?'

'Yes. He does now. It's none of his business of course.'

'And the children? Does Sebastos have their approval?'

'We're getting there. He really is lovely you know, Minty.'

'I'm sure he is. He sounds pretty much perfect. The kids will come round to the idea when they've met him.'

'They already have. We all went out for a meal last week. Pippa was a bit funny with him at first but I could see Sebastos winning her round. It's impossible not to like him. He's so… well. You know. I don't want to sound like I've lost my head. It probably won't last.'

I tell her off then for being negative, but the effort of being positive for someone else when I spend all day doing it for myself is exhausting.

When she's gone I sleep on the sofa until Simon comes home.

Life is very strange at the moment.

I have an email from Sarah. It's August 31st and the baby has come early. My heart thumps wildly as I read it, my palms are so clammy and shaky I can barely hold the phone.

It's a boy. They've taken a DNA sample and compared it with Jack's. Amazingly she's done all this without Gary knowing a thing.

'....thought you'd like to know that Gary is definitely the baby's father.'

I fall to my knees on the hard kitchen floor with the phone in my hand and sob and sob until there is nothing left.

16. Bridie

Digging

I'm late, as usual, trying to pull Martha's wellies on, the ones we bought from Gary's company, they've got black Labrador puppies on, they're too small really, but I don't have time to look for Theresa's old ones, which will be in the cardboard washing machine box in the garage along with all the other wellies, football boots, roller blades, trainers and the like, I really should sort through them, and Wes is slobbering all over me, desperate to get out.

Every year Kingsmead enters the Best Small Town Flowers Competition and this year we won it, hurrah, and Carol and I are part of the team that looks after all the flower beds and pots across the town and I'm supposed to be meeting her outside the library in, like, ten minutes ago, and Martha is getting as annoyed as I am about these stupid wellies. She has to come with me, she loves it, she's got her own little trowel.

Well, eventually I get there, and Carol of course has already started on the flower beds. She's kneeling on her polystyrene mat and getting stuck in. There's a pile of pulled weeds next to her. I tie Wes up with his extended lead to the silver birch tree and get started. Martha is complaining that her feet hurt.

'Her wellies are too small,' I explain to Carol, who looks fantastic these days, really great, years younger, she's had an expensive haircut and has started wearing more make-up, but it isn't just that, it's a light in her eyes. 'How's Sebastos?' I ask her. I've given up on any hopes of her and John getting back together.

She smiles. It's a smile that completely takes over her face, as if she has no control over it. 'Fantastic. Just great. I can't believe it really. I don't know what he sees in me I'm sure.'

'Oh, stop it. Look at you!'

'Exactly!' She laughs like a school girl. 'Good job he can't see me in these old leggings.' She tugs at a dandelion.

'And what about…no; Martha, don't pick the flowers, just the ones like this. And…what about John? And Shona? What's happening there?'

'I don't suppose Jeremy tells you everything, does he?'

'No, he doesn't.' This isn't entirely true and I say a silent prayer in repentance for my lie.

'She's in St Anne's.'

'The hospice?'

'John isn't handling it very well. Her family are being understandably possessive and you know what he's like about being in control. He feels like everything is out of his hands.'

I dig into the soil, thinking. 'Does he talk to you then?'

'He's been calling round more often. It's hard to turn him away when he's so obviously upset, but…well, you can imagine. It's confusing for me. Him coming back to the house all the time.'

'Yes.' So maybe there is hope after all. Maybe, if poor Shona dies, and if this fling with Sebastos burns out…

'But don't start thinking there's any chance whatsoever of us getting back together,' says Carol, tossing another weed on to the pile and dashing my hopes. 'Too much damage has been done. And I've changed.'

'Yes, well, that's hardly surprising.' I want to ask her if she's still taking all the medication, the anti-depressants and sleeping pills, but her phone rings, interrupting us.

Carol looks at the screen, then puts the phone back in her pocket. 'It's John. I'll call him later. I'm waiting for a call from Sebastos,' she says, digging out a small but tenacious thistle. 'Did you hear about the earthquake in Greece this morning?' I confess I haven't. News from the outside world has to battle its way into our house past the Disney Channels, Playstation Fifa and the rest. 'It was six point four on the Richter scale,' she says, 'and the epicentre was near the village where Sebastos' family lives. He's worried sick.'

'That's terrible.' I say another silent prayer.

Carols sits back on her heels and examines her work. 'He has a disabled brother, he's in a wheelchair, something to do with his spine that he's had from birth. They've been saving for years for an operation. And his father's not well.' She begins digging again. 'But Sebastos is always so optimistic, even while he's worrying about them. I admire him so much for that. He makes me feel incredibly ungrateful for all my good fortune.'

'Hey, that sounds like Catholic guilt, you're not allowed that!'

'It's true. So my husband left me, so what? I'm alive, healthy, my children are wonderful, I have more money than I know what to do with. Sebastos sends almost everything he earns back to his family. He's amazing.'

'Martha, what have you got in your mouth?'

'She's not eating worms I hope. Jonty used to do that.'

I fish a chrysanthemum head out of her mouth. She grins at me and I melt. 'Don't eat the flowers, darling.'

I'm thinking, Carol's really fallen for this man and it makes me strangely uneasy. It just doesn't feel right. Her husband is at the bedside of a woman who is dying of cancer and Carol has gone bonkers for a man she's known a matter of weeks. I thought John and Carol would stay together forever. I never saw it coming, none of us did, not even Carol. What a mess.

When her phone rings again she rips off her gloves to answer it. It's Sebastos. She's gets up and walks away out of earshot, the phone pressed to her ear as if she can't get close enough. Martha copies me turning over the soil and I tell her what a great job she's doing. Wes barks at a squirrel running across the library roof.

After a while Carol comes back. Her cheeks are glowing. She pulls her gloves back on and kneels down next to me.

'Everything alright?' I ask her, thinking about Sebastos' family out there somewhere, in the rubble, and all the others who might be underneath it at this very moment, buried alive, or dead. After this I will go and light a candle in the church.

Carol looks upset. Her gloved hands are resting on her thighs. 'They've lost everything,' she says.

'Oh, Carol, that's terrible…'

'But they're alive, at least.' She begins digging again, less constructively than before. 'He's going out there tomorrow.'

Martha wants to know who's lost everything, so I tell her about the earthquake, and Carol's friend who has family there. She doesn't know what an earthquake is so I try to explain without frightening her. Carol has gone quiet and is frowning at the flower beds, miles away I'm sure. Often after our gardening sessions she usually comes back to my house for tea and cake, but today she says she needs to get home, there are things she has to do.

'Will you out to Greece with him?' I ask her as we pack up our things.

'What? Oh, no, not just yet anyway. It's probably not the best time to be introduced to his family, just after their house has been reduced to rubble.'

'No, I suppose not.'

She stoops to give Martha a kiss, who tells her we have fruit scones at home.

'May I have one another day?' asks Carol. Martha nods, giving her gracious assent.

Martha and I stop off at the church and light a candle for Sebastos' family and all the other poor people who are suffering in Greece. Martha asks me if Carol is going to ask John to build her friend a new house. She knows John builds houses. It makes me smile, the thought of a John Dixon home in the middle of a remote Greek village.

'That would be nice, wouldn't it, darling?' I say.

If only life were that straightforward.

17. Carol

Folly, Fretting and Finding Out

I am going to help Sebastos.

I know John would disapprove, and so would the children, but this is nothing to do with them. In fact, the thought of their disapproval only convinces me further.

John left me rich, because he felt guilty I suppose, but also because he knows what divorce lawyers are like, and the last thing he wanted was to put money in their pockets as well as mine.

The house belongs to me, mortgage free, and so does the car. A huge sum of money, much more than I can ever possibly spend, was spread over various accounts and I've taken advice on the best way to invest. I've never been particularly extravagant and I think I could live on the interest alone.

I support a cat charity and another that brings fresh water to villages in Africa, I always give generously to comic relief/ sport relief/children in need and to any disaster that comes up in the news, but doesn't everyone? I've never found a cause that makes me truly burn with indignation at the audacity of tragedy, not until now.

Sebastos sounded terrible on the phone, really distraught, and I was touched that he should expose his vulnerability to me so early in our relationship. He has spoken to his mother but not his father, who is apparently helping to dig for survivors or bodies with his bare hands, and he's seventy-five years old. The disabled brother, Alexio, is lucky to be alive. His wheelchair has been crushed and all his other equipment is buried under twenty feet of bricks and concrete. All the money they were saving is also under the rubble, in cash, and payment is due for Alexio's operation which he is supposed to be having on Monday. Even if they eventually get to the cash it will probably be ruined. Water pipes have burst and much of the house, what's left of it, is flooded.

How could I not help? I asked Sebastos how much they needed for the operation. Fifteen thousand, he said, but because his parents will be staying in Athens while Alexio is in hospital recuperating they will have accommodation bills to pay, and then all the physiotherapy and drugs and everything on top of that. Sebastos was going to try and borrow some money but without a second thought I told him not to.

'I'll lend it to you,' I said. My heart was thumping, but in a good way. I felt excited and reckless but convinced I was doing a wonderful thing. Bridie and Martha were just a few yards away digging up weeds and Wes was barking at something. Cars went by, a lady in a blue dress came out of the hairdresser's across the road, just a normal day, but I was doing something extraordinary, I had the power to change lives, to save them possibly, and I was so exhilarated I felt like dancing, shouting, crying.

Sebastos refused. No way, he said, no way, and his refusal was so attractive to me that I wished he was right there beside me so I could hold him and smell him and tell him that he had no choice but to accept.

'It's only a loan,' I told him, knowing that it wasn't, knowing that I would never ask for it back, what would be the point in that? But I had to tell him it was a loan or he would never have taken it. He went quiet for a bit, then I heard funny little noises and I wondered if he was crying. He said he was sorry, and I asked him what for? Coming into your life, he said.

That's the kind of thing he says. That's what he's like. He worries about everyone else and never about himself. I have never heard him complain about the long hours he works, or having to share a house with three University students who come home loud and drunk and play music non-stop. He tells me these things as if they're amusing. He's a saint. A saint with the most beautiful hands, the most gentle touch. I quiver with pleasure when I think about his hands and what they can do to me, what they have done to me. But that's aside. That's just between me and him. Those intimate times we share will never be known by anyone else. When his face is close to mine, when he's whispering to me, nothing else exists.

Listen to me, like an infatuated school girl! This is exactly why I will never tell anyone how I feel. Not even Sebastos. It's too beautiful, too wonderful, too erotic to be felt by a woman of my age. I keep it secret.

This is how I can repay him for all the pleasure he gives me. It's an equal recompense. I can give his family some sort of a life back, just as he has done for me.

I asked him to send me his bank details so I could transfer the money to him. He stressed it was a loan, and I said yes, it's just a loan.

The text came an hour later, just as I was stepping through the door of my house, all his bank details as he had promised. It was followed by rambling, heartfelt thanks, then, a few minutes later, another text in which he told me loved me. The first time he's said it.

I leant against the Aga holding the phone to my chest. The words burnt through me. I had to look at the text again and again.

The bank has just called to say that there has been an 'unusual transaction' on my account. 'Twenty thousand pounds to a Sebastos L Hatzi, is that correct?'

'Yes,' I tell them, 'that is correct. When will the money be transferred?'

'The funds should reach Mr Hatzi's account within the next couple of hours.'

Later, when the transaction has been cleared, Sebastos texts me again - 'Thank you so much. My angel. X'

I swear I sleep all night with a smile on my face.

He's booked on an early morning flight. I sleep in until past eight o'clock and check the flight status, but there are so many flights leaving Stansted for Athens this morning, it could be any of them. Maybe he's gone from a different airport, he was vague about it. There are no messages on my phone, which means he must already be in the air. He wouldn't text me in the night, he wouldn't want to wake me and he knows I keep my phone switched on by my bed in case one of the children calls.

I make myself some breakfast, a poached egg on wholemeal toast, and rooibos tea. I switch on a news channel and see more pictures of the devastation caused by the earthquake. They show a group of women, varying ages, comforting each other as the men behind them help rescue workers search for survivors, or bodies, and I think, one of those women could be Sebastos' mother. I think of Sebastos there with his poor family, comforting them, being strong, and my heart goes out to him. Then I imagine how they will react to the news that he has all the money for the operation, and more. How will he talk about me? Will he tell them I'm just a friend? Or something more?

The reporter at the scene hands back to the studio.

I check my phone again. Still no messages. It's ten o'clock. I have an appointment with Minty at eleven. I decide not to check my phone again until I have come out of the salon. It's only making me fret. I send him a text asking him to let me know when he's arrived and then I put the phone in my bag.

When I see Minty she gives me an enormous hug.

'You look amazing,' she tells me, 'I'm jealous.'

'Don't be ridiculous,' I say, feeling pleased. But she has dark circles under her eyes and her hair is dull and lifeless, pushed back behind her ears. She leads me to the treatment bay and draws the curtains.

'How are you?' I ask her, quietly because Krystel is not far away.

'Shit.'

'Oh, Minty. Don't give up.' Then we laugh at what I've just said.

'But, you know,' she says, placing a fluffy towel over me, 'as Forrest Gump said, life is a box of chocolates, and all that. Is it just a leg wax today Madam or lady bits as well?' She raises an eyebrow at me.

'Same as before,' I say, blushing like a child caught out. Minty notices of course, and grins at me.

'So how is lover boy?'

'He's gone back to Greece this morning, his family were caught up in that earthquake.'

'Shit.'

'They're ok though, thank goodness. But the family home is a pile of rubble, and his brother was due to have a big spinal operation on Monday.'

I notice Minty's hands are shaking as she smooths the hot wax on my leg.

'Good job I'm not a brain surgeon,' she mumbles, reading my mind.

'You're doing great, Minty,' I tell her, 'I'm proud of you. It took some will power to come off all those pills Jeremy gave me I can tell you, and I was only on them for a few months.'

Minty presses the strips of paper on to the wax then whips them off, making me wince.

'I'm not out of the woods yet,' she says.

'Is Simon being supportive?'

'Amazingly. But then he always was. Pretty much the perfect husband really. He was always too good for me.'

'Rubbish.'

'But enough of my crap. Tell me more about lover boy. When's he coming back?'

'He's not sure.' I wonder if there's a message on my phone? I'd put it on silent when I got here but now I'm desperate to look. 'I suppose it depends on the state of things when he gets out there. They've lost pretty much everything.' I wince again as another strip is pulled off.

'And no insurance I suppose?'

'God, no, nothing like that. They're quite poor. Sebastos is the Big Provider.'

'They must adore him.'

'Yes. He is…quite adorable, I have to admit.'

We exchange a look of feminine understanding.

As soon I'm back out on the street I check my phone, taking it for granted that by now he will have tried to contact me. When I see the blank screen my stomach turns. Surely he must be there by now? And if he's still stuck at the airport waiting for a flight why hasn't he called or answered my text?

233

Perhaps the battery on his phone has died, or he's dropped it and broken it. It's stupid of me to worry, and what is it I'm worried about anyway?

I jump when I feel the phone vibrate, at last! But it's only Bridie.

I don't answer. She'll be wanting to know the latest on Sebastos and the earthquake. I'll call her back later.

I call in at the deli and buy some bread and olives before heading home, feeling weird, as though something terrible is happening to me and I don't know what it is.

I can't keep ignoring John forever. On his fifth attempt today I answer the call. I know what he's going to tell me and I feel hollow.

'She's gone.' I can tell that he's holding back tears but I can't express sympathy. 'She died at twenty minutes past nine this morning. It was…peaceful.'

'Where are you?' I ask him, for want of anything better to say.

'I'm in my car. In the car park at St Anne's. Where've you been? I've been trying to get hold of you.'

'My phone was on silent. I was with Minty.'

He sighs. We both endure a silence that I won't fill.

'She was thirty-two.'

'Yes. I know. Her parents must be devastated.'

'They wouldn't let me be with her you know, at the end, can you believe it?'

'Yes, I can actually.'

'What?'

'I'm just saying I understand how they must be feeling. She was their child.'

'For fuck's sake, Carol. Are you still so bitter? It doesn't flatter you.'

'Go fuck yourself.'

I'm shaking as I kill the call. I have never spoken to John like that. I don't think he's ever heard me swear. I expect him to call straight back, to tell me what he thinks of my attitude and my language, but he doesn't. I pace the kitchen with the phone in my hand, thinking about Shona, my rival, the marriage wrecker, the destroyer of my peace, lying dead in the hospice, and then I think about Sebastos, his beautiful hands, his whispering words, and none of it makes sense. I feel the madness descending again.

'He called me for sympathy,' I say to Bridie on the phone ten minutes later when I have calmed down enough to call her.

'I expect he's a bit confused right now,' she says, 'what a horrible situation. I don't know what to say to you, Carol. Why don't you come over? Minty's here, we're having pea soup for lunch.'

'Give me twenty minutes.'

It's half past one by the time I get to Bridie's house, and I still haven't heard from Sebastos. Bridie and Minty can tell I'm upset and they assume it's because of the phone call from John. Martha is dipping chunks of bread into a bowl of pea soup and getting it everywhere.

'He's got a nerve,' says Minty, 'I know it's tragic about Shona and everything, but I can't believe he called you of all people, feeling sorry for himself. Hasn't he got any mates for God's sake?'

'He lost a few when he left me.'

'Yes, well, serves him right.'

Bridie is serving up more pea soup.

'To be quite honest,' I say, holding out my bowl, 'John is not my concern right now. It's Sebastos I'm worried about.'

235

This gets their attention. The soup ladle hovers.

'Why, what's happened?' Bridie is dramatic about tragedy and she looks worried. She's only just digested the news that Shona has died and doesn't look ready for any more shocks.

'Are his family ok?' asks Minty.

'As far as I know. It's just that I haven't heard from him since yesterday and it's not like him.'

'But he's in Greece isn't he?' says Bridie, 'Maybe the earthquake has affected the phone signals or something…'

'What time yesterday did you last hear from him?' asks Minty.

I get out my phone. '16.04.' I show her the text. Minty squints at it because she refuses to wear glasses.

'What's he thanking you for? If you don't mind my asking?'

'I sent him some money.' I look down at my soup because I don't want to see the expression on their faces. I pick up my spoon and stir the soup idly. 'It's a loan, just until they can retrieve all the cash that's buried somewhere under what used to be their home-'

'How much?' Minty cuts to the chase.

'Twenty thousand pounds. It's just a loan.'

'Jesus, Carol.'

'Please, Minty, not in front of Martha,' chides Bridie.

'I'm *praying*, alright?'

'It's a just a loan,' I say, 'wouldn't you do the same under the circumstances? They've lost everything.'

They both stare at me as if I've grown horns. I feel my blood running hot with indignation through my veins.

'I wouldn't be able to afford to give anyone twenty thousand pounds even if I wanted to,' says Bridie cheerfully.

Minty is quiet and I know what she's thinking. It makes me furious. If only he would text. Please, Sebastos, please, get in touch.

Bridie's older children come back from school and we change the subject, but I can't get it out of my head, the way they looked at me when I told them about the money.

They just don't understand.

I can't bear the thought of going back to my empty house waiting for the phone to ring. A text comes though from John telling me he's sorry. Sorry for what? There is so much to be sorry for. I answer simply, 'me too.' I just want peace.

I drive away from Bridie's and without thinking about it I head out towards the Wisteria Lodge Care Home. The verges are thick with cow parsley and overgrown hawthorns. It's the best sort of late summer's day. I suppose it's even hotter in Greece right now. I imagine Sebastos with his sleeves pushed up, sweating as he helps the rescue efforts in his village. How stupid and selfish of me to expect him to think of me at a time like this.

At the care home I see that some of the residents are sitting in the garden at the side of the house. Maud, a lovely Glaswegian lady in her nineties, waves at me and I wave back.

'Lovely day!' she calls.

In the foyer the photo frame this week holds a picture of Arthur Henry Lott, who 'passed away peacefully'. Aged eighty four. 'Arthur loved music and gardening and had a cheeky sense of humour.' In the photo he's wearing a red checked shirt and thick rimmed glasses. He looks out at me as if he knows something I don't.

Linda greets me with the same burdened expression. Too many of the staff have taken their summer holiday at the same time, she says, rolling her eyes. I ask her if she enjoyed her recent stay in a caravan in Skegness with her family and she says it was alright, she'd rather be on a cruise round the Med but chance would be a fine thing.

The smell of the place fills my nostrils, it's worse than ever. A man I don't recognise, a new resident, is shuffling down the corridor with a walking frame. He looks lost. I say hello and ask him if he's alright. He says he's on his way to ask Linda if he can go home now. My heart breaks. Good luck, I tell him. Somewhere off in the distance I can hear Janine's distinctive voice asking someone if they want fish or beef for dinner. Fish or beef, she repeats, then louder still, FISH OR BEEF. From somewhere else comes a shout which I can't decipher, something like alarm. I feel my heart rate quicken as I reach Mum's room. How I hate this place.

Mum is sitting in her chair as usual but she's not fully dressed. She's wearing a full length petticoat with large, floral knickers on underneath, I can see them because the petticoat is crumpled up to her hips. She isn't wearing a bra and the empty, drooping breasts that once fed me and my sister hang like flaps of skin against her chest. Who has left her like this?

'Hello Mum,' I say, not wanting to startle her before I squat down and touch her hand.

She looks at me with those empty eyes and I try to suppress the anger rising in me but it grows fast and out of control. It's as if all the anger I should have felt over the last few years has suddenly decided to come out all in one go. I'm terrified of its effects as it gains momentum. It feels like a tsunami inside me. I take some deep breaths to try and calm myself down.

'Carol came to see me,' she says.

I could cry. 'Did she? That's nice.'

She nods. 'It was lovely to see her. I haven't seen her for ages. How's Michael?'

That's it. I can't stand it anymore.

I go over to the wardrobe and start pulling out clothes. I find a summer dress and carefully put it over Mum's head. She's like a compliant child. I put her arms through the sleeves of a white cardigan and then brush her hair. She smiles at me.

I unfold her wheelchair and bring it alongside her. I help her to stand, pulling the hem of her dress down as I do so.

'Is it cold outside?' she asks.

'No, it's a beautiful day.'

'I'd better bring a cardigan just in case.'

'You're wearing it Mum. There, that's it, now lift your feet, let's get these pedals up. Where are your shoes? Never mind, you can keep your slippers on.'

'Are we going out for tea?' she asks. There's a beady light coming into her eyes.

'No Mum,' I tell her, 'we're going home.'

Fortunately Mum decides to have a nap as soon as we get back to the house. I put her in the chair with her feet up on a footstool in the sitting room. The car journey and the strangeness of everything has tired her out. I have a lot of phone calls to make.

But first, I go on to the Google home page and in the search bar I type Sebastos L Hatzi Optometrist. I tap Enter and quickly scan the first page. I go on to the second page, and the third.

Is this a dream? A nightmare from which I will soon wake?

Then I call three home care companies and arrange for assessments to be carried out. I feel ruthless, efficient, strangely outside of myself. Then I answer a call from the manageress of the Wisteria Lodge Care Home, who wasn't in her office when I went sailing past Linda with Mum in her wheelchair. I made it clear to Linda that we weren't coming back and I felt like a girl from St Trinian's breaking free, I wanted to shout and cheer. The look on Linda's face was priceless. Helen, the carer who was the nicest, has left a concerned voicemail but I'll have to call her later, there are more important things to deal with, practical things.

I call Bridie and tell her what I've done. She's horrified at first, she's convinced I've gone completely mad, she may be right, but she's reassured when I tell her of all the plans I'm making. I tell her I need to speak to Jeremy, not expecting him to call me back until he gets home, but as luck would have it he's with her and she puts him on. I explain what I've done, and ask him if he could come out and examine her, just give her a bit of an all over health check. He checks his diary and we fix an appointment.

'And there's one other thing,' I tell him, 'I wonder if you could find something out for me, I'm at a bit of a loss.'

'I'll try. What is it?'

'I'm sure you've heard that I've recently been seeing a man called Sebastos.'

'Bridie told me, yes.'

'He's an optometrist.'

'So I understand.'

'He told me he works at Addenbrooke's, and also at a private clinic in Cambridge, I can't remember which one. But I've been Googling him and...' Oh God, don't start crying, don't. 'I can't find anything about him and I just wondered if...maybe...I don't know.' The tears are coming fast now and Jeremy talks to me so kindly it only makes me cry harder.

'I'll put some feelers out,' he says, 'see what I can find. What is his full name?'

'Sebastos L Hatzi. That's all I know.'

'Ok. I'll give you a call tomorrow.'

I want to lie on the floor and sob like a child but Mum wakes up and asks for tea. She's frightened in her new surroundings but smiles when she sees me. She asks me if Michael is coming.

'You'll be happy here,' I tell her, wiping tears from my cheeks, 'I promise you.' I squeeze her tiny hand, and it feels so fragile, like the skeleton of a little bird. 'I'll go and make some tea. Would you like the TV on? There might be a movie on somewhere.' Mum always used to like the old black and white films. I pick up the remote and switch on the TV, which goes straight to the news channel I was watching last night. More reports from the epicentre of the earthquake. I scan the picture, thinking I might see Sebastos there amongst the crowds. The reporter says she's in a village near Archanes, north of Athens. I remember, suddenly, as if someone has said the name in my ear, where Sebastos said his parents live.

'I'll back in a minute,' I tell Mum, going to the kitchen to open up my laptop. I put the name of Sebastos' village into the search bar. It comes up on Google Maps. I pan out.

It's nowhere near the epicentre of the earthquake. It's the other side of the country.

Jeremy calls me two hours later. I am sitting with Mum watching 'Bang! You're Dead!', the 1954 version starring Jack Warner. Mum appears to be engrossed. She keeps nodding to herself, as if she's seen it before.

'I think I know what you're going to say,' I tell Jeremy. I am prepared now.

'There's no record of him anywhere,' says Jeremy, sounding shocked himself. 'I'm so sorry, Carol.'

'Well, there's no fool like an old fool,' I say, knowing my light-heartedness is not convincing him. 'My mother always used to say that if something appears to be too good to be true then it probably is.'

Jeremy is stuck for words. He tries a little professional comfort but I'm not having any of that. It's time to move on. I've been a fool, but there's nothing I can do about it now. I thank Jeremy and tell him I have to go, it's time to get my mother's tea. And I won't be yelling FISH OR BEEF in her ear either.

Me and Mum. We're through with men, and anyone else who tries to take control and screw us over.

It's just the two of us now.

Epilogue

There's a car parked not far from the council house where Jules and Doug live. A large, bald man in his forties is sitting in the passenger seat drinking from a bottle of Coke. Next to him sits a woman of similar age with lank, black hair and mean eyes. She is wearing a navy jacket over a cream blouse which is gaping at the buttons. They don't say much. They look at the house where Jules and Doug live. The woman yawns without covering her mouth. The car is non-descript, like them, functional but probably not very comfortable, old enough to be unfashionable, a shade of undefinable green. The passenger window is open a few centimetres.

Jules comes out of the gate at the side of her house, pushing her bike. She has all her cleaning equipment in the basket as usual, as well as a bottle of orange barley water and a plastic lunch box which contains her sandwiches. She looks up and down the road before getting on her bike and cycling towards the town.

The couple in the non-descript car watch her go, then the man starts the engine and they follow her, like snakes in the grass after a mouse. All day they watch her go from house to house, each time taking her cleaning items out of her basket, and her slippers, which she changes into before going inside. She spends three hours in the first house, two in the second, and two in the third. She eats her sandwiches on a bench outside the library and admires the flowers.

The couple in the car take photos and make notes.

Three weeks later Jules has a letter from HMRC informing her that she is being investigated. It is their belief that she has been working for cash and not declaring her earnings. She will never know who tipped them off, but she suspects the Kings, who have gone to Cornwall to start a new life.

The 'For Sale' board outside Gary and Sarah's house has a 'Sold' sticker on it. A removal lorry is in the street, being unloaded. A man is looking up at the gutters and pointing something out to his wife, but she is more interested in the furniture and the boxes, and giving directions to the men. She looks excited but stressed. She looks at her watch. Only one hour until the children come home from school. Her husband lets the little white dog out of the car and takes it around to the garden at the back, where it frantically sniffs the perimeters of its new home.

Within weeks the house is transformed into a lively, noisy family home, with no trace of Sarah and Gary left in it at all.

Araminta is saying goodbye to Jack on the drive of their home. Jack has got a job in London and Simon is driving him to the station. Araminta hugs her son, and he doesn't pull away like he used to. Jenny comes running out, gives her brother a quick hug, laughs at something he says, then goes back inside the house. Music is playing, drifting out from a bedroom window. Araminta is looking good, still a bit weighty, but fit and healthy, her hair cut in a new style, her skin tanned from the long walks she takes in the park to help distract her from the cravings. She is wearing a long red dress and the bangles on her wrist make a pleasant jangling sound when she moves.

She stands on the pavement and waves until the car out of sight.

Carol's mother sits looking out of the window. It's her favourite pass time. The lady across the road, the one who spies on her neighbours, finds it disconcerting to be the one who is now spied on. Tables have been turned. Carol's

244

mother is doing well, she's more alert, more aware, and seems happier now that she is living with Carol, who she recognises sometimes. Carol takes her into town now and then, for cake at Kate's Tea Rooms, or to Minty's salon to have her nails done. They avoid Kirsty's gift shop. John has taken himself off to Australia for a few months, to rethink his life, he said. He's staying with his brother. He phones and skypes Carol regularly and hints at them getting back together.

Carol says hell will freeze over first.

There is laughter coming from Bridie's house, and the sounds of a party. Twenty children are in the garden playing party games, some of the parents have stayed 'to help' but mostly they stand around chatting and drinking tea. There are paper plates, paper cups, sandwiches, slices of birthday cake, cards with the number 5 on, presents piled on the sofa, coloured balloons, Twiglets crushed into the carpet, jam on the door knob and grass brought into the house on little shoes because Jeremy cut the lawn yesterday for the first time in three weeks. It would have been better, Bridie thinks, if he had left it until after the party, but he was trying to be helpful. Jeremy is late and Bridie wonders if it's deliberate. These parties are always so exhausting but the children are happy, and therefore so is she.

The other Mum's say she's a saint.

Sally is often asked if she's heard from Sarah, and she says no, not for weeks. All she has is an email address, but since the house has been sold there's been no more communication. Everyone knows she had a baby boy and they imagine her in some blissful domestic situation in Canada, in a nice house, with doting in-laws on hand. Sarah lives an ordinary life but because they can't see her, and because they know nothing about her, they imagine it be much more interesting than it really is. They speculate. There are rumours about Sarah and Karl Huth, about the baby not being Gary's, but they die out. The Huths are oblivious of course. They just get on with living life. Then one day they announce that they're going to live in Germany, Karl has got a job there, one that will pay him much more money, and soon they go too, and the house comes on the market, and Araminta hopes the new neighbours will be nice.

Expensive cars cruise up and down the High Street. Minty's salon has fairy lights in the window. Kate's Tea Rooms has the biggest and brightest hanging baskets. Kirsty's gift shop where Carol was caught shop lifting is having a sale. Hambletons Estate Agents has the Huth's house in the window. Pupils from Kingsmead School amble and giggle down the street. An elderly lady waits to cross the road at the pelican crossing. A young mother is struggling to get her pushchair over the step into Oxfam.

Someone is laughing, and someone is crying.

END

Printed in Great Britain
by Amazon